Cold Turkey Guide to Marriage, Family and Deng mal,

Vol. 1,2

If There's a Will

There's a Way-sequel to If There's a Will

Books are available on Amazon.com in paperback or kindle.

What readers are saying about *If There's a Will*.

What a great first novel from this author. I laughed, I cried, I couldn't put it down...A Minnema.

Our book club loved this book. It was entertaining and took us to new locations. We can't wait to read his second book. Amazingly well written...Nancy

This book will keep you awake...Yooper

One of my favorite reads of the new year, this book had me laughing one minute and on the edge of my seat the next...D. Maloney

Wonderful fast-paced story grabs you and doesn't let go until the very end. Even after finishing each chapter, you are left reflecting 'what would I have done?' 'Could I have done that?' Masterfully woven story, full of action, adventure, and ethics. Anxiously awaiting the sequel...K Downs.

The author has quite the imagination with all of the twists and turns in the story...Amazon customer

I wasn't an insomniac until I started reading this book. "Just one more chapter, then I'll go to bed..." Adriatic C.

John Ingalls has a knack for multi-layered creative plots, good narratives and coherency. When I finished reading the book, I felt like I had caught the tail of a good dragon and had enjoyed a wonderful ride...Maggie from Ontario

THE WOMAN IN THE EMERALD CASKET

Michael

Believe

[signature]

JOHN W INGALLS

ISBN: 9781796448863

Imprint: Independently published, KDP.com

Cover Photo: Wood Water Wall (Thailand)/Shutterstock.com

www.johningallswriter.com
johningallswriter@gmail.com

For
My Parents

Those tired, overworked, unsung heroes preparing the next generation with the hope of making the world a better place. There is no greater challenge, nor higher position than that of a parent entrusted with the love and care of a child.

A father's goodness is higher than the mountain, a mother's goodness is deeper than the sea.
-Japanese Proverb

Contents

CAST OF CHARACTERS

Maggie O'Reilly, 77-year-old widow, lives alone in Peterville, a dying farm community in western Minnesota. She is impulsive, energetic and prefers to live outside the box.

Mary, oldest daughter. Iron willed like her mother, the nut doesn't fall far from the tree.

Tommy, second child, brother to Mary, serving a ten year prison sentence in Waupun, Wisconsin.

Freddie, middle child. He's married to Therese. Therese likes credit cards and shopping.

Eliza, the fourth child and the second daughter. She was the cream that rose to the top, but she was too busy saving the world to have time for her mother.

David, the youngest child.

Mick Torkelson, retired, semiprofessional mini-golfer.

Patrick Murphy is a lonely widower, struggling to get over the death of his wife, Ethel.

Goldie Finkelstein is the wife of Arthur Finkelstein.

Velma Gladwell is Maggie's look-alike.

Sally McTavish and **Mabel Feely** are widows and members of St. Michael's Parish.

Father Shamus Muldoon is the priest at St. Michael's Parish.

Vinny Maldonado is a mortician and owner of Maldonado's House of Eternal Rest in Chicago.

FOREWARD

Writing a novel is a bit like driving in the fog. The author has a general idea about the direction of travel but a multitude of surprises lurk along the road. There are waysides and overlooks, potholes and ruts, detours, speed bumps and unexpected creatures ready to pounce. We long for the straight and narrow path but the way is seldom smooth and never straight.

I set out to tell a story of a lonely widow near the end of her life, searching for answers from her disengaged children. It wasn't a complicated question; she wanted to know if her children loved her unconditionally; an admirable quest and one I'm sure many of us would like to discover. It's a black and white question with a many-colored answer, like sunlight through a crystal water glass. Like art, we can't define it but we know it when we see it. Sometimes.

My father's life was an inspiration for this story, though he will never know it. He died December 8, 2015, after a short battle with cancer. The cancer didn't win and he didn't lose, it was just his time. If it wasn't the cancer it would have been something else. But that's another story for another time.

In all my years of knowing him I don't recall hearing the words "I love you" but he said it over and over, in other ways, but I didn't understand until it was almost too late.

Here is a short essay I wrote after his death. It is a good representation of how he communicated and it sets the stage for Maggie O'Reilly's search for answers. Enjoy.

How's Your Car Running

Communication between people appears simple. One speaks, another answers, and the information shared, leads to the next response. However, as we add layers and layers of complexity on top of the simple word exchange, the task of communicating effectively, becomes more difficult. Wavering hands, voice inflections, body language all in the context of the immediate environment can change the meaning of a sentence or words significantly. Toss in an idiom, mix in a metaphor alongside a generational difference and you set the stage for misunderstanding. Such was the case with my father. It took me many years to finally understand the intent of his words but when I did it made all the difference.

On October 8, 2015, I had the unenviable task of letting him know about the cancer. In just 3 months' time it went from a small spot to everywhere. With little hope of effective treatment, he took a simple approach of foregoing further treatment, choosing to enjoy what days he had left with as much enthusiasm as he could muster. He looked me straight in the eyes and asked for the truth, "Do I have 2 months?" I wanted to be generous and dispense hope but there was little to do but nod and wipe my own tears. I grasped for words but there were none. He was the one to offer comfort. There was no use fretting about it; that was just the way it was. Ironically, it was 2 months to the day, almost to the hour, when he took his last breath.

Shortly after getting the news Dad asked me to speak at his funeral. "Just 5 minutes" he said and he didn't want anyone else speaking a bunch of foolishness. I paused trying to visualize the situation. It wouldn't be easy. I knew He wanted me to speak and I considered it a great honor.

"I don't know if I can do it," I said.

"If you can't, I understand." He looked to the side avoiding direct eye contact.

"The speaking part is simple," I said, "I just don't know if I can find any stories I can repeat in church."

I learned a lot about him just by observation. I learned that he is a very caring person, genuinely interested in you. He loved people and loved to be around friends. Although outgoing, he was reserved. He could openly discuss his health and bodily functions with total strangers but he wasn't one to just say "I Love You". He said it in his own way.

I was attending the University of Wisconsin in Madison in the 1980's and my parents came to visit. I predicted to my wife what my father was going to ask, "He's going ask how my car is running."

She thought that was ridiculous. "Why would he ask how the car is running?"

I had pondered this for some time. I asked my brother about this and he confirmed the same conversations had taken place in his life. For years he would ask me that very same question and I finally realized that was his way of saying "I care about you". After their arrival and the greetings and initial small talk had subsided, not 10 minutes had passed; he turned and asked me "How's your car running?" Since then I have heard it many times and I knew he really cared. It was his own reserved way of reaching out and once I understood what he was saying it made all the difference to me.

I learned many other things about him as well. In honor of his 80th birthday I had the privilege of being the chaperone on a fishing trip with dad and his two brothers, Earl and Ole. I had a difficult time convincing them to go. Dad complained, he was too old and too slow. He had a thousand excuses. "What if I have to go to the bathroom and we are out in the boat? What if I can't go to the bathroom? What if we hit a rock? What if we get lost? What if the plane goes down? What if..." and the list went on.

I tried to reassure him that the place we were going was a small slice of heaven on earth. In the mornings the staff will make you hot coffee and cinnamon rolls and eggs and pancakes and anything else you want. Every evening when you return, they will feed you steaks and baked potatoes and turkey and chicken and more hot delicious food than you can eat. Every day on the lake you will eat beans, fried potatoes and more walleyes than you dreamed possible. And you will catch fish until your arms ache from catching fish and your cheeks hurt from smiling so much.

We all went and I learned that if you spend a week eating beans and fried potatoes with the Ingalls brothers you better sit in the front of the boat so you get some fresh air. He caught more fish than he had ever caught in his life. The most memorable moment for me came during the last hour of the last day. It was a perfect summer day, blue skies, calm winds and warm, the kind of day you dream about in winter. Comfortably tired from a long day on the water we decided to stop in just one more place. Dad with his stiff arthritic wrists couldn't cast his bait so he simply dropped it over the side of the boat and let the rocking of the boat move his bait around. In the final minutes he caught 3 trophy walleyes on three successive casts. Completely worn out and satisfied he threw up his arms and looked up to the sky and announced "Saint Christopher, you can take me anytime."

I hate cancer but I respect it for what it gives you. It is a formidable enemy, one I wish we could defeat. Sometimes we gain ground and sometimes we lose ground, in the battle. All too often it wins the war on the body but it can't destroy the spirit. When I told him, he had a short time to live he took the news in a matter-of-fact manner. No time to waste, he cleaned the shed, the basement, the yard and got everything in order. He gave away tools and rain barrels and personal things. Going through his woodshed he brought out five fence posts and said he wanted me to have them. I had a big garden and would need to fence out the deer. A week later he took me back into a wooded area behind his house and told me where he had some old powerline poles cut up into lengths and these would make some great fence posts. Another week passed and as he was getting weaker, he reminded me about the fence posts so they didn't go to waste sitting back in the woods as they had for the past 20 years.

During the last few weeks of his life I felt guilty. When I wasn't at his side, I felt guilty for not being there and when I was there, I felt guilty for not wanting to be there. I hated to watch his once strong body convulse with pain and waste away. His voice became weaker and you had to listen carefully to what he wanted to say. Almost a whisper, he would strain to speak and sometimes wave his finger to come closer if he wanted to say something.

Somewhere in the last few days of his life he motioned for me to come closer. I leaned in straining to hear his words. This is the moment of wisdom, the moment of truth, the father and son talk we never had. He's finally going to tell me where he buried the gold.

Getting weaker with his eyes half open he took my hand and said "Did I ever tell you about those fence posts in the back yard?"

I nodded.

He paused to catch his breath. "How's your car running?"

CHAPTER 1

*In the city a funeral is just an interruption of traffic;
in the country it is a form of entertainment.*
— George Ade

Maggie O'Reilly died on a Wednesday because she planned it
that way. But that's not the end of the story, and it isn't the beginning either.

Maggie was a good Catholic widow. She had six children,
gave generously to the church and never drank Guinness on Sundays. Everyone knew she was loaded. She had money too. She
smoked cigarettes but they were low tar. On Fridays, she ate fish,
wore a black dress and she went to confession.

"Father, forgive me for I have sinned."

The confessional was claustrophobic. Maggie could hear rustling through the vented wall where the priest sat, alone in the
dark. There was no answer so she waited for a few moments.

There were only three of them remaining in the parish that
still went to confession. Old Mabel Feely, Sally McTavish and herself, Maggie O'Reilly. It's not like Father Shamus couldn't tell who
was talking. Everyone knew, that he knew, who did what, but it
was easier to confess when you didn't have to look him in the eye.

Patrick Murphy was too good to sin or he was too proud to
confess, Maggie wasn't sure which but for the last 13 years, she seldom saw him darken the door of the church during the confession
hours. Ethel, his wife, died a few years ago and Mabel Feely was
the first one over to his house with a huckleberry pie. Ethel was

probably still twitching when the door-bell rang. But Patrick was too good for Mabel or anyone else for that matter. He went to the church and lit three candles every day in her memory, and only set the cuff of his shirt on fire once, that Maggie could recall.

They were the four remaining regulars at St. Michael's Parish. The others were sporadic attenders, seeking prayers when a family member was sick or needed money or the usual church holidays of Easter and Christmas. On a really busy Easter Sunday they might have thirty or forty in attendance but most Sundays it was just Mabel, Sally, Patrick, Maggie and a couple strays.

Mabel had a squeaky old voice that cracked like a seagull choking on a dead fish. At least that's the way Maggie pictured it. Sally wasn't much better. Maggie thought Sally was flirting with dementia. For the past ten years, whenever they met, Sally told the same stories and showed the same photos of her children and grandchildren and sometimes her late husband, Richard. The one of him stretched out in the casket was the creepiest. Maggie was tired of nodding and listening to the old bat. But she was a good Catholic woman so she listened without complaining and reviewed a mental shopping list and her plans for the upcoming week until Sally ran out of things to say. Then Maggie would cough and look at her watch and say, "Look what time it is. I must be going." It was the same every week.

Maggie knew Father Shamus could tell the difference between them, anyone could if you had half a brain. She cleared her throat and coughed. Her voice sounded like Lauren Bacall after a late-night party and too little sleep.

"Father forgive me for I have sinned." This time she said it with a bit less conviction because she wasn't convinced, she had sinned, at least not yet.

From the dark recess beyond the vent she heard, "Go on my child, share what the Lord has put on your heart."

Maggie thought it was funny when Father Shamus called her 'child' because she was seventy-seven years old and had grandchildren almost the same age as the priest. But that's what priests do, they call people children.

But she didn't think of her own children as children. They were leeches, every one of them, except maybe Tommy and David. Eliza was more of a worm. Freddie was nice some of the time but Maggie was hard pressed to say anything good about Mary. She was the oldest and the worst. David was her favorite, but she didn't like to admit it in front of the others. Maggie hoped Tommy could visit next year, if he gets parole.

It was Albert's fault the kids turned out the way they did. He had been dead for seventeen years and he was on the road twenty years before that, but it was still his fault. He was a lousy husband and father. He was never home. Always working, always doing business but when he had a stroke at fifty-nine, he had a big life insurance policy and money in the bank. But it was still his fault. Everything.

"Go on my child." The voice from the dark reminded her of the reason for her visit.

"Forgive me Father for I have sinned."

"You already said that."

"I'm planning to kill myself and I need your help."

CHAPTER 2

Every man is sociable until a cow invades his garden.
-Irish Proverb

There was a long pause in the dark confessional. Maggie heard Father Shamus take a deep breath and exhale slowly. She heard him take out a handkerchief and blow his nose twice then he sniffed. "My child, surely you don't mean what you said."

"Father, I didn't mean it that way."

"What did you mean?"

"I'm sorry. I need to go." Maggie pushed open the door of the confessional and darted across the narthex as fast as an old woman could dart. She was relieved that Sally and Mabel were already gone but she her heart skipped a beat when the door of the church swung open just as she reached for the handle.

"Patrick?" she asked. "What are you doing here?"

"I was...well..." He said, "Um..." He held a small bouquet of flowers in his right hand. He quickly shifted them to his left and then back to his right.

Maggie didn't wait for an answer. She pulled her black scarf up to keep her just-permed hair from flapping in the wind. Stepping around Patrick, she disappeared into the late autumn afternoon before she met anyone else.

"That was stupid," she muttered to herself as she walked through the cemetery behind St. Michael's. "What's Father Shamus going to think of me now?" *I'll do the rosary and put an extra twenty into the offering.* She kept her head down as she walked and a low hanging branch caught her scarf and nearly choked her. She stopped to adjust the scarf. Regaining her composure, she continued on to Albert's grave in the right front corner, closest to the gate near the street.

She found the wrought iron bench near Albert and sat down. She crossed her legs and her top foot bobbed up and down. It always bobbed when she was agitated or worried what others would think. The tall engraved O'Reilly family monument was lichen encrusted and silent. There was an angel cherub on the top with his finger pressed to his lips as if keeping a secret. To the front and sides, three generations of O'Reilly's rested in peace. But Maggie wished she could disturb their peace, just a bit.

"Albert, it's all your fault. You left me alone with all those kids and I didn't know what to do." She coughed when she was done speaking like she always did when she raised her voice. Maggie didn't wait for an answer, she didn't want one. Whatever Albert had on his mind, it was too late and she didn't care. She got up from the bench and picked up a broken tree limb that had fallen into the path. Getting a good grip with both hands she swung the limb and hit Albert squarely on the headstone. The branch cracked. Albert said nothing. She left through the gate and headed home.

#

Mary Tucker turned north on highway 13 heading out of Baxter to Peterville and her mother's house like she always did on Saturday. The first color of autumn could be seen in the maples along the road. The summer traffic had passed and the highway seemed abandoned. Farmers were preparing their equipment for the harvest. Pumpkins and squash were stacked alongside help-yourself vegetable stands and there was a chill in the air. Mary cracked open her car window to enjoy the freshness of September.

The white picket fence around the O'Reilly house was faded and chipped. Moss and lichens grew on the boards along the ground and the rest was mottled gray like the faces of the parishioners at St. Michael's. The brick house stood on a rise near the center of Peterville. There weren't any hills here or anywhere within sixty miles. A rise was as good as you could get.

Peterville was named after Peter O'Reilly, father of Albert O'Reilly Sr. and grandfather of Maggie's husband, Albert Jr. The business center of the town was built around the train station but as the railroad faded into history most of the town died with it. Any new businesses sprang up along Highway 13 going north and south out of town. The center of town was like an ancient oak, strong appearing but rotting in the center. All that was necessary to end the misery was a strong wind and Peterville would become an asterisk in a history book. A generation back, there were plenty of O'Reillys running around but now, Maggie was the only one left.

Back in the 1800's when the town was in its infancy, Peter O'Reilly was the sheriff and judge. He owned the mercantile and was one of the founders of St. Michael's church. Then came Albert along with eight siblings. Three of them died in early childhood from diphtheria or measles, Mary was never sure which and she didn't want to ask. Apparently, Albert didn't amount to much and being the son of the sheriff and judge he had a get-out-of-jail card whenever he needed it. He got a girl pregnant and became a reluctant member of a shotgun wedding. Albert Jr. was the result, Mary's father.

Mary flipped a strand of red hair out of her face as she turned off the highway into Peterville and parked in the driveway of her childhood home. Before she opened her car door, she paused and took a deep breath as if she was getting ready to jump off a cliff into ice water. She was never quite sure of the depth of the water. Sometimes she could swim, sometimes she was drowning. Today she felt confident because she had a letter in her purse. A letter from David.

CHAPTER 3

Just living is not enough...
one must have sunshine, freedom, and a little flower.
– Hans Christian Andersen

Patrick jerked his head up as he met Maggie at the door.

"Maggie..." he started to say but the words caught in his dry throat and it came out like an awkward hiccup. He shifted the flowers from his right hand into his left and broke one of the stems. The red carnation fell onto the floor and Maggie crushed it with her foot but didn't seem to notice.

"Patrick?" she asked. "What are you doing here?"

"I was...well..." He said, "Um..."

Maggie paused for a moment as if giving Patrick a chance to speak then hurried out the door. The cool September air mixed with the dank musty smell of the old church narthex and it swirled about extinguishing the candles lit in memory of loved ones.

Patrick looked down at the flowers clutched in his hand. Three carnations, one stem bent like his bad knee, one straight and one crushed on the marble floor at his feet. It didn't matter anyway. He twisted the remaining flowers into a bunch and dropped them into the trash can behind the front entrance to St. Michael's.

He dug into the deep pockets of his tweed jacket and pulled out three fresh votives and placed them onto the stone shelf on the right side of the church. He struck a match and the head burst into flame with a pop and a sizzle. He held the flame to the first wick.

His hand trembled, not enough to interfere with his candle lighting task, but enough to annoy him.

"Ethel, there's something I need to ask you." Patrick moved his shaky hand from the first candle to the second. He paused as if waiting for her response. "I've been thinking...you know it's been four years and a month since you left."

There was a slight noise in the back of the church. Patrick turned toward the sound as the match burned closer to his finger.

"Patrick...I thought it was you." Father Shamus said. "Here to light another candle for Ethel, are you?"

Patrick jerked his hand as the flame touched the tip of his index finger. "Son of a..." he started to yell but caught himself in front of the Father. As he snapped his wrist the flaming end of the match flipped through the air and burned a small hole in the left arm of his jacket. The same jacket Ethel bought for him on their 40th wedding anniversary, in Dublin. He slapped the smoldering hole with his right hand and turned away from Father Shamus.

"Patrick, are you alright?" The priest rushed forward inspected the arm of the old man. It was obvious no harm was done but Shamus treated the remaining members of the flock with the same care as a kindergarten teacher putting colorful bandages on little owies.

"I'm fine," Patrick muttered. He turned to leave.

"Did you come for confession?"

"I've nothing to confess, Father." Patrick looked down at his scuffed shoes, embarrassed by his verbal outburst still echoing in the recesses of the church.

"Whatever the Lord lays on your heart. Perhaps just a talk then?"

Patrick shifted his weight from his left foot to his right and back again. He swayed like a tall building in the early stages of an earthquake. "I'd like to ask something but I don't know if you can help me... being the way you are and all."

"I'm not sure I understand." Shamus motioned with his right hand toward the church pews. "Would you like to sit down a spell or would you prefer the confessional?"

"This is stupid" Patrick mumbled.

"Please sit and tell me what's on your mind."

As if on autopilot, Patrick shuffled to one of the church benches and slumped down into the usual spot where he sat every Sunday morning, seven rows from the front on the right side. He hung his head and started speaking.

"Ethel's been gone four years and a month, you know." He began. "I know she was homely but I loved her just the same. We would have been married fifty-two years next week."

Father Shamus cleared his throat softly as if to acknowledge he was listening but he didn't want to interrupt.

"Anyway, I've been having some feelings, not that you would understand, being a priest, the way you are." Patrick paused. He shifted his feet about and rubbed his left index finger in his ear trying to dislodge the ball of wax.

"Why don't you think I would understand?"

"Well...because...you know...you're celibate and all."

"I see."

"I want to move on but I don't think Ethel would approve."

"Patrick, Ethel is dead. She's been gone over four years. There is nothing inappropriate about moving on, as you say."

"I know that, it's just...I don't know how to do it anymore."

"How to do what?"

"How to talk to a woman. After fifty years, you know what the other person is thinking. We didn't need to talk. Every morning she made oatmeal and coffee. I read the paper and she did the crossword puzzle. Every night we had a casserole. She cleaned up the kitchen and I did something in the garage until it was time to watch our shows. We turned on the TV, leaned back in our recliners and fell asleep. When one woke up, we would poke the other and head off to bed. That was the last ten years of our lives together. I don't know how to do it anymore." Patrick took in a deep breath and stopped talking. He rubbed his eyes to wipe away the tears before they made tracks on his face.

"How to do what?"

"You know...be a man, be normal, talk to someone as if they're interested in what you might have to say."

It was deathly quiet in the church. Neither spoke for several minutes. Father Shamus cleared his throat again and said, "I think the best way to learn is practice. Why don't you start by talking to some of the ladies here in church?"

"I couldn't do that. What would they think if I said something to them? I knew you wouldn't understand." Patrick stood up as quick as his bad knee would allow and limped out of the church."

Father Shamus sat quietly for a few minutes before getting up from his seat. He walked to the crushed carnation lying on the floor near the door. He bent and picked it up, turning it over several times in his hands. Speaking softly to himself he said, "Yes, I think I do understand."

CHAPTER 4

The fear of death follows from the fear of life. A
man who lives fully is prepared to die at any time.
-Author unknown

Mary saw her mother's face peek through the parted drapes covering the front window as she opened the door of her silver Toyota. She saw her mother's lips move, likely muttering something about foreign cars. Mary took a deep breath and adjusted the strap of her Coach handbag on her right shoulder before stepping toward the house.

Maggie pulled the front door open as Mary reached the top step of the porch. "Mary, I'm so glad you stopped by. No one ever visits me anymore."

"Mom, I come every week."

"But not for a real visit. No one cares anymore. You feel obligated because I'm old."

"You know that's not true." Mary slipped the handbag from her shoulder and took off her sweater. "I came last week and I know Freddie and Therese were here last month." Mary could feel the pulse in her temples already and she was barely inside the house.

"But you were here only ten minutes last week."

"That's because you argue about everything."

"No, I don't. You're the one arguing. Look you're starting already."

"Mom..."

"You're just like your father."

"Mom..."

"I remember the day you were born he said you were going to be trouble."

"Mom, knock it off."

"Even Father Shamus wonders why none of my children attend church with me anymore."

"Mom, will you just shut up for a minute."

"Don't tell me to shut up. Your father never taught you to respect anyone. Now he was a good man, God rest his soul." Maggie jerked her hands in the form of a cross and her eyes darted upward.

"Mom, when dad was alive you never had anything good to say about him. You fought like cats and dogs." Mary hung her jacket on the hook in the closet and pushed her way past Maggie and went into the kitchen. "Do you have any coffee?"

"Is that what you came for? This isn't Starbucks." Maggie crossed her arms and walked into the sitting room. Mary followed and sat awkwardly on the edge of the chair as if preparing to sprint out of the room.

"I went to visit Tommy last week. He's getting along okay." Mary tapped her right foot. "He's up for parole review next month and could be out by spring if everything goes well."

"I should have whipped that kid when he was little." Maggie said. She paced the length of the sitting room and finally placed herself in the corner chair where she could look out the window toward St. Michael's. "I should have whipped all of you."

"You did," Mary looked away.

"Well...I should have done it more often. I wish Tommy would have been more like David."

"Can we change the subject? I didn't come to rehash the past." Mary asked, "Why are you so angry at me? At all of us? What did we do wrong?"

"No one comes to visit me anymore."

"I do every week."

"It's only because you feel obligated or you want money. I'm never sure which."

"That's not true and you know it." Mary checked her watch. So far, she stayed longer than her last visit. "If you want us to visit more, why don't you act happy to see us. At least fake it for a few minutes."

"Like you do?"

Mary shook her head no. It was quiet in the house for several minutes until Roger the cat strolled into the room and began rubbing against Maggie's leg. His purring seemed to defuse the tension. She looked around the sitting room. There was dust on the framed photos and the piano top.

"I saw Mick Torkelson at the corner gas station," Mary said. "He mentioned having dinner with you last week."

"What's Mick blabbing about now?"

"Nothing really, we were just making small talk."

"Well, don't believe everything you hear. He thinks he's a big shot in town, but he can't handle his putter like he used to."

"Mom?"

"St. Michael's bake sale, bazaar and mini golf tournament. I beat him. He was the champion three years in a row, but not anymore."

Mary felt the tension in her shoulders release. "I thought he was Lutheran?"

"He is, but that's not the worst of it. At the potluck he sat next to me and rested his hand on my thigh, under the table. I felt my heart flutter."

"What did you do?"

"I faked a seizure so he would leave me alone. Now he feels sorry for me and calls every day to see if I'm okay."

"See Mom, people really do care about you. I'm sure he just wants to be friends. That's great."

"You don't know Mick. He's after one thing and it isn't pot roast."

Mary checked her watch again. Thirty minutes and she hadn't thrown anything. "I don't know Mick that well, but it's good to have companionship, isn't it?"

"It's getting worse. Yesterday I met Patrick Murphy coming into St. Michael's with a handful of carnations. It wasn't for Ethel and I know it wasn't for Father Shamus."

"He was bringing you flowers? That's sweet of him."

"He's not as sweet as he lets on. He's the reason Mick lost the tournament. On the fifteenth hole, Patrick and Mick started arguing. Mick poked Patrick in the chest with his putter. Patrick grabbed it and bent it over his knee. It was his handmade putter autographed by Arnold Palmer."

"Are you in the middle of a Peterville love triangle?" Mary couldn't help but smile, just a bit.

"There's no love in this triangle." Maggie stood abruptly and went into the bathroom. From the sitting room, Mary could hear her having a coughing fit.

Maggie coughed into a folded tissue and when she pulled it away from her face there was small spatters of blood. She stared at the blood for a few seconds then quickly crumpled it and tossed it under the bathroom vanity into the trash. When she returned to the sitting room she said, "Mary, I need to go."

"But we were finally having a good conversation. Why the hurry?"

"If you must know, Mick is taking me to the Peterville Pub & Grub for Taco-Tuesday."

"But today's Monday."

"What's the difference? It's the same menu every day, anyway."

"Before I go, have you heard from David recently?"

"David? Why?"

"I was just wondering, that's all." Mary leaned forward and took an envelope out of her purse. "He sent me a letter."

Maggie returned to her chair in the corner. She coughed again into her hand but there was no blood this time. "I remember when he announced about becoming a priest. Albert and I were so proud."

"We were all proud of him." Mary's hand trembled slightly as she handed the letter across the room.

"I wish Tommy and Freddie could have been good boys like David." Maggie said as she took the letter. "Why did he write to you and not to me?"

"He's afraid to talk to you."

"Why?"

"He left the church and moved to San Francisco."

CHAPTER 5

Finding love is like making crème brulee.
It may take a few times before you get it right.
-Crystal Woods

Mick Torkelson snapped a Rod Stewart cassette into his old stereo and cranked the volume. He sang along with a cracked voice, *"Wake up Maggie, I think I've got something to say to you. It's late September and I really should be back at school..."* In his basement workshop he could sing as loud as he pleased without risk of discovery. When the song ended, he continued to hum, even as he picked up his Arnold Palmer autographed putter with the bent shaft.

He held the putter up to the light and peered down the shaft with his good eye. The bend was obvious. He feared any attempt at straightening it would likely break the shaft. *Time to hang it up.*

Mick had driven to Augusta, Georgia in 1964 to watch the Masters. He couldn't afford the admission to the final round but he got tickets to watch the practice rounds. That's when Arnie signed his putter. Ten years ago, Mick had a right knee replacement then a left hip replacement. After that, his golf game failed miserably and Mick was embarrassed to be seen in the clubhouse. He went from a scratch golfer to a twenty-seven handicap on a good day. He quit golfing but every year for St. Michael's bazaar and mini-golf tournament he pulled out his beloved putter and had a few moments of glory. Until last week.

He clenched his jaws and ground his dentures together as he took one last look down the bent shaft. Surprisingly, he felt little anger over the putter's demise. It was Maggie O'Reilly that put a song in his heart. She was the first one to beat him in the mini-golf tournament in four years. He remembered the touch. Mick recalled unfolding his dinner napkin and laying it across his lap. He slipped his left hand under the table and rested it on her thigh. The response was electric. She jerked and her whole body shook for a minute but when Father Shamus Muldoon came to her aid, she announced that she was alright.

Mick put the bent putter carefully on the shelf next to his workbench and turned off the lights. He would win Maggie's heart and if a bent putter was the price to pay, so be it.

#

Shamus Muldoon began his week the way he always did, walking around the town of Peterville. As he walked, he prayed. It helped to clear his mind and after the confession of Maggie O'Reilly a week ago, last Friday, his mind needed clearing. It was obvious that Father Shamus knew it was Maggie in the confessional. But her words kept coming back to haunt him. He barely made it through the Sunday Mass because of what she said. *"I'm planning to kill myself and I need your help."* On Sunday morning he avoided eye contact with her or she avoided him, either way no words were spoken which was odd for a congregation attendance of 13 people.

It didn't make sense to him. He wasn't certain of her age but guessed it hung somewhere between seventy-five and eighty years. When he talked with her, she always seemed perky and vivacious, sharp and witty. He knew she had issues with her family but he didn't know their side of the story, only what she told him. Killing herself seemed out of character. He couldn't believe she would actually do it and struggled to think she would even consider it.

"Good morning Father."

Shamus was jerked back into the present. Patrick Murphy stood on his front step in his bathrobe and slippers. He leaned on his cane as he bent to pick up the Monday edition of the daily paper on his front porch.

"Good morning Patrick. It's good to see you up and about this fine day."

"Good morning to you too, Father. I'm sorry for the way I acted at the church the other day." Patrick looked away as he spoke.

"Think nothing of it," Shamus added, "If you have something you want to talk about, let me know."

"Thanks, it's okay now." He waved and stepped back inside his home with the folded newspaper in his hand. Shamus waved in return and he continued his early morning walk. He had chosen a different route today because it would bring him past the house on the hill, Maggie O'Reilly's home. He checked his watch, 9:20. He hoped it wouldn't be too early to call on Maggie.

As he approached the house, he noticed the front door slightly ajar and Roger the cat was sitting on the front step. "Hello Roger, is Maggie about?" The cat yawned and looked away.

Father Shamus knocked several times. No response. He pulled the door open slightly and stuck his head inside. "Hello Maggie, it's Father Shamus." He listened but heard nothing. "Maggie?"

He walked into the sitting room. No Maggie. No sound. "Hello?" Nothing.

He walked into the kitchen. It was quiet, he heard no sound, no movement. "Maggie?" Father Shamus found his heart beginning to pound. *She wasn't serious, was she?* Then he saw it on the floor, a drop of blood, then another and another leading down the hall. *Oh God, I pray I'm not too late.*

He dashed down the hall following the drops to the bathroom. He burst through the door...

Maggie sat naked on a folded towel over the edge of the bathtub putting a bandage on her leg, just above the ankle. She jerked her arms in the air and lurched backwards. A murderous shriek echoed down the hallway. She landed with a thump, on her back, inside the bathtub, her arms and legs kicking straight up in the air.

"Maggie!?" One part of him was thrilled she was still alive and the rest of him was mortified at what he saw.

Father Shamus stood shocked and frozen. He hesitated between bolting out the door or helping Maggie out of the tub. Naked Maggie with her arms and legs flailing about, searching for a grip.

"I thought you killed yourself."

"Oh, for the love of Pete! Don't you believe in knocking?" She reached up with her right arm toward him. "Well you've seen me in my birthday suit, now help me out of here." Her hands and arms were still slippery from lotion and his grip was tenuous, but he wasn't certain he wanted to grab anywhere else. Shamus bent forward to assist Maggie out of the bathtub. His foot slipped on the wet floor and he pitched forward. There was a dull thud as his right cheekbone struck the far side of the clawfoot tub. Maggie gasped for air as she felt his heavy limp body collapse on her.

Maggie squirmed and pushed but she was too weak to move Father Shamus. His unconscious body pinned her against the side and bottom of the wet bathtub. She grunted and pushed but she couldn't free herself.

"Father Shamus, are you okay?" There was no response. "Father Shamus?"

She could hear his labored breathing. *At least he's alive.* She cocked her head as far to the left as her old neck and the side of the bathtub would allow, trying to get a look at him. His right eye was already nearly swollen shut. His head was pressed against her chest and she could hear his nose making sucking noises when he inhaled and whistled when he exhaled. She manipulated her own anatomy to allow him room to breathe. The newspaper headlines of tomorrow flashed through her mind: *Priest Suffocated in Bathtub by Naked Woman.*

CHAPTER 6

Life is the art of drawing without an eraser.
– John Gardner

Maggie was trapped and for the moment she had no options. She couldn't wiggle free. She couldn't push Father Shamus out of the way and he remained unconscious. She considered yelling but was afraid of who might respond. She had no phone in the bathroom and even if she did, who would she call? Not Mick or Patrick. Not her children. The police? Never. They would file a report. Sally or Mabel? Certainly not. In the end she decided it was better to die naked under a priest than to be found alive in this condition. Minutes passed and Father Shamus was no closer to recovery. She thought there was a noise from the front room but with her grunting and his breathing she couldn't be certain. She paused and held her breath again. Then she heard it.

The doorbell. Her front door creaked opened.

"Hello? Maggie?"

"Who's there?" Maggie yelled as best she could. It sounded like she was yelling from deep in a cave.

"It's Sally. We have our beauty shop appointment today. It was my turn to drive. Remember?"

Maggie could hear her walking about. She pushed as hard as she could against Shamus but he was dead weight. He suddenly made a loud snoring noise as if sucking in his last breath. His head jerked back and it clunked against the side of the bathtub.

"Aunnnngggh." He groaned so loud it sounded like the Angel of Death had come to call.

"Maggie are you okay?" Maggie could hear Sally's footsteps in the hall, approaching the bathroom.

Maggie yanked her right hand free and slapped it over his mouth. "I'm fine. Just a bit of constipation."

"I heard you groaning. Are you hurt?"

Father Shamus began to struggle. He jerked his head trying to breathe. *She's going to hear him.* Maggie pressed harder. *I have to get rid of her.*

"I need a laxative," she yelled.

"I have some at my house, do you want me to get it?"

"Yes...No. Go to Olson's Drug store and get something."

"What do you want? I use Milk of Magnesia but Richard liked prune juice. I never did like the taste of prune juice. He always said..."

"Richard is dead. I don't care what he said. Just go, I need it bad." Maggie pressed her hand tighter. Shamus started to mumble and groan louder. *Say something, cover the noise.* "OH, SAY CAN YOU SEE, BY THE DAWN'S EARLY LIGHT..." Maggie belted out the lyrics as loud as she could.

"Maggie why are you singing? Are you watching a football game in there?"

"I always sing when I'm constipated. Hurry..."

Maggie heard the front door close. She relaxed her grip over his mouth and removed her hand. She could see the blanched outline of her fingers pressed into his cheeks and lips. Shamus blinked and thrashed about.

"Father Shamus, wake up."

It was another minute before he was functionally conscious. He stared blankly out of his left eye. His right eye was swollen shut. Suddenly he pushed himself off of Maggie and struggled to climb over the side of the bathtub.

"What happened?" He asked.

"If you don't remember, I'm not going to tell you." Maggie pushed herself into a sitting position.

"Let me help you," he said.

"You've done enough helping. Just hand me that towel." She pointed toward the big white towel hanging on the back of the door.

Shamus handed her the towel and exited the bathroom as gracefully as he could. Maggie wrapped the towel around her body and headed to her bedroom down the hall. She knew Sally was slow but it still didn't give them much time. She toweled off and threw on some clothes. She pulled her wet hair back and wrapped an elastic hair tie around it. No time for makeup.

When she was properly covered Maggie took a deep breath and walked down the hall. Father Shamus had already cleaned up the drops of blood on the floor. He blushed when their eyes met. Maggie couldn't help laughing.

"Oh, Father Shamus. It's the most excitement I've had in years. That should get the girls at the parish talking."

"I pray they will never know." Shamus took a damp wash cloth and dabbed his forehead. "Maggie, I am so sorry."

"You won't be able to keep it a secret."

"Why?"

"Your face looks like an overripe eggplant." Maggie took a small gel icepack from her kitchen freezer and handed it to Shamus.

"You didn't mean it did you?"

"What? About keeping this a secret?"

"No. What you said in confession... about killing yourself. I saw the blood on the floor and I thought..."

"You thought I killed myself?" Maggie giggled.

"What would you think? You said you were going to kill yourself and then I saw blood on the floor." Father Shamus adjusted the ice pack over the throbbing purple mass on his right cheek.

"I can't tell you now. Sally McTavish is coming back with a jug of prune juice. If she sees you like this, you'll have to leave town."

"Prune juice?"

"You wouldn't believe me if I told you." Maggie pulled back the curtains in the front room and watched for Sally's green Buick. "Here she is now. Wait ten minutes and go out the back door, and for Pete's sake, don't let anyone see you."

"But..."

Maggie was already heading out the front door before Sally could come to a complete stop in her driveway. She could see the look of surprise on Sally's face.

"I have your prune juice. I couldn't find the Milk of Magnesia so I bought some Ex-lax. I hope that's okay."

Maggie glanced back at the house as she climbed into the passenger side of the car. Roger the cat was still on the front step. "It doesn't matter now. Everything passed."

"I'm impressed. I'm going to try singing the next time I have trouble."

#

Father Shamus walked back into the bathroom, trying to piece together the morning's events. The last thing he recalled was leaning forward to help Maggie. His head throbbed. He looked into the mirror to assess his situation. His hair was matted. His shirt was wet and there was blood on the right shoulder. His face was worse.

The right side of his face was a giant plum gone bad. It was a dark, pulsing purple with a blood-filled blister forming over the cheekbone. There was a shallow cut over the eyebrow and blood ran down his cheek and onto his shirt. He winced as he tried to pry open his eyelid. When he got his eye lids far enough apart to see light, he was satisfied. At least he wasn't blind.

It took him a few minutes to find the bandages. He stuck two of them on his eyebrow the best he could and headed out the back door.

A dog barked near the street and he heard a snarl from Roger. Father Shamus ducked around the side of the house as Roger rushed past, followed by a wiener dog, dragging a short leash.

"Father Shamus?"

He squinted with his good eye to see the owner of the wiener dog, chasing the free end of the leash.

"Patrick?"

CHAPTER 7

I made my money the old-fashioned way.
I was very nice to a wealthy relative right before he died.
-Malcolm Forbes

Freddie O'Reilly checked the return address on the envelope as he pulled a letter opener from his top desk drawer. He didn't know why he was opening it, he already knew the contents. Another late notice on his car payment and his checking account was overdrawn. He grabbed the next envelope and tore it open. The credit card statement glared back at him. The total was only $4789. 67 but the minimum payment due was $119.75 plus a $35 late fee and his interest rate was bumped to 25.9%. There was a list of recent charges by Therese for three new pairs of shoes and dinner plus a tip at the Kyoto Sushi Bar and Steak House.

Fred dropped the letter back onto his desk and reached for his phone. He touched the speed dial icon for his wife, Therese, then hit cancel. He dropped the phone back on his desk and cradled his head in his hands. *It isn't working. It's never going to work this way.*

Vodka was his friend when he was alone. It lied to him every day, promising a pain free life, but it never delivered. Therese said she loved him but he was never sure if it was genuine or if it was conditional. He wondered about his mother too. *Does she love me? Does she really care?*

It was nineteen years ago when he and Therese were married. They met their first year in college. She was the cute girl with all the answers. She sat near the front during lectures and was the first one to raise her hand for questions. Fred sat in the back and slept most of the time. He came late, left early and listened to Bon Jovi on his iPod during class. She always completed class assignments on time and he procrastinated until it was too late.

In the spring of their senior year he proposed and she accepted. Both families went through contortions trying to dissolve the relationship, ironically for the same reason. He was Catholic and she was Southern Baptist. His mother, Maggie threatened to disown him and barely mentioned his name for a year after they were married. Therese's parents seemed a bit more accepting but only because he started attending their church, the Second Baptist Church of Crowley, Iowa. But that didn't last very long either because the church was praying for the Catholics, ranking them between heathens, Hell's Angels and aboriginal headhunters. Fred was confused and stopped attending altogether.

Two years later they moved to Baxter to be nearer to Maggie. After Albert died, Freddie felt an obligation to be closer to his mother but Therese wasn't happy. Their marriage was tepid at best. He worked. She spent. He complained about her. She ignored his ranting. He visited his mother. She didn't.

Over time, he tried talking with his mother and sporadically attended Sunday Mass with her at St. Michael's Parish. Their relationship was amiable but never warm. He and Eliza were the middle children, the forsaken ones. Mary was the strong willed one. David was the chosen one. As far as Maggie was concerned, David couldn't walk on water yet, but sainthood was certain to follow. Freddie could barely slog through mud.

Freddie knew that brooding over his middle child status wasn't going to solve his problems. He was deep in debt and needed money. He and Therese asked her parents for money several years ago. They chastised him for being lazy and not providing for his family. Therese was crying, her father was stern faced and her mother tried to smooth it all with tea and cookies. In the end Freddie and Therese received a thousand-dollar loan but they had to sign an agreement and pay it back with interest. From that day on, Freddie decided he would rather have a root canal without anesthesia than ask her parents for a dollar.

Winning the lottery wasn't likely. Crime didn't suit him like his older brother, Tommy. That left his mother as the only logical source for a bailout. But he couldn't bring himself to ask her. He decided to ask Mary to ask their mother for help, but felt ashamed. He was forty-four years old and he couldn't get ahead. He couldn't break even. He poured a glass full of cheap vodka and took a deep swallow.

#

David O'Reilly checked the caller ID on his iPhone and turned off the sound. He turned his head and looked out the restaurant window toward Fisherman's Wharf. His friend, Steven drained the last drops of his Paso Robles Chardonnay from his glass and furrowed his brow as he stared at David.

"Aren't you going to answer your phone?"

"It's my mother."

"You don't want to talk to her?"

"You wouldn't understand. When I went to seminary to be a priest, my parents acted like they won the lottery. They had a backyard party bigger than my sister's wedding reception." David turned his eyes down and was quiet.

"What have you told her?"

"I haven't talked to her in six months. Not since this spring when I was home." David picked up his phone to see if there was a voice mail notification. There was.

"What are you afraid of?" Steven asked, "Are you embarrassed about us or the fact you left the church?"

"Are you my therapist?" David asked.

"When you moved to San Francisco you said 'it's the happiest day of my life'. But for the past week you've been moody and short tempered. I don't care if you talk to your mother or not. Just deal with it."

"Let me ask you a question. When do you stop being controlled by your parents? When you're twenty-one? When you're thirty? When you're fifty?"

"Never."

"Are you serious?"

"Not even when they are dead," he said. "Look at it this way. When you are a baby you want to please your parents. When you are a child you seek their approval by giving them crayon drawings and hugs before bedtime. It doesn't change as you get older. You choose friends and careers and living arrangements, subconsciously motivated by your desire for parental approval."

"That's a crock. Where did you hear that?"

"I read it in Good Housekeeping."

"So, you think everything we do is motivated by our subconscious relationship with our parents?" David shook his head.

"Of course. Why are you running away from her?" Steven asked.

"I'm not running away from anything."

"Then maybe you should talk to your mom. She obviously wants to talk to you."

His phone beeped again. His mother had called three times in the past week and she was calling again. He didn't want to talk to her. Not now. Maybe not ever.

CHAPTER 8

Given the choice between the experience of pain and nothing,
I would choose pain.
-William Faulkner

Maggie sat in the straight-backed waiting room chairs thumbing through old magazines. People to her right and left, hacked and sniffed and wheezed on each other until the nurse called their names. She watched one old man make three trips to the restroom in the past twenty minutes. On the other side of the room a teenage boy looked sullen with his ankle in a brace and a pair of crutches leaning against his leg. Patrick Murphy sat in the corner of the waiting room with a dogeared Readers Digest in his hand. He stared at Maggie but every time she glanced toward him, his eyes darted away.

Maggie tried to quell the urge to cough. She held the tissue ready in her left hand but the tickle in her chest slowly subsided. Maggie nodded toward Patrick but he turned away. She shifted her position so she could look at him without turning her head but every time their eyes met, he seemed to jump. *Why is Patrick acting strange?* Maggie checked her watch. She had been waiting for nearly a half-hour. She looked up as Patrick's shadow passed over her.

"I wrote to the Bishop," he said.

"That's nice," Maggie replied. "I hope Bishop O'Connor is well."

"I don't think you understand. I wrote to the Bishop about Father Muldoon."

"What about him?" Maggie gripped her tissue, feeling another tickle in her chest.

"I think you know," Patrick said. He slowly raised his right hand and touched his right eye.

"What is that supposed to mean?" She mirrored his actions and touched her own right eye. Maggie's heart skipped a beat as she recalled the events of the past week. In a flash, she knew that he knew. But how much did he know?

"I saw him come out of your house. You can't deny it." He smiled. His broken front tooth mocked her.

"Father Shamus was helping me out of the bathtub when he fell in," she said. Maggie held the tissue to her mouth and squelched the cough once more.

"You're lying. Father Shamus would never do that." Patrick took a step back trying to grasp what she just said.

"Believe what you want." Maggie picked up the newspaper again as if the discussion was over.

"Then why did you leave with Sally through the front door and he went out the back door? Huh? Tell me that one." Patrick started to shake. His voice got louder and the other patients in the waiting room stopped reading old magazines and focused on Patrick. "Do you think I don't know what's going on between you two?"

"Are you spying on me?"

"I live down the street. I can see your house from my front window."

"I know what you're thinking but there's nothing going on between us."

"Then what is it?" His finger shook as he pointed directly at her face. His nose and cheeks flushed and his face went from a ghostly white to a ruddy blue cast. "I want to know the truth."

"What would you do with the truth? Would you bend Mick's putter again? You're just a jealous old man still living in the past. Ethel is dead and you can't deal with it."

Patrick's face went blank and he stared at Maggie. He dropped his arm and stood still, unblinking in the middle of the waiting room. The other patients waiting for their turn to be called, became silent. One young mother grabbed her toddler and retreated to the corner. The receptionist stopped checking insurance cards with her hand poised over the phone as if to call 911 for police backup. The nurse opened the side door to the examination area without speaking and motioned toward Maggie. She stood up from her chair and stared into the bulging eyes of Patrick Murphy. "What if I told you I was dying and Father Muldoon was there to give me my last rites? What would you do about that?"

"You're lying."

"If I am dying, you aren't invited to the funeral." She stepped past Patrick and went through the door.

#

"Hello?"

"David? This is Mary."

"Hi Mary. I suppose you are calling about mother." David sounded subdued. "How did she take it?"

"Better than I expected," Mary said. "I gave her the letter."

"What did she say?"

"First, she seemed angry, then she went quiet and her face got really pale. I thought she was going to faint." Mary was quiet for a few moments as she organized her thoughts. "She didn't swear or yell or throw anything. She paced around the house for a few minutes but didn't say much. At least she wasn't picking on me."

"She's called my phone three or four times over the past couple days but I didn't answer." David's voice trailed off as if he was walking away.

"David, you need to talk to her, soon. How would you feel if something happened to her and you missed the chance? She's getting old, anything could happen." Mary realized how much she had become the surrogate parent for her siblings.

"She'll never forgive me. She and dad bragged about my plans for seminary and now..."

"Now what? This isn't the end of your life. Most people make career changes."

"Not if you're a priest."

"What do you want?" Mary asked.

"I'm not sure. I feel like I destroyed her trust in me and I guess I just wanted to make her proud. That's all I've ever wanted." The phone was quiet for several minutes, neither Mary nor David spoke.

"Do you care about her?" Mary asked.

"Of course. She's our mother."

"Have you told her?"

"No, but she's never said, 'I love you' to me either and I've never heard it from you or anyone else for that matter."

"Some people express their love in different ways. In our family we yelled and argued all the time. If we didn't kill each other, that meant we loved each other. Does that make sense?" Mary wondered at her own words. It didn't make sense. She was making excuses for her mother and herself.

"Alright Mary, let me ask you a question. If Mom had a stroke and needed to live with one of us, would you do it?" David asked.

"Do what?"

"Take her in and care for her?"

"Are you kidding me? She'd be in a nursing home before she hit the floor." As she ended the call she wondered if her own children would say the same about her.

CHAPTER 9

Never go to a doctor whose office plants have died.
-Erma Bombeck

"What seems to be the problem today, Mrs. O'Reilly?" The young nurse with a long pony tail and a Halloween pattern scrub top wrapped the blood pressure cuff around her left upper arm and started pumping without waiting for an answer.

"I have a cough."

"What was that? I couldn't hear you when I was checking your blood pressure."

"Then don't ask a question until you're ready to listen." Maggie picked up another tissue and coughed into it.

"It sounds like you have a bad cough," the nurse said. She jotted down the blood pressure reading on the intake sheet, 147/89, pulse 78.

"A cough? I hadn't noticed. I came in for a pregnancy test."

"You're not serious, are you?"

"I'm dead serious and I don't know who the father is." Maggie coughed again.

"Then I need to ask some more questions. Have you ever had an STD?"

"A what?"

"STD, sexually transmitted disease."

"I could only hope..."

"Okay then. You'll have to pee in this cup and then get undressed and put this paper gown on. The doctor will be in shortly."

"Honey, look at me. I was born before the Korean War. The last time a man touched my leg I went into convulsions. I'm not going to strip naked and wrap myself in paper towels. You can tell the doctor what you want. And take that cup with you."

"Maybe you're depressed?"

"I wasn't when I came in but I'm moving in that direction."

"Have you lost interest in things you once found enjoyable?"

Maggie thought for a moment. At seventy-seven, she had lost interest in nearly everything she once found enjoyable; friends, family, food, sex, shopping, she couldn't think of anything to say. *If I say yes, they'll have me in counseling and on drugs before I walk out the door and if I say no, they'll know I'm lying.*

"Mrs. O'Reilly, have you lost interest in things you once found enjoyable?"

"On second thought, let's do that pregnancy test. And leave the paper gown."

Maggie stripped down and tucked the pink paper gown around her lean but sagging, one hundred-twenty-five pounds. The doctor opened the door in a whoosh, sending Maggie's paper fashion statement fluttering like a napkin in a wind storm. The front of her gown blew open and the breeze rushed through the arm openings. Her skin puckered at the cold intrusion.

"Mrs. O'Reilly, I'm Doctor Smith." He barely made eye contact as he logged into the computer terminal sitting on the desk. "What seems to be the trouble today?"

"Didn't the nurse tell you?" She asked.

The doctor flipped through a couple sheets of paper which had been clipped outside the examination room door. "You think you're pregnant?" Doctor Smith asked. "Are you serious? At your age?"

"How old do you think I am?"

"It says you're seventy-seven. I hate to tell you, but that's beyond the normal childbearing years, Mrs. O'Reilly."

"Why don't you tell that to the little tart who put me in the room." Maggie waited for an answer and watched Dr. Smith type something into the electronic medical record under her name. She couldn't read everything from her perch between the stirrups but she did see *delusional and anti-social behavior.*

"Mrs. O'Reilly I'm giving you a prescription for an antidepressant. Start taking it at bedtime and if you aren't feeling better in six weeks, come back and see me." He scribbled something on a gray prescription pad and handed it to her.

Maggie took the prescription, she folded it once and ripped it twice. She let the paper fragments flutter to the floor. "Doctor, let's get something straight. I came in here with a simple problem and no one listened to me; not the receptionist, not the nurse and certainly not you. I didn't get undressed for nothing. When you get done running your hands all over me, I'll tell you the real reason and not a minute before. Understand?"

"But Mrs. O'Reilly..." He stuttered for a few minutes. "I should get a nurse to be in the room with us."

"You can get the janitor and the UPS driver if you want but I'm not leaving until it's done."

When Doctor Smith was done with the examination, he washed his hands and dabbed the sweat from his forehead. Maggie pulled out a tissue from her purse and held it open to the doctor. A smudge of dried blood rested in the creases. "This is the reason I came in," she said as she handed it over to him.

"How long has this been happening?" he asked.

"It happened three times over the past two weeks."

After a handful of additional questions, Dr. Smith returned to his computer terminal and started punching the keys. "You need more tests. I ordered a CT scan, blood tests and a referral to a lung specialist.

"What's your opinion," Maggie asked.

"I don't want to alarm you but it could be serious."

"Don't do the song and dance with probabilities and statistics. Just give it to me straight."

"It could be as simple as a ruptured blood vessel or an infection."

"Or...? She asked.
"It could be lung cancer."

CHAPTER 10

What butter and whiskey won't cure, there is no cure for.
-Irish Proverb

Father Shamus Muldoon stepped slowly to the front of the church. The purple remnants of his visit with Maggie were migrating down his face leaving a widening puddle of yellow and green below the spot where his cheekbone met the bathtub, but his eye was open and he could see the faces of the parishioners staring back at him. He looked from Sally to Mabel to Patrick and finally he rested his eyes on Maggie O'Reilly. He felt his face flush, amplifying the tenderness of his cheek.

"In the name of the Father, and the Son and the Holy Ghost. Amen." He waved his right arm in the shape of the cross.

"Amen," they said in unison. Maggie coughed.

Mabel Feely leaned toward Sally and whispered as people on edge of deafness whisper, "What happened to Father Muldoon?" In the cavernous bowels of the church the hoarse whisper reverberated across the empty pews. The question on everyone's mind was asked.

Father Muldoon was facing the altar when he heard the whisper. A tremor went through him as if a magnitude 4.1 earthquake just cracked Peterville. Before turning toward, the congregation, he waited to see if there was an aftershock. He counted the throbbing pulse in his swollen cheek as his brain filed through his premeditated responses.

"It's her fault." Father Muldoon turned to see Patrick Murphy on his feet, pointing at Maggie. "I caught him coming out of Maggie's back door with a black eye."

Sally and Mabel gasped in unison. Several of the Sunday Mass visitors fidgeted in their seats as the St. Michael's family drama unfolded. The candles on the altar flickered from an unseen breeze and two of them went out.

Father Muldoon raised his right hand and said, "Let us pray."

"You'd better be praying," Patrick announced. "I wrote to Bishop O'Connor about this."

"Patrick, how can you be so mean?" Mabel twisted her head to the left trying to take in the glowering menace from the seventh row. "I'm sure there's a good explanation." She turned back to face Father Shamus. Everyone waited for the good explanation.

Maggie spoke up. "Father Shamus is innocent of whatever your perverted minds can conjure."

"Then why did you leave by the back door?" Patrick was starting to shake again. "You're guilty, I know you're guilty."

"Guilty of what?" Sally asked. "When did this happen?"

"Monday, I was walking Pickles, my wiener dog. I dropped her leash and she ran behind Maggie's house. When I got there, Father Muldoon was coming around the corner with a black eye and he was alone."

"Monday? The day I picked you up for the beauty shop?" Sally asked as she turned toward Maggie.

Maggie said nothing.

"I heard a noise in the bathroom," Sally said. "Maggie was singing the Star Bangled Banner. When I asked what was wrong, she said she was constipated." Sally stopped talking and turned toward Maggie. Her eyes opened wide. She held her right hand over her open mouth. "Father Shamus was in the bathroom with you, wasn't he? That's why you wanted me to go to Olson's drug store to buy a laxative."

Sally's face went pale and she slumped forward until her nose hit the back of the pew in front of her. There was a gentle crack, the same sound you get when cracking salted peanuts at Christmas. Blood spurted out of her left nostril. Sunday Mass at St. Michael's Parish ended early.

#

Mick Torkelson perched on the red vinyl, round topped stool at the breakfast counter. Main Street Café was his customary haunt on weekdays. His favorite was the greasy hash browns and salty omelets, topped with a healthy dose of local gossip. It was Monday morning but instead of the usual five or six people the place was abuzz with activity and chatter.

"So, what's the news?" he asked the waitress as she sloshed some weak coffee into a chipped mug and pushed it in front of him.

"You haven't heard?"

"What?" Mick took a long slurp of his coffee and set in down beside the menu.

"Old Sally McTavish got her nose broke in church. They called the police and the ambulance."

"Sally? Not surprised. She's probably nippin' at the communion wine." Mick said.

"Not what I heard." Mick turned to see who was talking. Gus Rasmussen, a local farmer sat at the table behind him. "Did you see his face?"

"Who?" the waitress asked.

"The priest, Father Muldoon." Gus looked around to make sure people were listening. He raised his voice a bit. "His cheek looked like a purple cabbage run over by a tractor. I heard Muldoon said something to Sally and she hit him with her cane, then old Pat Murphy punched the priest in the face. That's what I heard."

"My mother, Mabel attends St. Michael's and she said there's a love triangle between the priest and Maggie O'Reilly and Patrick Murphy." Tim Feely the local barber nodded toward his fellow breakfast diners. "I guess Shamus Muldoon and Patrick Murphy got into a fight over Maggie and Sally got in the middle of it."

Mick perked up when he heard Maggie's name. "Love triangle? With Father Muldoon?"

"Yep. Mom said Sally caught him and Maggie singing songs together in the bathroom last Monday. I think the priest was getting frisky and Maggie laid him out with a single punch." Tim picked up his fork and took a big stab at his hash browns and poached eggs. "You never can tell, can you?"

"Is Maggie okay?" Mick asked.

Another local spoke up, "Maggie's fine, nothing happened to her, but I heard Sally got airlifted to Rochester."

"Not true," Barney Middleton said. "My daughter works in the ER in Baxter. I guess her nose was more crooked than a politician but they had a specialist come in and give her a nose job."

"In Baxter?" someone else asked. "I didn't know they could do nose jobs in Baxter."

The chatter gradually shifted from Sally's nose and the Catholic love triangle to Botox in Baxter. Mick gobbled down his bacon and cheese omelet and left a generous tip on the counter.

It was time to visit Maggie.

CHAPTER 11

Good judgment comes from experience,
and experience comes from bad judgment.
-Rita Mae Brown

Shamus Muldoon stood alone in the middle of St. Michael's. The only remaining sound was the ringing in his ears. The EMT's and first responders were gone. He had given his statement to the police. The last of the meager congregation had long since departed and he just finished wiping down the church pews with hydrogen peroxide.

He walked toward the altar of the church and stopped before a statuette of the Virgin. "I'm innocent you know," he said to her as he raised his eyes toward heaven. Her porcelain lips were silent, her glazed eyes unmoving. He regretted not defending himself but there was no time. The accusations, the rumors, Sally's encounter with the back of the church pew and it was over. There was a heaviness in his heart, not just for Sally but for all of them. He liked it in Peterville. The Bishop was fair and would hear his side of the story but he doubted he would be allowed to remain after the scandal. He glanced again at the Virgin. There would be no miracles today, at least not for Father Shamus Muldoon, parish priest for St. Michael's in Peterville.

#

Mary reached for her reading glasses to study the photo on her computer screen. Facebook was full of junk. She posted occasionally but she wasn't one to display the trivia of her life for the rest of the world's entertainment. However, she was a browser, lurking in the shadows, living vicariously through the quips and comments of others.

A former high school classmate still living in Peterville posted a photo of Father Shamus Muldoon. His face was disfigured and with an iridescent shade of violet over the right cheekbone. His eye was nearly swollen shut and his mouth formed the word "no" as if he were reacting to the one holding the camera. His good eye was wide and there was no mistaking his thoughts. It wasn't a selfie.

But it wasn't just the photo that captured her attention, it was the comments that followed. Suspected love affair at St. Michael's. Father Shamus Muldoon and church member Maggie O'Reilly were discovered together in her bathroom, last Monday, by another parishioner. Rumors have been flying around Peterville regarding the nature of his injury. All of this led to an argument in Sunday Mass and one of the ladies of the church, Sally McTavish, was seriously injured and taken to the hospital. Following the post were 173 comments. Like sharks in a feeding frenzy, most of the comments were crass and degrading. Some of the comments were in support of Father Muldoon. None of the comments supported Maggie.

#

Maggie spent Sunday afternoon in a fitful state. She stayed in her home with the drapes pulled and the lights off. Her television was turned off and she didn't listen to the radio or music. The only sound was the creaking of her hardwood floor as she paced and the monotonous drip of her kitchen faucet.

She pulled out some stationary and started a letter, first to Bishop O'Connor and then to the church in general. After writing several drafts, she crumpled the letters and tossed them into her trash. *It doesn't matter. They aren't interested in the truth.* But as distressed as she was about the events in Sunday Mass, it was her own fate that gave her the greatest concern.

She was scheduled for a CT scan of her chest this coming week and was to see the pulmonologist the following day. She no longer coughed up any blood but in her mind the boneyard was looming. Maggie pulled a pack of cigarettes from her purse and lit one, but after three puffs she snuffed it out.

I'm going to die and nobody cares. She picked up her phone and called St. Michael's. After seven rings the answering machine answered. "This is Father Shamus Muldoon. I'm not able to take your call but please leave a message and I will call you back as soon as I can. Have a nice day and God bless you." She didn't leave a message. Next, she tried his cellphone. Again, no answer but after the beep she said, "Father Shamus, this is Maggie. I need to talk to you soon."

Ten minutes later her home phone rang.

"Maggie, I'm sorry about what happened."

"I don't care about that. Let the rumors fly."

"That's easy for you. My reputation is ruined."

"You never did anything wrong. I'll swear on a stack of Bibles, on your behalf but I need you to help me first."

"Maggie, I'd do anything to help you. You're the only one who believes me. How can I help you?"

"Meet me at the Baxter bowling alley, tomorrow for lunch."

"Is it urgent?"

"Yes."

"What are you planning?"

"It's about a dead body and I need you to lie about it."

CHAPTER 12

*I have left orders to be awakened at any time during
national emergency, even if I'm in a cabinet meeting."*
— Ronald Reagan

Dr. Grant Smith sat at his desk and looked up at the framed
Hippocratic Oath hanging above his desk. He was bound ethically
by the oath and he was bound legally by current privacy laws but
internally he struggled with the idea of breaking the confidence of
a patient for the good of the patient.

He logged into his computer and pulled up the medical file of
Maggie O'Reilly and reviewed the past entries. It appeared Maggie
probably drank too much alcohol, she smoked cigarettes and
wasn't interested in quitting. She was in the clinic on average, once
or twice a year to check her blood pressure and cholesterol but she
refused all medications. She was usually evaluated by one of the
physician's assistants. He had seen her only once in the past two
years and that was for an accidental cut on her hand from a
kitchen knife. On the positive side, she got a flu shot every year.

He found no entries regarding depression or delusional behavior, but he couldn't forget her recent clinic visit. He remembered feeling startled and intimidated by the skinny old lady. He
had agreed to do the pregnancy test only because she demanded it.
If his colleagues knew he ordered it, he would be laughed out of
town. He later cancelled the order so it wouldn't be in her records,
citing error as the reason for the original order.

He found her next of kin in the demographics file and jotted down Mary's phone number. Twice he dialed the number and twice he cancelled the call before anyone answered. On the third time he waited.

"Hello?"

"Is this Mary O'Reilly, daughter of Margaret O'Reilly?" Dr. Smith asked.

"Mary Tucker is my married name, but yes, I'm her daughter. Is something wrong?" Mary sat down as if preparing for bad news.

"This is Dr. Grant Smith. I'm a physician at the Baxter clinic. Your mother came it to see me a couple days ago."

"Is she dying?"

"I don't think so, at least not yet. But that's not the reason I'm calling. I need more information." Dr. Smith adjusted a yellow legal pad on his desk and picked up a pen. "How would you describe your mother?"

"She's about 5'4" tall. She seems..."

"I'm sorry, I meant mentally, you know...psychologically."

Mary was quiet for several minutes before speaking. "Doctor, I assume you understand statistics."

"Yes, of course."

"If most of us are average, my mother is two standard deviations from the mean."

"Do you think she is unstable...at risk?"

"At risk for what? Too much alcohol?"

"Would you consider her a vulnerable adult so that someone could take advantage of her?"

"Mick Torkelson has been trying to take advantage of her for years."

"I'm sorry, who is Mick Torkelson?"

"He's an old Lutheran widower living in Peterville. He got his putter all bent out of shape during an argument over Maggie."

"So...you think she is vulnerable?"

"I don't know how to answer your question. There was just a thing posted on Facebook about her being involved with the priest of St. Michael's Parish. One of the other women of the church supposedly caught my mother singing the Star-Spangled Banner in the bathroom with Father Muldoon, the parish priest." Mary stopped to clear her throat. "There's a photo of the priest with a big purple bruise on his cheek."

"Is this normal behavior for your mother?"

"Like I said, she's two standard deviations from the mean."

"Is your mother promiscuous?"

"She's been a widow for many years."

"Please let me explain. When she was here at my office, she requested a pregnancy test."

There was a long pause in the conversation, finally Mary said, "My mother is a strict Catholic and she's proud of it. Promiscuity isn't in her vocabulary." She paused again. "Are you sure this is what she wanted?"

"I'm certain. The nurse heard it too. She wanted a pregnancy test and a complete physical exam to make certain. And she said she didn't know who the father was." Dr. Smith cleared his throat. "I have a couple more questions if you don't mind. Does your mother have financial resources?"

Mary said, "She's a frugal as a monk but she's got plenty of money. My father died young with a generous life insurance policy. I don't know if she has a will. I've tried talking to her about it, but she always seems vague and doesn't answer my questions."

"Mrs. Tucker, I have some serious concerns about your mother." Dr. Smith paused and scribbled notes as he spoke. "I'm worried about her mental state. She could be developing dementia, she could have a brain tumor or she could just be suffering from mental illness, or all of the above."

"What should we do?"

"Keep this confidential but write down your observations. If you see a pattern of abnormal behavior that you consider risky, then you will have to petition the court for a competency evaluation."

"I'm not sure I understand." Mary's throat was dry. She felt her pulse rising.

"This is a psychological assessment signed by two different physicians declaring a person incapable of managing their own resources or even incapable of caring for themselves. The court would then appoint a guardian to manage the estate and make decisions on her behalf."

"I know my mother, and she would never consent to any of this voluntarily."

"That's the problem with these cases. If someone has a diagnosis of dementia or mental illness, they may not know they are a risk to themselves or others. Common problems are loss of memory, aggressive or hypersexual behavior, impulsiveness, giving away large amounts of money to strangers and so on."

Mary thanked Dr. Smith for his concern. When the conversation was over, she took two ibuprofen and poured herself a cup of coffee with a generous shot of Bailey's Irish Cream. She went over her list of siblings trying to decide who was going to be the first one to call. David had his own issues, Tommy was in prison and Freddie had marriage and money issues. That left Eliza who was saving the whales, somewhere in Portland.

Mary dialed the latest number she had for Eliza and left a message.

"Liz, this is Mary. I'm calling about Mom. I got a call from a local doctor. He thinks her cheese has finally slipped off her cracker."

CHAPTER 13

The hardest thing to learn in life
is which bridge to cross and which bridge to burn.
-David Russell

Baxter Lanes was a business that lingered outside the margins of prosperity. It was located on the end of a side street, so far
out of the main avenues of traffic that it remained obscure to many
locals and unknown to travelers. It had eight lanes but two of them
were damaged from a leaking roof and never repaired. They had
cheap beer and great bacon cheeseburgers which made a good
lunch stop for those who knew how to get there and it was a good
place to meet without attracting suspicion.

The fall bowling league was just forming and several clip-
boards hung on the wall awaiting team signup. Maggie recognized
most of the names. They were the same, year after year, changing
only when someone died. Over the years many of the teams had
shrunk in size, merging with others until just a few diehards remained.

Father Shamus was a bowler but he wasn't great. He had a
163 average which wasn't bad for Baxter but the serious bowlers
wouldn't consider him as a competitive team member. The main
forms of recreation in the Peterville and Baxter area were hunting,
fishing and drinking, not always in that order. Bowling was somewhere in the top twenty. Other than Wednesday night bingo, Shamus didn't have many social outlets. He wanted to feel like he was

part of the community so bowling became a way to meet new people outside of St. Michael's Parish.

Maggie wasn't a bowler. She tried it a few times but her hands were small and her wrists were weak. She couldn't get a decent grip. She had more gutter balls than strikes and wasn't invited to be in the women's bowling league which suited her just fine. She never held a great fascination with rolling heavy balls at wooden pins and preferred playing bridge because she could hold a glass of Jameson in one hand and her cards in the other without spilling a drop.

Maggie arrived at the bowling alley a few minutes before Father Shamus and found a table in the corner. She saw him enter through the side doors next to the end of the bar. Several other patrons glanced up from their hamburgers but barely acknowledged his presence. He spied Maggie across the room and wound through the tight dining area to her table.

The bruise on his face had shrunk slightly but, other than his nose, it was his most visible feature.

"Hello Maggie," he said as he pulled out a chair from the round pub table. He caught the eye of the waitress across the room and gave a quick wave. She grabbed two menus from the bar and headed in their direction.

"Father Shamus," Maggie said. "Thanks for coming. I was afraid I might scare you away." She was halfway through her second Guinness when Father Shamus arrived.

The waitress rattled off the daily lunch specials and snapped her chewing gum as she pulled the pen from behind her right ear and scribbled down their orders. Shamus ordered the soup and sandwich special with a cherry-coke and Maggie had her usual bacon-cheeseburger with extra fried onions.

Once the waitress was out of hearing range Shamus scooted his chair closer to Maggie and drummed his fingers on the table top. "A dead body?"

Maggie glanced around the room. No one seemed remotely interested in them. "I have a plan," she said.

"I'm dying to hear all about it."

Maggie rolled her eyes slightly. "I'm going to get a dead body and stage my own funeral so I can find out if anybody cares about me."

"Are you crazy? You can't go around borrowing dead people."

"It isn't as difficult as it seems."

"But why?"

"I want to know the truth if my children love me."

"Do you believe they don't?"

"Money," Maggie coughed slightly, "It's all about money. My kids are lurking in the shadows to get my money. They say things to make it sound like they care but I don't believe them."

"Maggie, it says in the bible that the righteous shall live by faith."

"Righteous? What's that got to do with it?"

"That's not the point. Sometimes you just have to accept people at their word." Father Shamus scratched his head. "If I said I loved you as a friend, would you believe me without needing proof?"

"Of course, you're a priest. You can't lie." Maggie took another big suck on her beer and wiped the foam from her upper lip.

Their lunch arrived. The waitress clunked the dishes on the closest edge of the table and gave them a calculated shove. The plates stopped in perfect alignment with the guests. A handful of paper napkins were dropped on the table. "Okee-dokee. If you need anything, just holler." She retreated to the kitchen and reappeared with another armful of platters.

"I've made some arrangements and I need your help." Maggie said.

"Maggie, you've been very gracious with me over this. I owe you."

"I want you to handle my funeral."

"You aren't dead yet and I hope you aren't serious about suicide." Father Shamus stopped eating and dropped the spoon back into his bean and ham soup. "You know I can't let you do this."

"You can't stop me," she said. Maggie set her cheeseburger down and wiped a streak of catsup and grease from her chin.

"If you force the issue, I will stop you or at least I will let your family know what you are intending."

"This might change your mind." Maggie pulled an envelope from her handbag and handed it to Father Shamus.

The envelope had a return address for Nixon, Dixon, Filbert and Tripe, Attorneys at Law. Inside was a copy of the Last Will and Testament for Margaret M. O'Reilly. The recording date was five days ago.

"Look at the first attachment," Maggie said.

Shamus flipped through the pages until he came to the first attachment. He waded through the legalese and raised his eyebrows when he found his name in bold print. "What's this?"

"You're the best priest I've known in sixty years."

"Well...that's very kind but I don't understand."

"You have a good chance of being dismissed or reassigned because of what happened."

"What happened?" he asked.

Maggie said nothing but put her finger beside her cheekbone and tapped three times.

"But Maggie, nothing happened. I did nothing wrong."

"Patrick wrote to the Bishop. You can bet there will be questions."

"You wouldn't say anything against me, would you?" Father Shamus asked. He pushed his half-eaten sandwich away.

"What if something bad happens to me? I don't want anything bad to happen to you. This way you will be taken care of for the rest of your life."

"What's going to happen to you, Maggie?"

"I can't tell you yet. I need you to be my eyes and ears with my children." Maggie took another gulp of Guinness. "They won't lie to you."

"I still don't understand."

"Talk to them, listen to them and report back to me what you learn. I want to know if they've changed or if they're still jerks like their father was."

"But Maggie, answer me straight. Are you serious about killing yourself?"

"That depends..."

CHAPTER 14

There is always some madness in love.
But there is also always some reason in madness.
– Friedrich Nietzsche

Mick Torkelson popped a breath mint into his mouth and checked his hair in the rearview mirror. He rearranged the hair on his sparsely populated scalp with a fine-tooth comb until he was satisfied then took a deep breath and opened his car door. A gust of autumn wind left his comb-over in disarray and for a moment he contemplated jumping back into the car, but he held his ground. He was on a mission and it was too important and too late to turn back.

Her front room lights were on and there was a light in the hall upstairs so Mick assumed she was home. He checked his watch, 7:19 PM. *I'm giving up Monday Night Football.* He was a block away from Maggie's house as he locked his car door and started down the sidewalk. The words of Rod Stewart's song chorused through his head. *Wake up Maggie, I think I've got something to say to you...* He tried skipping but his artificial knee clicked. He scaled the five concrete steps to her front door and knocked, tentative at first, then louder. He was here to see Maggie.

"Mick?" was all she said as the front door swung open.

"Maggie," he stuttered and fidgeted. "Um...ah...I thought I would stop by and see how you're doing."

"I'm fine. Why the sudden concern?"

"Oh, I don't know. I heard some people talking and I wanted to make sure you were okay. That's all." Mick danced around on the front porch like a third grader doing the full-bladder-waltz.

"People were talking? About what?" Maggie stood squarely in the doorway making certain Mick didn't sense a free pass to the kitchen or anywhere else in the house.

"I don't know. People are just talking that's all. You know how people are."

"Did you come to hear the truth or are you like the rest of the gossip hounds ready to start barking as soon as you get a whiff of something?" Maggie crossed her arms and clenched her jaw. If Mick was going to cross the threshold, he knew it would be on her terms or not at all.

"Maggie, what happened on Sunday?"

"You tell me what you've heard and I'll tell you if it's true or not."

"It's all over town. Some people said it's on Facebook. You're caught in a love triangle between the priest and Patrick Murphy." Mick stopped pacing on the front step and stuck his hands deep into his pockets. "There, I said it... I want to know if it's true."

"I'm not going to tell you out here on the porch. I've got a pint of Jameson in the kitchen and a chicken pot-pie in the oven." Maggie stepped aside and let Mick into the warm house. Before going inside, she looked across the street and down the block toward Patrick Murphy's house. As she stared in his direction, his front curtains suddenly closed and his house went dark. She stepped inside and pulled the door closed behind her.

#

Bishop O'Connor was awake every three hours like most old men. He was troubled about the letter and when he couldn't sleep, he decided to make good use of his time and use the bathroom whenever he was awake. When he first received the letter from Patrick Murphy, he dismissed it as a disgruntled parishioner but then he got a tip from another church about the Facebook post.

Bishop O'Connor wasn't on Facebook and he had no desire to jump into the social media cesspool but it was a convenient way to check on his area churches. He didn't trust most of the junk posted but he couldn't ignore a priest with a purple swollen eye.

There had never been any complaints about Father Muldoon since he took over St. Michael's Parish seven years ago. Many young priests were ambitious and requested placement in larger churches, but not Shamus. He was humble and content with little. He loved people and they loved him right back so an incident like this involving Shamus Muldoon, showing up on Facebook was concerning, and demanded his attention. He checked his schedule and decided early November was a good time to make a visit to St. Michael's Parish in Peterville. He wasn't looking forward to the weather but he had nothing else to do and he wanted to deal with it before Christmas.

#

Patrick Murphy trembled as he pulled his curtains shut and flipped off the light. He stuffed his Nikon binoculars into the crack between his sofa cushions and sat down. *I knew it. First Father Muldoon and now Mick Torkelson.*

He sat alone in his living room with the lights off. Pickles, his wiener dog, snuggled in against his leg and drifted into a happy dog dream with twitching and yipping. Patrick reached over to the end table next to his sofa and picked up a framed photo of Ethel. He held it at an angle so her smile caught the thin beam of light from the street, leaking through the cracks in his drapes.

"Ethel, I don't know how to tell you this. Since you've been gone it's just me and Pickles. I've been lonely but now there's someone in my life and she cares about me, I know she does." He stopped talking and gently placed his hand on the sausage shaped dog jerking by his side. "I keep the ten commandments and I go to mass every Sunday." He laid Ethel's photo on the table face down. "I don't want to embarrass you so I'm going to put your picture away until it's done."

Patrick got up from the sofa and turned on the floor lamp. He walked down the dimly lit, narrow hallway and opened the door to the hall closet. He found it in the third box along with his old police uniform. He held his trusty .38 revolver in his shaking hands. He held it up and sighted down the barrel at a target symbol on the side of a box in his closet. In over thirty years on the police force and he had never fired it at a real person. But he knew he could if he had to.

CHAPTER 15

An archaeologist is the best husband a woman can have.
The older she gets, the more interested he is in her."
— Agatha Christie

"How do you know if someone cares about you?" Maggie asked Mick as she placed the chicken pot-pie onto a trivet in the center of the small kitchen table.

"Are you asking if I care?" Mick scrunched his eyebrows together.

"Not just you, anybody. How do you know if someone cares or if they're lying"? Maggie asked. She handed a dinner plate to Mick and sat down opposite him.

"Ask them."

"Too easy to lie."

"I think you can tell if someone is lying." Mick said. "Look into their eyes."

"Alright, say something and I'll look into your eyes." Maggie poured a shot of Jameson into a glass with ice and took a sip.

"What do you want me to say?"

"Say whatever it is you came to say." Maggie dipped the serving spoon into the crust of the pot-pie. Steam and gravy oozed out. She scooped out a generous serving and dumped it onto Mick's plate.

Mick took nip of his own Jameson breathed deeply. "Maggie, you're a special person."

"Say it again, you blinked."

"Maggie you know it's true."

"You're lying. You didn't come over here to play cribbage. You came to play house but I'm not playing."

"But Maggie, we're old. We live alone. I like you. I want to spend time with you."

Maggie took another sip of Jameson. "Okay Mick, help me with a project and we'll spend time together. What do you say?"

"I'm all yours."

"I'm dying."

"Don't say that Maggie, it isn't true."

"We're all dying, it's just a matter of time. So, here's the deal." Maggie held her napkin to her lips and coughed. "I want to know if my family cares about me or if they're just after my money."

"That's sad."

"What? That I'm dying?"

"It's sad if you don't know if your children love you."

"It's probably my fault. I was basically a single parent and a bad one. Before Albert died, he was gone all the time. He was married to his job. When Albert died, I was angry. I drank too much and I didn't care. I blamed him and then the kids. I pushed them away and I don't know how to get them back."

"Have you seen a counselor?"

"That's like talking to a house plant. Not going to happen." Maggie paused for long time. "But I have a plan and I need your help."

"If it will help you get back with your family, I'm in. Just tell me what to do." Mick smiled. "I really do care."

"Yeah, yeah."

When dinner was done Maggie picked up a two-month old copy of Time Magazine and opened to page 13. She handed it to Mick.

"Read this and tell me what you think."

"This is about unclaimed bodies in Los Angeles. What's that got to do with you?"

"Look at the numbers. They have over six hundred bodies waiting to be claimed. Many are identified but some aren't. They have so many, they do a mass cremation every few months to get rid of people."

"So?"

"It only costs $200 to claim a body. That's cheaper than pee-wee hockey equipment." Maggie leaned forward and pointed out areas for Mick to read.

"This doesn't make any sense. You're planning to scare your family with a dead body?" Mick poured himself another shot of Jameson whiskey.

"Better than that," she said. "Think about it. After someone dies, people start saying the truth about the deceased because they no longer need to pretend. When the shock of someone's death wears off people reveal what's really in their heart and not some cockamamie story. I'm going to claim a body and stage my own funeral."

Mick closed his eyes and didn't move for several minutes. Maggie wasn't sure if it was the Jameson or her words that sent him into a catatonic state. Finally, he stirred, blinking and rubbing his eyes before turning toward Maggie.

Mick shook his head. "You can't be serious."

"I'm dead serious."

"Oh, that was a bad one. It will never work. You would have to find someone who's already dead and looks like you, a skinny 77-year-old Irish grandmother. Don't you think if someone's grandma died, they might want to have their own funeral?"

"I think I have that one figured out too." She turned to page fifty-seven of the Time Magazine and laid it in front of Mick. "Clara Alverez, age 79 has been in the Los Angeles morgue for three months because her family doesn't have the money to claim the body or pay for a funeral. She even resembles me."

"Did you really look at her? Clara Alverez is Hispanic, she's five feet tall, a hundred-sixty pounds and she has black hair." Mick pushed the magazine back across the table.

"This photo was from ten years ago. Maybe she lost weight."

"They're going to lock you in a rubber room and throw away the key." Mick shook his head.

"It's simple. I pay the money to rescue Clara from the freezer, we borrow the body for a week, maybe two tops, then when we are done, we ship her back to LA and her family can have their own funeral. I'll pay the expenses and everyone will be happy."

"Do you want my opinion?"

"Only if you agree with me."

"You're crazy. You will never convince your children that you are Clara Alverez and Clara is you. Besides, you would need to have a mortician and a priest agree to the whole thing, which means they would have to lie. It isn't going to happen." Mick got up from the table and stretched. "It's not ethical and it's probably illegal."

"That's the pragmatic Norwegian talking." Maggie said, "I need you to think like me."

"You want me to think like a crazy Irish-Catholic woman who drinks too much and doesn't trust her kids?"

Maggie ignored him. "Albert had a cousin who married a mortician, in Chicago. I met him many years ago. Manny Maldonado was his name. I think he died but his son, Vinny took over the business. As I recall, they specialized in cremations, probably to destroy evidence. Anyway...morticians are experts with makeup. If they can make dead people look good, why couldn't they make a Mexican woman look Irish? Maggie drizzled some more Jameson in her glass and pushed it back toward Mick.

Mick sat down and poured himself another round. The warmth of the kitchen and the whiskey started to work their magic. He struggled to argue against Maggie.

"Could we go to jail for this?" Mick asked.

"I'm not proposing anything illegal."

"Maggie, if your kids don't trust you now, they will never trust you after this."

"It'll give them something to talk about after I'm gone."

"If I did this to my kids, they'd kill me, cremate me and dump the ashes down the garbage disposal."

"Don't worry Mick. This is good for everyone. We get some excitement before they click the lid shut. They get to bury granny and I get to hear my kids tell the truth."

CHAPTER 16

*Your siblings are the only people in the world who know
what it's like to have been brought up the way you were.*
-Betsy Cohen

It wasn't the probability of Maggie going off the deep end that
worried the siblings, it was Mary's heavy hand if they didn't respond to her beck and call. Mary inherited her mother's iron will.
In the early years of the O'Reilly family, Mary naturally accepted
her role as surrogate mother. When Maggie was busy bottle feeding the babies, Mary was the sheep dog, nipping at the heels of the
young flock to keep them in line.

David said goodbye to his friend and took the red-eye flight
out of San Francisco the next day. There were plenty of direct
flights to Minneapolis but the late-night flight with stops in Phoe-
nix and Aberdeen, South Dakota saved him $369 round trip. He
was convinced his mother's impending demise was his fault, since
he left the church and moved in with Steven. He retained some
vestiges of the priesthood and hoped for reconciliation before his
mother went totally bonkers. But he doubted the sibling reunion
would lead to anything positive.

Eliza left Portland soon after Mary had called but drove her
Toyota hybrid through the Rocky Mountains and across North Dakota rather than fly because driving was easier on the environment. Even the final cracking of her mother couldn't induce Eliza
to increase her carbon footprint in the world. She considered herself well informed, having received reports of her mother's

behavior from Mary in the past. Eliza assumed her mother was in the early grips of senility and if it was due to Alzheimer's disease, it was irreversible and progressive. Life prolonging measures didn't make sense to her and there was little incentive to break the speed limit.

She and her mother had argued about every major social issue since Eliza was old enough to debate. Maggie neither believed nor supported anything Eliza did and the feeling was reciprocated. To Maggie, global warming was a hoax, carbon footprint was a black smudge on the carpet and empowerment of women was a communist threat to destabilize the west. If Maggie was losing her marbles then the sooner, they nailed the coffin shut, the better. Eliza wasn't quite ready to say goodbye to her mother but she also wasn't against pulling the plug when the time was right.

Freddie received the news with tainted remorse. An elderly mother with an unstable brain could be very expensive. If Maggie required any long-term custodial care, the cost would run into thousands of dollars each month. The hope of an inheritance, even a meager one was waning unless something tipped her over the edge. Guilt weighed on him and he felt trapped between loyalty to his aging mother and his wife, who controlled Freddie and everything in his life.

They came together on a Thursday, at Mary's home, in Baxter. The agenda was simple; share the doctor's concerns and discuss a plan to get Maggie declared incompetent. Then they would fight over who would be the guardian.

Mary was the first to speak. "I know this is difficult but we need to be ready when the time comes," she said. "I'm afraid things might be worse than I originally thought."

Fred and Eliza remained stoic in their positions around the living room. Only David stirred but he was quiet. There was a box of tissues within easy reach but no one needed any.

"Dr. Smith called me last week about Mom. She went into the clinic for a pregnancy test and insisted on a complete physical."

She pulled out some papers and glanced over her notes before continuing.

"Do you mean she just wanted a checkup or the whole thing?" Freddie asked.

"The whole thing."

"But, what's wrong with getting a physical? Isn't that a good thing to do?" David asked.

"Yes, but not a pregnancy test, when you're seventy-seven years old," Mary said. "She told the nurse she didn't know who the father was."

"Are you sure Dr. Smith didn't get her mixed up with someone else?" David asked.

"I doubt it. He had her birthdate, address and phone number and he described her perfectly. There couldn't be two Maggie O'Reilly's in the world."

"Did you call Tommy about this?" Eliza asked.

"I did better than that. I drove to Waupun and we talked, face to face."

"What does he think?" Freddie asked. "He's up for parole after the first of the year."

"He told me that Mom sends letters every month and visits a couple times a year. He witnessed nothing to make him suspect she was losing her marbles," Mary said.

"I've been doing some research on dementia," Eliza said. "First of all, we don't know if she has dementia or if she's mentally ill, or if she has cancer. She smoked like a chimney since we were kids. She could have something growing in her head. Shouldn't we let the doctor run some more tests before we start calling the guys in the white coats?"

"I agree with Eliza," David said. "Let the doctor do some more checking. Why the rush?"

"It was the doctor who called me. He was the one concerned."

"We can't do much about dementia anyway," Eliza said.

"It's not her mental state that worries me," Freddie said. "If we can't stop her from going crazy, maybe we can stop her from ruining our lives."

"What do you mean by that?"

"What if she suddenly gets married to some loser and he takes control of all her money? Or she gives it all to some homeless shelter?" Freddie shifted in his chair. "I think the doctor is right, she's a vulnerable adult and if she isn't capable of taking care of herself, then maybe we need to step in, sooner rather than later."

"Has Therese maxed out your credit cards again?" Eliza rolled her eyes and turned away from Freddie.

"Shut up, Liz," Freddie clenched his jaws and folded his arms across his chest.

"Knock it off. I think we need to make a plan." Mary flipped her papers over so everyone could see a detailed list on the other side.

"This is stupid. Do you expect us to just walk into Mom's house and declare her wacko?" David asked. "Why don't we all sit down with her and have a nice heart-to-heart talk. We might learn something by listening."

"In the past thirty years, have you ever had a nice heart-to-heart talk with Mom?" Mary asked. "If she isn't playing with a full deck, what makes you think it's going to happen now?"

No one answered.

"The doctor suggested observing and keeping notes on her behavior. If something appears irrational then it could be evidence for the judge to declare her incompetent. But we need to be subtle and we should start immediately." Mary looked around the room, making eye contact with each sibling. "I think it's going faster than we realize or she knows something she isn't telling."

"Like what?" Freddie asked.

"I stopped by her house two days ago." Mary tapped her iPhone and displayed a photo of Maggie. "She was reading an article on how to plan your own funeral. She had brochures from

Maldonado's House of Eternal Rest and she cut and dyed her hair, jet black."

CHAPTER 17

Most of us spend the first six days of each week sowing wild oats;
then we go to church on Sunday and pray for a crop failure.
-Fred Allen

Father Muldoon prepared himself for Friday afternoon confession like he always did. He lit a candle, he read his bible and he knelt before the altar to confess his own sins. There were three things on his mind and confession wasn't one of them. He prayed for quick healing for Sally's broken nose. It was still askew but the swelling was improving. Unfortunately, her crooked nose would always be a quick reminder of that fateful Sunday morning.

He winced as he touched his own cheek. It was settling down. He never went to the doctor for x-rays to determine if his cheekbone was broken. Like Sally, he accepted what he had and wasn't overly concerned. But he was concerned about the Bishop.

Shamus knew Bishop O'Connor to be a wise and fair man but if there was hint of a scandal at St. Michael's Parish, Shamus didn't want to be the cause of it. If Rome was the center of the Catholic world, St. Michael's in Peterville was teetering on the outer reaches of the church. With a dying congregation and no evidence of young families moving in to revive the church, it would soon be shuttered anyway. Whether he stayed or was forced elsewhere probably made little difference to the Bishop, but it did make a difference to the few remaining in his flock.

Maggie O'Reilly was an enigma. Feisty and energetic she never seemed worried or frustrated. If it was cloudy outside, she was a ray of sunshine. If someone was lethargic, she was a goad in the side. If the world threw lemons at her she made limoncello. Eccentric and indomitable, she was the reason Father Shamus wanted to stay in Peterville. But her words still haunted him: *I'm going to kill myself and I need your help.*

He heard a stirring in the narthex and glanced down at his watch. It was soon time for confession. He raised his right hand in the shape of the cross and eased into a standing position from the kneeling bench before the altar.

"Good afternoon Father."

"Mary, how wonderful to see you back in church. Are you visiting Maggie?"

"I came to see her, but she wasn't home. I expect she will be in for confession."

"Maggie hasn't missed Friday confession in several years."

"Before she comes in, can I have a few words with you?"

"Certainly." Father Muldoon escorted her into a side office and shut the heavy oak door behind them. "Is there something wrong?"

Mary condensed the family meeting and the conversation with Dr. Smith into a few minutes. When she was done with the summary Father Muldoon took a deep breath and sat back in his chair. He reached up and gently massaged the bruise on his cheek. "It's starting to make sense," he whispered to himself.

"What's making sense?" Mary asked.

"Mary, you understand what is said in confession is held to be sacred and confidential."

"I understand, but if there is something putting my mother at risk, you should share it with us."

"I took an oath before God. I won't break that oath," he said, "but when Maggie comes in for confession, she might be willing to share her thoughts."

"Father Muldoon, I love my mother very much and I want her to be safe. If you're withholding harmful information, we need to know."

"Why don't you wait here. Confession rarely takes much time, I have so few parishioners remaining. When Maggie comes in, we can talk."

The first person to arrive was Sally McTavish. Her nose pointed slightly southwest and her raccoon eyes had changed from black to a light shade of avocado green but she seemed in good spirits. If she harbored any malice against Father Muldoon it wasn't apparent. Shamus was the one with anxiety as he stepped into the confession booth and closed the door behind him.

"Father forgive me, for I have sinned," she began.

"If you're faithful to confess your sins God is faithful to forgive you."

"I was angry with my husband once," she said. "He was always late from work, one day. I got mad and dumped out his bottle of Jack Daniels."

Father Shamus yawned and relaxed. He had heard it all before. He let her prattle on while he focused his thoughts on other things. It was several minutes later when he realized she was no longer talking.

"Father did you hear me?"

"Yes, my child. Your sins are forgiven. Your husband has passed into new life and there is nothing to fear." He checked his watch. Twenty minutes had passed.

Sally left the confessional and exited the back of the church. Father Muldoon waited patiently for someone else to arrive. It was quiet. He returned to his office to visit with Mary as they both awaited the expected arrival of Maggie. A delay in her arrival wasn't unusual but her absence was out of the ordinary. Finally, the back door of the church swung open and a gust of cold autumn air unrolled across the tile floor.

Patrick Murphy stood in the entrance, his long gray overcoat unbuttoned and his thin comb-over hair in disarray. Pickles the portly wiener dog trembled at the end of the leash, her sides heaving from exertion. A brisk walk on five-inch legs was almost more than she could endure.

His eyes darted around the church, from the altar to the confessional. He ignored the table of candles available to be lit in memory of lost loved ones, and displayed no concern with the small puddle of water forming around his feet from Pickle's incontinence.

Father Muldoon and Mary stepped from his office to greet Patrick. "Good afternoon Patrick," he said.

Patrick's right hand trembled as he raised it and pointed directly at Mary. "Jezebel. She's made a deal with the devil."

"Patrick, what are talking about?" Shamus asked. He looked from Patrick to Mary and back. Mary was silent.

Patrick lowered his arm and turned toward the priest. "I was wrong about you Father Shamus. I beg your forgiveness. It was her, wasn't it?"

"You're forgiven, Patrick. Would you like to sit in the confessional?"

"It's too late."

"It's never too late to confess your sins." Shamus stepped toward Patrick and motioned in the direction of the open confessional.

"It's too late for Jezebel."

"Who are you talking about?"

Patrick pointed again at Mary. "She's gone."

"Are you talking about my mother?" Mary asked.

Patrick shook his head and began to weep.

CHAPTER 18

To die, to sleep -
To sleep, perchance to dream - ay, there's the rub,
For in this sleep of death what dreams may come...
— William Shakespeare, Hamlet

"She's gone."

"Who?"

"Mom. Patrick Murphy came into the church and told us she left this morning before sunrise, in a U-Haul truck with Mick Torkelson."

"You're joking, right?" Eliza asked.

"Tell the others and meet me at the county sheriff's office in Baxter."

"Do you think she's in danger?"

"I'm going to file a missing person's report and get the district attorney to call Dr. Smith. We need to assume she's irrational." Mary gritted her teeth and stared through the streaked windshield. Her tires thumped and screeched as she drove over the edge of the curb and into the street.

The old brick courthouse served double duty as the county seat and the sheriff's office. Three people were waiting in line to pay parking violations. Another deputy brought in a young man wearing handcuffs. His hands and clothes were greasy and all the way down the hall Mary could hear him professing his innocence because he didn't know the car was stolen.

Officer Bill Thompson was the first to see Mary and listen to her story. "Don't you think you're over reacting?" he asked as he tried to digest the confusing mess of events.

"You don't know my mother."

"That's true but have you ever had reason to suspect she was a bit daffy, in the past?"

"My mother has always been eccentric, but she never misses confession on Friday and I can't remember the last time she left Peterville without letting me know." Mary checked her phone for messages. There were none.

"You said she left with Mick Torkelson. What do you know about him?" Officer Thompson turned to a fresh sheet on his yellow legal pad and readied his pen.

"I don't know Mick that well but I think he's harmless. I know he's divorced and he has a couple kids living around Alexandria. Mom said he was a semi-professional mini-golfer. I didn't know there was such a thing."

"Have you ever seen him agitated or violent?"

"Just once, when he got his putter bent." Mary shook her head at the absurdity of it all.

Bill's eyes widened a bit but he wrote down the details as best as he could explain them. "Look Mary...I understand your concern. I have a mother whose bubble is a bit off level but I'm not worried about her running off with a Norwegian mini-golfer. Your mom probably bought some furniture and enlisted the help of Mick Torkelson to haul it home. Don't you think that makes more sense?"

"I know that makes sense to you but..."

"Mary, I know the district attorney and the judge. They aren't going to issue a missing person report yet. She may be eccentric, as you say, but there's no evidence of foul play and no evidence that she's in trouble. Give it some time. I bet she'll be back this evening with a new lazy-boy and there'll be nothing to worry about." Bill stood up from the desk. The meeting was over.

Mary returned to the waiting area in the county courthouse. Eliza and Freddie were waiting. Mary dabbed at the corners of her eyes with a tissue as she walked out.

"Not good?" Freddie asked.

Mary shook her head. "They don't believe me."

Eliza spoke up, "There's only two logical things to do. We can wait and see what happens or we can try and follow her."

"How are we going to follow her if she left at daybreak in a rented truck?" Freddie asked.

Eliza was busy tapping the screen of her iPhone. "There are three U-Haul rental places within thirty miles of Peterville. If we can find out where she rented the truck then we have our starting point."

"They won't tell us anything," Freddie said. "They have privacy rules to follow just like everyone else."

"Then we tell them she has dementia and probably won't return the truck. That will get their attention."

Mary spoke up, "Before we start interrogating some poor rental clerk, why don't we start at the house and see if we can find some answers."

The key was under the loose brick by the back door as it had been for as long as any of them remembered. They let themselves in but hesitated in the hall. The spirit of Maggie saturated the air around them. If they were uncomfortable in her presence, they were doubly so without her. They dutifully took off their shoes by the door and shuffled about in stocking feet. The old oak floorboards creaked at their intrusion.

The house had a cold mustiness, the smell of old people and stale air. The throw rugs, the furniture, even the knick-knacks on the shelves were unchanged over the past fifteen years. Their father's photo was framed and sat on the top of the old upright piano in the corner. There was dust on the keys.

"Where do we start?" Freddie asked. There was a small pile of unopened mail on the kitchen counter, one of them was a bank statement. Freddie picked it up and held it up to the light as if hoping to see hundred-dollar bills fall out the side. Next to the mail on the table, was a photocopy of the church calendar. Upcoming Lenten services were highlighted otherwise the calendar was blank.

Eliza opened the refrigerator and took a mental inventory. There was little food. About a third of a chicken-pot-pie remained, covered with plastic wrap. There were small jars of mayo, catsup and mustard and one jar of orange marmalade, four eggs in a carton, a half stick of butter, but little else. In the produce drawer were two grapefruits, one was soft and had the beginnings of a green overcoat. She gently removed it and dropped it into the kitchen trash can under the sink. "It doesn't look like she's stocking up for the winter."

Mary was drawn to the flashing light on the answering machine. She bought it for her mother over ten years ago in hopes it would improve their lines of communication, but it gave Maggie less incentive to answer the phone. Now instead of talking to her mother she heard a younger rendition of her own voice from the initial set up at Christmas, many years prior.

She pressed the button, eleven messages. The first was from three weeks ago, Mick Torkelson asking her out for a fish fry at the VFW. Several more were nothing more than a beep and silence, probably telemarketers. But the last few messages caught her attention.

"Mrs. O'Reilly, this is the radiology department from Baxter hospital. I'm calling to remind you of your CT scan scheduled tomorrow. You need to be fasting, nothing to eat, but you need to drink a small glass of the contrast at six o'clock in the morning, four hours before the scheduled scan. If you have questions, please give me a call." Mary jotted down the number and checked her calendar. The CT scan was scheduled four days ago.

The next message was from later the next day. "Mrs. O'Reilly, this is Dorothy at the Baxter hospital. You missed your scheduled CT scan. We contacted your doctor about this and he was very insistent that you reschedule. Please give our office a call as soon as you can."

The last message was two hours ago. "Mrs. O'Reilly, this is Dr. Smith calling about your CT scan. I know you were reluctant to have further testing but coughing up blood is something that should never be ignored. Please consider rescheduling or come into my office so we can discuss alternatives." Dr. Smith left his office number and also his personal cell phone number.

Everyone was quiet until Mary spoke. "My doctor has never left his personal number. This can't be good."

Eliza was checking with Google about coughing up blood. She read from her screen, "The top three causes of coughing up blood in an elderly smoker were pneumonia, emphysema and cancer. WebMD said it was cancer until proven otherwise."

Mary picked up the brochure for Maldonado's House of Eternal Rest and opened the cover. Casket options were detailed on the second page. There was a black circle around the mid-priced one.

CHAPTER 19

Every man must do two things alone;
he must do his own believing and his own dying.
– Martin Luther

Father Muldoon was uncomfortable. It was the first time he had heard the name "Jezebel" used against one of his parishioners, and his most loyal one at that. Without Maggie here to defend herself, Father Shamus did his best to deflect Patrick's anger, or at the very least, try to understand it.

Patrick was clearly distraught. After Mary, Freddie and Eliza left the church, he collapsed into the church pew and sobbed. It was twenty minutes before he regained enough composure to speak coherently. Father Shamus invited him into the confessional and Patrick followed without resistance.

Once inside the confessional, Patrick seemed to relax a bit and his voice was less strained. He chattered on about Ethel for several minutes, rehashing old stories and feelings and Father Shamus began to relax. Ethel had been gone several years but the same issues resurfaced whenever Patrick attended confession.

"She's in league with the Antichrist. She needs to be stopped."

"Who are you talking about?"

"Jezebel."

"Who is Jezebel?" Father Muldoon asked.

"You know who I'm talking about. She needs to be stopped."

"Stopped from what? What is Jezebel going to do?"

"She needs to be stopped."

"Patrick, you've said that three times. Who is Jezebel and why does she need to be stopped?" Father Muldoon felt the tension in his voice. He coughed once and wiped the film of sweat from his forehead.

Pickles growled softly. If there was fear or anger or something else in the air, Pickles sensed it. Patrick reached down with his left hand and gently stroked the hair behind her ears. Her throaty growl eased and her tail wagged at her master's touch.

Patrick said no more. He snapped the leash on the stubby dog and opened the door to the confessional. He pulled his leather gloves from his coat pocket. The cuff of his glove caught on something and there was a soft metallic sound as it fell to the floor.

Looking through the small lattice opening from where the priest sat, Father Shamus saw the light glint off the shiny brass casing of the .38 pistol bullet.

"Patrick?"

There was no answer. Pickles tugged at the end of the leash as they opened the back door to the church and stepped into the late afternoon air.

#

By the time Maggie's children were done snooping through her mail, phone messages and anything else they could find, it was too late to contact the U-Haul rental office. The sun had set and the thin light from the street lamps filtered through the windows.

"We need to get out of here. If Mom comes home and finds us going through her stuff, she'll write us out of the will," Freddie said.

"What if she doesn't have a will?" Eliza said. "What if she's already off the deep end? What if she's marries old Tick Torkelson and he controls the money?"

"It's Mick Torkelson," Mary corrected.

"Rick, Tick, Schmick, what's the difference?" David asked. "If she catches us here like this, it's the end of our happy family."

"Let's lock up the house," Mary said, "and meet at my place in Baxter in a couple hours. I'll order pizza and we can talk about the next step. Maybe we'll know something more in the morning."

There was no dissent. Eliza and David were staying with Mary anyway and Freddie's wife was visiting friends in Palm Springs. He wrote a text to Therese about the phone messages they found at his mother's home but at the last minute deleted them. There was no sense in getting her hopes up.

#

Mick exited interstate 90 onto West Cermak Road and drove until he turned left on S. Damen Drive between the Lower West Side and Heart of Italy, suburbs of Chicago. Maldonado's House of Eternal Rest was a nondescript brick building half covered in ivy. It was tucked between a men's clothing store and La Belle Vie restaurant. The red neon open sign in the restaurant's front window flickered in the early darkness.

The off-street parking was in the back. Mick maneuvered the panel truck into the narrow drive and parked out of view. The light over the main entrance was on, which meant they had a customer inside or they were expecting Maggie, or both.

"Are you certain you want to do this?" Mick asked.

"If I was certain of anything, I wouldn't have to do this," Maggie said. "But my mind is made up."

They entered through the dark side door of the mortuary into a brightly lit foyer. A tall man with slicked black hair and a neatly trimmed moustache stood beside a podium with the guest registry. His shiny black pin-stripe suit was immaculate and his brass cufflinks glinted in the light.

"I'm Vincent Maldonado. You must be Maggie." He stepped forward and offered his right hand. The large diamond ring on his little finger pressed into her hand but he was gentle.

"I'm Maggie O'Reilly and this is my friend Mick Torkelson." Vincent shook hands with Mick and pointed toward the small conference room adjacent to the foyer.

Maggie and Mick followed into the room and sat in the tall straight-back maroon Italian leather chairs around the mahogany table.

"Can I get you anything? Coffee? Wine? Grappa?"

"Grappa for me," Maggie said. Mick shook his head, no.

Once they were settled around the table, Vincent took a seat at the end. "Mrs. O'Reilly…"

"Please call me Maggie."

"And friends call me Vinny." He cleared his throat, "Maggie, you have a very interesting idea. After you called me last week, I spent some time considering your dilemma wondering if we could pull this off." He looked from Maggie to Mick and back again. "I think it would be an interesting project."

"Do you actually think this crazy idea would work?" Mick asked.

"I don't believe this is as hard as you think," Vinny said. "When a loved one dies, people tend to idealize things. They see things as they want to see them, not as they really are. How many times have you heard someone describe a dead body in a casket, 'they look so natural, like they're sleeping." Vinny raised his eyebrows and sat back in his chair. "They aren't sleeping and they don't look natural. They're dead."

"But do you think it will bring out their true feelings?" Maggie asked.

"That's up to you. We can paint the stiff… I'm sorry." He took a sip of grappa. "We can provide the deceased with appropriate makeup but we can't make anyone talk, not the way you want them to talk."

"You're really going to do this Maggie?" Mick asked.

Maggie looked at Vinny. "Where do we start?"

"What do your children know?"

"About this? Nothing."

"You realize, you might gain some information but it could cost you the chance to rebuild a relationship with them afterward."

Maggie ignored his warning. She took out the Time Magazine and handed it to Vinny. He glanced at it and handed it back.

Vinny took out a business card. "This is the county coroner in Chicago. We've done business together in the past. Go see him tomorrow and tell him I sent you. Explain what you are looking for. Chicago has just as many unclaimed bodies as any other major city and you don't have to drive as far."

"I rented a U-Haul. I was expecting to drive to LA and pick up someone." Maggie said.

"I don't want your family to get suspicious. I have an antique writing desk in the back that I picked up from a customer who didn't pay his bills. Take it home with you. Sell it if you want, it's worth a couple grand."

"But what about picking up a body?" Maggie asked.

"If you go up to the coroner's office in a rental truck the cops might ask some questions. My friend's name is Sal. He'll help you pick out your twin sister. Once you get the number from the toe tag, I'll send one of our boys down with the hearse. Clean and natural."

"Is this illegal?" Mick asked.

"Of course not," Vinny said. "We are a licensed funeral home. You're just good Samaritans providing a Christian burial for some poor forgotten soul."

After reviewing a few more details the meeting was over. As they stood up to leave, Vinny took Maggie's hand in his own. "Thank you for coming, Maggie. Family loyalty is very important to us here at Maldonado's House of Eternal Rest. I know it's important to you too."

"I hope I'm doing the right thing," Maggie said.

"Don't worry." Vinny said. "You're a good mother. I like the way you think."

CHAPTER 20

Put a silk on a goat and it is still a goat.
-Irish Proverb

The days following his meeting with Maggie at Baxter Lanes left Father Muldoon strangely unsettled. He had a hard time studying and he didn't have any prepared sermon notes for Sunday Mass. At noon he wandered downtown and sat at the counter in the Main Street Café.

"What'll you have Padre?" Emily, the lunch time waitress was always friendly.

"Give me the usual."

"The hot turkey sandwich with gravy is the special today." She nodded toward the chalk board as she poured him a glass of ice water.

"Sounds good." He took a quick swallow of water. "No wait. I'll take the corned beef hash and two poached eggs instead."

Emily scribbled the notes. "Coffee?"

"Never mind," he said.

"No coffee?"

"No. Cancel the order, I'll just have coffee if that's okay."

"No problem. Everything alright?" she asked.

"Yes, everything's fine." He nodded in her direction but everything wasn't fine. It was as far from fine as he had ever experienced and he wasn't sure how he got here.

Maggie's last will and testament troubled him. It was ethically wrong to accept an inheritance from a parishioner. He worried how it would affect his judgement. He was called to be a shepherd to the small flock at St. Michael's but how could he not show favoritism when one of the flock was offering a large portion of their estate. *What exactly was Maggie expecting of him? I can't spy on her children. I can't lie to them or to her.*

His phone vibrated in his pocket. He pulled it out and studied the screen. It was a number he had called twice in his years at St. Michael's Parish. The number belonged to Bishop O'Connor's office.

He let the phone ring.

#

"I'm sorry I'm late." Dr. Smith dropped his reading glasses on his desk as he collapsed into his chair. "I wouldn't normally meet with a family on short notice but I understand some of you are from out of town."

Mary spoke first. "This is my sister, Eliza from Portland, my brothers Freddie and David. David lives in San Francisco. We have another brother who isn't able to be here."

"Doctor, can you give your opinion of our mother's mental state?" Eliza asked.

"Declaring someone incompetent is very serious."

"Are you saying she's incompetent?"

"I'm not sure. As I mentioned before there can be many reasons for confusion, disorientation, delusions and so on. She has chronic lung disease from smoking but other than that she seems remarkably spry." Dr. Smith adjusted his glasses and looked over some of Maggie's information.

"Could depression cause this?" David asked.

"Of course."

"It's my fault." David said to everyone in the room. "I should have never left the church."

"Wait a minute. Mom's been playing three cards short of a full deck for years," Freddie said. "I doubt you're the reason for any of this. If that's true, then we are all guilty."

"What about her lungs?" Mary asked.

"I think that is the most serious issue," Dr. Smith said. "I explained, why she needs more testing but she hasn't returned my calls and she didn't show up for her CT scan. Either she doesn't want to do anything or she doesn't understand."

"What if we talk to her?" David asked.

"That's good, but the same issues apply. If she understands the seriousness of her condition and decides to do nothing, that's fine. We call that informed consent. But if she doesn't understand or can't understand, then we may have an obligation to make that decision for her."

"Can't we make that decision now? Let's force her to do the CT scan." Mary spoke for the group.

"It isn't that easy," Dr. Smith said, "I'll give you an example. If you have a child who has strep throat frequently and the ENT doctor suggests getting the tonsils out, you make a decision on behalf of the child to do the surgery, because the child isn't capable of doing it. But if the same thing happened to you now, would you want your mother to make that decision on your behalf?"

"Absolutely not," Eliza said. "Only if I'm unable to make it,"

"Exactly, which is why we need to figure out if she's refusing treatment or if she's incapable of making that decision." He closed the file on desk and leaned back. "Unfortunately, we don't have much time."

"What do you mean?" Mary asked.

"She reported coughing up blood. From a medical perspective we have to assume this is cancer until proven otherwise." He looked from person to person. The gravity of the situation was reflected in their faces.

"How much time?" Freddie asked.

"I'm making some assumptions here but if you do nothing...six months to two years."

"And with treatment?" Mary asked.

"Maybe the same, but we can't determine that unless we have more information."

When the meeting was over the group was quiet as they filed out of the clinic and into Mary's minivan.

"We need to force mom to get the CT scan as soon as possible." Mary said.

"What gives you the right to force this issue?" Freddie asked. "It's her decision."

"What if she can't make that decision Freddie? What if she wants to live but she can't understand? Do you want that guilt hanging over you while Mom's in Purgatory?"

"Didn't the Pope abolish Purgatory?" Freddie asked.

"I say, let it be. You heard what the doctor said, six months to two years no matter what you do," Eliza said.

"I think she's depressed. It's all my fault," David said.

"Knock it off. You're making me depressed," Mary said. She hit the brakes but it was too late. The highway patrol pulled out behind her and flipped on the flashers. Mary slowed down and eased to the side of the road.

"Are you in a hurry?" he asked as he reached through the open window. Mary held her driver's license and insurance card for the officer.

"I didn't realize I was speeding. It won't happen again," Mary said. She sounded contrite.

Officer Bergman returned to his squad car and after several minutes reappeared at Mary's window. "You were fifteen miles per hour over the speed limit. Do you realize the fine for that is $360?"

"I don't normally drive like this. We were discussing our mother, who has health issues and she's losing her mind."

"I understand what you're saying. After my father died, my mother married an exotic male dancer and moved to St. Thomas."

"Are you serious? What did you do?"

"We visit every February. They have a great guest room and it's free."

"I'm sorry about your father," Mary said.

"I'm sorry too. Did you know your driver's license is expired by three months and your insurance policy lapsed?"

"There must be some mistake."
"I radioed for a tow truck You can come with me."

CHAPTER 21

All men are cremated equal.
-Mortician Humor

The antiseptic smell made Maggie nauseous. All she ate for breakfast was an English muffin and coffee but she was worried about losing it in the lobby and she hadn't yet laid eyes on a corpse. She folded her hands together to keep them from shaking and her palms felt moist. She held the business card she received from Vinny and handed it to the receptionist.

"One moment," the receptionist said. She punched a number on her phone. "Sal, I have someone here to see you."

"I'm busy." Maggie heard him yell through the phone receiver.

"They were sent by Vinny Maldonado."

"I'll be right down." The phone clicked.

In less than two minutes a short fat bald guy appeared through the side door. His white shirt sleeves were rolled up and he had grease stains around his collar. There was a cigar in his left breast pocket and a black ballpoint pen behind his right ear. Maggie could read the writing on the pen, *House of Eternal Rest*.

"Sal Bonacelli" He smiled and offered to shake hands.

"Maggie," she said. "Maggie O'Reilly, and this is my friend, Mick Torkelson."

"What brings you to the morgue?"

"Is there a place we can talk in private?"

"Certainly, follow me." They followed Sal down the hallway and took the elevator up two floors. The sign on his office said Facilities Director, Chicago Medical Examiner-Salvadore Bonacelli.

"Now what can I do for you? A friend of Vinny is a friend of mine."

Maggie looked around the office. It was typical government issue work space with a gray metal desk and three filing cabinets in the corner. There were several uneven stacks of papers on his desk and a signed Chicago Cubs baseball in a glass display case.

"I'm looking for a woman about my age and size."

"What's her name?"

"I don't know her name and she's dead."

"I'm not following you. You're looking for a dead woman but you don't know her name?"

"This isn't easy to explain. I am looking for a body that looks like me."

"I don't want no trouble. We keep everything above ground here." Sal started to laugh. "That's a joke, above ground." He laughed again.

Mick leaned forward. "Maggie wants to claim an unclaimed body and give it a Christian burial."

"But the body needs to look like you?" Sal typed his password on his computer. "We have five hundred thirty-seven people in the freezer. Only two hundred and three are women."

Maggie asked, "What happens to the people who aren't claimed?"

"When someone dies, we make every effort to contact the next of kin, but if no one claims the body the county coroner has the authority to make a decision for proper disposal. After ninety days the corpse is cremated. Vinny got the bid for the city of Chicago."

"And you have hundreds of bodies?"

Sal nodded. He hit the print button on his keyboard and several pages came out of his laser printer. "Here is a list of women who might fit your description. About half of them have documented next of kin. They have ninety days. The other half are homeless or came from drug houses. We may have names but no one to claim them. There are over twenty women still being identified." He handed the list over to Maggie.

Out of two-hundred dead women, maybe thirty or forty were about the same age or size. She tried to swallow. Her throat was dry. She wanted to stand up but her legs felt weak. *I could use a cigarette.* "Can I have a drink of water?"

Sal went to the small wet bar in the corner of his office and pulled out two bottles of water. "Have you ever been in a morgue before?"

"Only to identify my husband Albert, when he had a stroke." She took another gulp of water. "That was seventeen years ago."

When Maggie signaled she was ready, she and Mick followed Sal to the elevator and into the basement of the building. When the door opened, she was asked to sign the visitor registry. Sal took her list and handed it to one of the lab techs. "She's looking for a loved one. Make sure she finds what she's looking for."

Sal turned back to Mick and Maggie. "I think you'll find your sister. When you do, record the number on the toe tag and I'll have Vinny pick her up." Sal turned and left.

The tech headed toward the locked double doors. He handed each of them a long white lab coat. When the doors opened Maggie felt dizzy. The smell of antiseptic and dead flesh poured into the hallway. She reached for Mick and held onto his arm and as they stopped before a large stainless-steel freezer door. Number 102 was stenciled onto the front panel.

The tech grabbed the latch. There was a loud metallic click as the door swung open. Cold fog gushed out from the freezer and rolled across the floor. Maggie felt the air of death gather around her ankles. He pulled out a long tray, like an oversized meat drawer in a refrigerator. A stark frozen body poked out from the freezer drawer into the room. From under the fringe of the sheet, Maggie could see thin gray hair peeking around the shroud of death.

In a matter-of-fact manner the tech raised the sheet. An emaciated grandmother with a toothless grin and shrunken cheeks stared back with unseeing eyes. Her wrinkled skin was frozen in time, like lifeless wax. Her nose was long and was bent slightly to the left. She had a cancerous growth on her right cheek that appeared ready to resume growing as soon as it was freed from its arctic rest.

Maggie closed her eyes and turned away. "Does she have a name?"

The tech checked his list. "First name is Rita. We don't have a last name. She died in a homeless shelter."

Maggie shook her head no and the meat drawer slid shut and locked into place. Maggie realized this wasn't going to be as easy as she expected. She looked toward the closed double exit doors down the hall and wanted to run. She hesitated as the tech went to the next drawer.

The second woman had thick black hair, a wide nose and a double chin. She wasn't Irish. With each drawer, each click of the freezer latch, each encounter with mortality, her uneasiness ebbed.

At the thirteenth freezer she knew. The meat tray slid open and Maggie lifted the sheet herself. She saw herself ten years younger. Gray streaked, unruly auburn hair framed a thin face with faded freckles. Her skinny frozen arms were folded across her naked body. The tag on her toe read 138.

"What happened?" Maggie asked.

The tech flipped the paper on his clipboard. "Ward of the state. Died in a nursing home. No family. No one wanted her."

"Does she have a name?"

"Velma Gladwell."

Maggie took a deep breath and sucked in the cold air of death. She coughed and a small speck of blood landed on Velma's cheek. Mick raised his arm and gently put his hand against her shoulder.

"She's the one."

CHAPTER 22

We wallow greedily at any lie that flatters us,
but sip only little by little at a truth we find bitter.
-Denis Diderot

It had been two days since Patrick reported the U-Haul leaving Maggie's house and Mary was anxious. The police treated her like a girl who couldn't get a prom date and she wasn't ready to file another missing person's report. She accepted the forty-eight-hour waiting period but forty-eight hours was an eternity if you're the one waiting.

After the family meeting everyone agreed to write notes. She reviewed her notes so many times she could recite them verbatim. Eliza had contacted the U-Haul rental place but it wasn't a one-way rental so no destination was recorded. However, it was rented for seven days which seemed very unusual. *What would two old people do with a rental truck for seven days?*

They tried coming up with ideas but none of them made any sense. The idea given by the police officer, about buying furniture, made the most sense but it wasn't consistent with Maggie's character. The last time she bought new furniture was when Albert died. Maggie had the kids drag his recliner out to the curb and hang a free sign on it. She replaced it with another sitting chair but no one ever used it. Seventeen years later, aside from the dust, it still looked new.

The thought occurred to them, Maggie might be helping Mick move something but why enlist the help of a skinny old woman with osteoporosis if you needed to use a truck to move something.

Then again, Maggie may have been going along for the ride and not expected to do any lifting.

Mary left her phone number with Patrick Murphy with careful instructions. He was to notify her with any suspicious activity around Maggie's house. Maggie recalled his giddy grin when he took the phone number.

#

Patrick arranged the drapes on his front windows so he could sit back out of sight yet have a clear view down the street to Maggie's house on the hill. He was back on the beat, a stake-out and it was the best he felt in years. He sat on one end of his couch with a thermos of coffee, a sandwich, a bag of potato chips and his police-dog Pickles on high alert. Twice he caught himself nodding off and he slapped his face to shake off the heaviness of his eyelids. He leaned close to the window with his binoculars and double-checked Maggie's house to make certain he hadn't missed any activity. *Nothing*. He jotted down the time and observations in a small breast-pocket note book.

Patrick was dedicated to his post. He allowed himself breaks only to eat and use the bathroom. When Pickles needed exercise, he clipped a short leash to her collar and they walked toward Maggie's place to get a closer look and see if Pickles could sniff out some wrong doing.

It was the third day in the late afternoon. Patrick and Pickles were half-way back from patrol when he heard the panel truck turn the corner, two blocks away. He jerked Pickles from her dutiful inspection of the neighbor's mailbox post. Pickles' ears sagged and her tail went between her legs as if she was being chastised for inattentive guard duty. She wet on the sidewalk.

"Get ready, Pickles. They're back." Patrick half dragged the sausage shaped dog down the street until they were safely positioned in their own living room. He grabbed his binoculars and peered through the parted drapes. He checked his watch and scribbled in his notebook.

4:17 U-Haul arrived. Mick driving.

4:23 Maggie exits truck with package in hand

4:30 Called Mary. She's on her way.

After Patrick reported the new activity at the house, he clipped the leash on Pickles, slipped his .38 revolver into his coat pocket and started down the street. Pickles was nervous and trembled when they stepped into the cold evening air. Patrick nudged her forward but she held back resisting the pull of the leash. 100 steps. 150 steps. Pickles hunched up and fertilized the neighbors flower garden. 200 steps. Patrick hesitated. He considered returning to his house but the front door opened at Maggie's house.

Patrick picked up his pace and stopped in her drive beside the U-Haul. Mick came around the corner of the garage and took a quick step back.

"Patrick?" Mick asked. "Are you okay?"

"Where have you been Mick?" Patrick asked in a low voice. His hands were in his coat pocket. The loop of Pickles leash was around his right wrist.

"Nowhere special."

"Ethel said to watch."

"Were you talking to Ethel?"

"She said to watch. I have a report right here." Patrick opened his jacket and touched his breast pocket where he kept his tiny notebook.

Mick could see Patrick was wearing his old police uniform. The shirt no longer fit and a button had popped over his stomach. His white paunch and lint filled belly button peered through the gap.

Maggie appeared from the house and stood behind Mick. "Patrick? Are you okay?" She asked.

He said nothing. Car lights appeared in the early evening and turned the corner at the end of the block and stopped against the curb. Patrick slipped the leash from his wrist and his hand closed over the handle of the .38 revolver. His thumb felt for the hammer and his index finger curled around the trigger. He took several quick breaths and stepped toward Mick. When the car stopped behind him, he turned and blinked his eyes in the beam of the headlights. Patrick seemed confused for a moment then turned his back on the gathering crowd and limped down the sidewalk toward home with Pickles leading the way.

"Mom, where have you been?" Mary stepped from her Toyota and walked toward the U-Haul. "We've been worried sick." David got out of the passenger side and followed along with Eliza and Freddie.

"David?" Maggie asked. "Why are you here?" Maggie stepped toward her children. "Eliza?"

"You went missing and we didn't know where you were." David said. "Mary called us."

"Why don't you let us know where you are going so we don't worry." Eliza said.

"Let you know what I'm doing? You haven't come home in three years and now you're worried? I'm fully capable of taking care of myself. I don't need to wear an ankle bracelet so you can keep track of me."

"What are you doing with the truck?" David asked.

"You're behind this aren't you Mary? Always trying to control my life. You're just like your father."

"I'm not trying to control you. Just forget it If you don't want us to care about you, then we'll all leave and let you die in peace, gasping for breath, all alone in your bedroom."

"Gasping for breath? What are you talking about?" Maggie asked.

David cut in. He walked up to Maggie and gave her a quick kiss on the cheek. "Mom, it's good to see you again."

Maggie touched his thick hair on the back of his head and she pulled away. "Why are you here? The last time we were together was Christmas Eve, five years ago."

"We're just concerned about you, that's all." Freddie said. He walked around the U-Haul and opened the back door. "Why are you renting a truck?"

"I'm planning a surprise party for the whole family," Maggie said, "and if you don't attend, you're out of the will."

"You have a will?" Freddie asked.

"I'm not dead yet, Freddie. Tell your wife not to get her hopes up," Maggie said. "Since you guys are here, will you help me unload my new desk."

As David and Freddie unloaded the antique desk she received from Maldonado's House of Eternal Rest, Eliza pulled Mary aside and spoke in hushed tones. "Isn't this what the police suggested?"

"I'm not overreacting. I know what the doctor said. Why would anyone rent a U-Haul and drive all the way to Chicago to get an old desk from a funeral home. You call that normal?"

"It's out of the ordinary but it isn't crazy."

"What about the other stuff Dr. Smith mentioned? Coughing up blood and having a pregnancy test. You don't think that's crazy?" Mary asked.

Eliza shrugged her shoulders. As they turned to follow the others inside, they found a sheet of paper on the ground near the passenger side of the truck. Mary picked it up. It was an itemized invoice from Maldonado's House of Eternal Rest, funeral expenses for Velma Gladwell. All of the items were checked off and at the bottom of the page, written in red letters, "Paid in Full, $29,500.00". The signature at the bottom of the page was Margaret R. O'Reilly, dated yesterday.

"Who's Velma Gladwell?" Eliza asked.

Mary looked from face to face. "I doubt they went to Chicago to buy a desk. If mom doesn't give us some straight answers, I'm hiring a lawyer tomorrow."

CHAPTER 23

*There was never a scabby sheep in a flock
that didn't like to have a comrade.*
-Irish Proverb

Sally McTavish and Mabel Feely sat in their usual spots in church, the third row back, near the right side. Patrick was seven rows back on the inside, near the aisle and Maggie with four of her children occupied the fifth row. Across the aisle sat an older man, wearing black with a young assistant at his side. Bishop O'Connor neither frowned nor smiled but kept his focus on the actions of Father Muldoon.

Father Muldoon's hand shook and the candles on the altar flickered as he lit them. He tripped and nearly fell against the kneeling rail when he went from one side to the other. His face was returning to near normal. The swelling was gone but a residual dull green, like thin week-old guacamole, on his right cheek was ample evidence of the recent past.

"In the name of the Father and the Son and the Holy Ghost. Amen." He moved his right hand in the shape of the cross and turned toward the congregation.

It was a near sell-out crowd with Maggie's children on one side and Bishop O'Connor with his assistant on the other side. Patrick was stoic and quiet in row number seven but Mabel and Sally whispered more than usual with the excitement of guests in church.

When it was time for holy communion they filed up to the front of the church and knelt along the rail before the altar. St. Michael's Parish was rooted in tradition and with few members to influence any change, it had remained unchanged for years. Communion was offered in the common cup. Sally McTavish was first then Mabel Feely was offered the cup. Her nose was running and she attempted a quick sniff before sampling the wine. Unfortunately, she sucked in the wine at the same time sending her into a convulsive sneeze. Purple droplets splashed onto her face and blouse. Father Muldoon blinked to avoid getting wine in his eyes but he couldn't avoid the communion shower. He continued as if nothing happened.

He tried to wipe the rim of the cup with a napkin but it sloshed over the edge and ran down his arm to his elbow inside his robe. Father Muldoon offered the hastily wiped cup to Freddie. Freddie glanced sideways toward his mother as if he feared offending her. He shook his head side to side and got up from the kneeling rail. The wafer alone was enough communing for him. The others followed in his wake. Bishop O'Connor never got up from his seat but checked his watch several times.

Before the last person had returned to their pew, Patrick stood and pointed a shaky finger toward Maggie. "She did it," he announced.

All eyes turned from Patrick to Maggie. Sunday Mass was over, there was no purpose in trying to squeeze in a benediction. Maggie stood and glared at Patrick. "Have you been talking to Ethel again?" She asked.

"She's the reason I wrote the letter." Patrick continued pointing at Maggie but twisted his head in Bishop O'Connor's direction. He gripped the pew in front of him as he trembled and his face turned from pale to ruddy.

"Stop. Both of you." Father Muldoon stepped forward and gripped Patrick's arm and gently escorted him to his side. "We must learn to live as brothers and sisters in this world."

"Would someone please tell me what's going on?" Mary asked. She looked from face to face searching for clarity.

Before anyone could answer, Patrick swung his cane in an arch over his head. Father Muldoon was still gripping Patrick's left arm but was focused on Maggie and the brass handle of the cane struck him squarely on the crown of his head. His scalp split open and blood ran freely down the back of his neck and under his clerical collar. He crumpled to the floor, stunned but not unconscious.

David jumped over the back of his pew and wrenched the cane from Patrick's hand before another blow could be delivered. Maggie bent to the floor and pressed her small handkerchief on the oozing blood coming from the priest's scalp.

"Is this the way you conduct Sunday Mass?" Bishop O'Connor asked. He extracted his ample girth from between the pews and into the aisle alongside Father Muldoon.

"Since he got caught singing in the bathtub with Maggie," Mabel spoke up. "Nothing seems right anymore."

"Did I drive you to this?" David looked at his mother.

"Get over it, David," Eliza said. "At least Father Muldoon has the guts to stand up to people in his parish. You just tuck your tail between your legs and run off to California."

"What is going on here?" Mary asked her mother. "Patrick is clunking the priest with his cane. You get caught singing the Star-Spangled Banner in the bathtub with Father Muldoon after he gets knocked unconscious. Then you run off to Chicago with Mick Torkelson in a U-Haul to get an antique desk." She pulled a paper from her handbag. "And who is Velma Gladwell?"

She hesitated before answering. "Never heard of her."

"$29,500 for funeral expenses and you don't know who she is?" Mary crumpled the invoice in her hand and waved it in the air. "What Dr. Smith said is true, isn't it?"

"What did Dr. Smith say and why are you talking to him about me?" Maggie left her blood-soaked handkerchief plastered to Father Muldoon's head and stood as tall as she could. "You have no business talking to him about my health."

"I have every right to talk to anyone I please about you," Mary said. "You're going senile."

"There is nothing wrong with my mind."

"Listen to what's going on around here. You're all crazy." Mary held her arm out and turned in a circle. Several minutes passed with no one speaking. It was as if the reality of Mary's words registered in their minds.

Bishop O'Connor slipped his arms into his overcoat. "Shamus, get your head fixed and get some rest. I'll stop by your office tomorrow with my final decision."

"Don't blame him for anything. It's all my fault," Maggie said.

"I'm sorry Mrs. O'Reilly. He shouldn't have been in your bathtub and he has no control over the Parish. Many things are happening in the Church that shouldn't be happening. I have no choice in this matter."

"No choice?"

"Unless you can convince me otherwise, Father Muldoon will be suspended from conducting services for three months and undergo psychological analysis. If he's deemed fit for the priesthood, his case will be reviewed and then I will make a decision regarding his long-term fitness."

"But you can't." Maggie said.

"Why not," Mary asked.

"What if I die? Who's going to do my funeral?"

CHAPTER 24

Death is more universal than life;
everyone dies but not everyone lives.
– Alan Sachs

Monday.

"Dr. Smith would you please advise us on the next step?" Mary rubbed her eyes and smeared her makeup. "I think this is worse than expected."

"What's happening?"

The four siblings spent the next thirty minutes describing the detailed events of Sunday Mass. They described the sneezed upon communion wine, the confrontation between Patrick and the priest and Maggie's pleading request to allow Father Muldoon to remain so he could perform her funeral.

Dr. Smith jotted notes and nodded as they spoke.

"And then I confronted her about this." Mary held out the paid invoice for funeral services for Velma Gladwell. The signature clearly belonged to Maggie.

"And she had no recollection about this?" He asked.

"She denied it. It's not like her to lie so I assume she didn't remember."

"This is exactly what I was concerned about," Dr. Smith said. "We have to treat her as a vulnerable adult."

"She doesn't seem very vulnerable to me," David said.

"Vulnerable in the sense that people can take advantage of her such as bogus charities or sob stories about needing money."

Dr. Smith paused and leaned back in his chair. "My own grandparents were suckered into giving thousands of dollars to a young couple begging on the streets because they couldn't afford to feed their children. It turned out, they didn't have children. It was a scam."

"Do you think this is what's happening to our mother?" Eliza asked.

"Anything's possible. You might want to start with the funeral home and see what you find out." Dr. Smith clicked his ballpoint pen and slipped it into his pocket. "I think the next best step is to have her evaluated by a memory clinic, a specialist who focuses on identifying and treating dementia. If we can get another opinion regarding her competence then we could petition the court to get her declared incompetent. They would appoint a guardian or power of attorney to manage and protect her resources."

"She'll never agree to go to a clinic like that," Mary said.

"And if we trick her into it, she'll never forgive us," Freddie added. "I vote to forget this whole thing and wait to see what happens."

"If you love someone you do what is best for them, even if it's difficult," Mary said.

"Are you suggesting I don't care about Mom?"

"I never said that, but walking away isn't the answer either."

"Do you want the risk of permanently destroying her just to prove a point?" Eliza asked. "If she has dementia you can't change it. If she has cancer, then the clock is ticking with or without treatment. There's no clear benefit either way. Leave her alone. You don't care about her. You're just trying to save money or make yourself feel better."

Mary's face reddened at the accusations. She stood and put on her jacket. "I don't care what any of you say. I'm taking her to a memory clinic and if she hates me for it, that's a risk I'll take."

The meeting was over.

#

Vinny Maldonado checked his list of new clients for the month. Chicago was in the grips of an early influenza season and unvaccinated people were bearing the full fury of the virus. Twenty-three deaths were recorded in the city and it wasn't even the first of December.

Monday was delivery day. When the residents of the morgue had exceeded their stay and no one came to claim them, the county coroner terminated their lease and they were evicted. But the last ride wasn't in the back of a shiny black Lincoln Continental. Vinny used a large panel truck with the words, "Wendell's Flower Shop" stenciled on the side to avoid creeping out the neighbors. The frozen bodies were unceremoniously stacked in the back and delivered to the crematorium before 10 AM.

Maldonado's House of Eternal Rest also provided services for traditional funerals. Unfortunately, he was preparing funeral services for his mother's second cousin's half-brother and his wife. Alfonse and Fiori Romano were killed in a traffic accident and their children insisted Vinny provide the services because he was family. Cremations were quick and lucrative, traditional funerals took time and effort but Vinny was up to the task. He was a professional and if he couldn't deliver it would be a mark against the family. The urgency of so many deaths demanded additional help. He and several other undertakers in the region shared labor when schedules became excessive. It was a classic "you scratch my back, I'll scratch yours" arrangement and it worked. But today was different.

Velma Gladwell was released from the morgue and she was coming in style because Maggie O'Reilly insisted. Officially she was listed as Velma Gladwell; cause of death-heart disease. But unofficially she was Margaret O'Reilly and he had the printed false death certificate to prove it. The bill was paid in advance, but money wasn't the issue. Vinny had plenty and his contract with the county insured a steady flow of customers. He was intrigued by Maggie's plan and was honored to be part of it. Velma Gladwell-

Maggie O'Reilly was his project and he couldn't let the hired help in on the secret.

Vinny opened the image files on his desktop computer and studied the digital photos of Maggie. Vinny had insisted on a photo session with one of the local portrait photographers so he had some quality references for comparison. She was small but stood taller than her actual height. Her face was thin but not gaunt, she was nicely aged, like a fine wine, but not old. Her naturally wavy gray-streaked auburn hair was surprisingly thick and was dyed black and cut short just above her shoulders. She had nice cheekbones and a fine chin, not overbearing and jutting like some.

In the close-up photos, Vinny could see her teeth, strong and straight but tobacco stained with slightly receding gums. She had fine creases extending outward from her eyes like rays of sunshine breaking through a cloudy sky. Her skin was fair and lightly freckled but he didn't see any cancerous growths or age spots which would be difficult to reproduce. In another life she could have been an aging movie star. She was an original work of art soon to be duplicated by the artist. Vinny was ready for the challenge.

He heard activity in the parking area behind the mortuary. Vinny parted the venetian blinds and peered out. The panel truck had arrived and the black shiny hearse was right behind. He took off his Versace jacket and silk tie and rolled up his sleeves.

Time to go to work.

CHAPTER 25

Everyone's just dying to have their own funeral.
— Anthony T. Hincks

"How's your head?" Bishop O'Connor tugged on the sleeves of his overcoat and hung it on the hook behind the door of the priest's office at St. Michael's Parish.

"It's been better." Shamus gingerly touched the stitches poking out from the top of his head. The swelling had reduced to half of a goose egg with generous applications of ice. "Five stitches."

The Bishop grunted as he dropped into a chair across from the desk. "You're lucky."

"How so?" Father Shamus folded his hands together and leaned forward resting his elbows on his desk.

"These people like you and I can't find anyone to take your place, at least not for the next several weeks."

"What are you saying?"

"You have a generous donor and if it wasn't for him or her, we couldn't afford to keep this church open. If I ship you off to Sweet Grass, Montana we risk losing that donor and then the church would close."

"I promise things will run better in the future." Father Muldoon felt the tension in his shoulders relax.

"Don't make promises you can't keep. You're on probation. If I hear of any improprieties or even a hint of a scandal in the next ninety days you can pack your bags."

"Thank you."

"Now do you have any Jameson around here. We should celebrate your new beginning."

Shamus went to his office file cabinet and pulled out the drawer. The bottle clinked behind some manila folders. As he lifted it out of its hiding place, they heard the main church door close in the narthex. Father Shamus tucked the bottle back into its place and went to investigate. Patrick Murphy was standing beside the memorial table lighting a candle.

"Patrick, how are you today?" He asked.

"Father Shamus, nice to see you up and about," Patrick said. "Don't mind me, I'm here to light a candle and pray for Ethel."

"About yesterday..." Father Shamus said. "I forgive you."

"Forgive me for what?" Patrick stepped closer to Father Shamus and stared at the bandage on the top of his head. "What happened to your head?"

Shamus hesitated for a moment. "Oh, nothing. I bumped my head and it needed a couple stitches. I'm fine."

"Well you be careful. There's plenty of those dope-seeking gangs around here. I wouldn't want any of them cracking your noggin' for a jug of communion wine. Don't you worry Father, I'll be watching for you."

"Thank you, Patrick. I feel safer with you around."

#

When the meeting with Dr. Smith adjourned there was obvious discord between Mary and the others. Eliza and Freddie voted to leave Maggie alone. Eliza was anxious to return to Portland and save the whales or trees or sea slugs or whatever was the threatened species of the week. Freddie was overdrawn at the bank and had little hope of financial security unless he divorced his wife, filed bankruptcy and won the lottery. Or his mother died.

David was more tepid than old dishwater. He wiped his eyes and blew his nose three times driving from the doctor's office back to Mary's house. "It's all my fault."

"Just shut up. That's the thirtieth time you said that." Eliza clenched her jaws and stared out the side window of the car.

"Mom thinks she's dying. Don't you remember what she said after church? She's talking about her funeral. Instead of treating her like a criminal she needs our love and care." David blew his nose again.

"If she needs our love, she has a funny way of showing it," Mary said.

"I don't care what any of you do but I've decided to treat her nice because I don't want to get cut out of the will," Freddie said.

"What if she doesn't have a will? Do you know what will happen, Freddie? The estate will go to probate, the lawyers and government will take half and by the time we get done fighting over the rest, you won't have enough to leave a ten-percent tip at McDonalds." Everyone knew Eliza was right.

Mary flipped her blinker and turned left into her driveway. "If she has a will, we need to find it soon because if she's getting dementia, anything signed from now on could be contested on the grounds of incompetence." She turned the key and her car came to a rest.

"Then maybe we shouldn't pursue the competency issue." Freddie added.

"What about the coughing blood stuff that Dr. Smith talked about. She's dying or going bonkers or both. We don't have much time." Mary unbuckled her seatbelt.

"Let's decide the next step before we do anything else," Eliza said. "Mary, are you going to arrange the memory clinic thing?"

"Not yet," she said. "There's a private investigator I hired to spy on my ex-husband. I'm going to have him put a listening device in Mom's house so we can check on her."

"But that's illegal and unethical," David said.

"Not if you don't get caught."

"Mary, you need to take a close look at Mom the next time you see her," Eliza said.

"Why?"

"Because that's you in twenty years."

#

"House of Eternal Rest," Vinny heard the secretary answer the phone in the front office. There was a long pause and Vinny could hear her scribbling notes. "I'll let Mr. Maldonado know right away." The phone clicked.

She turned from her desk and walked into Vinny's private office. "Mr. Maldonado, I have some sad news. That was the county coroner. Arthur Finkelstein's wife died last night."

"Goldie? How did she die?"

"He said 'she's gorked from a blood clot'. Anyway, they want you to do the funeral but they want it done before the Sabbath which is Saturday. What should I tell them?"

"They're Jewish. Why do they want me to do this?"

"He said you made a deal on some diamond jewelry a few years ago in trade for a deal on a casket."

"I vaguely remember the conversation." He went back to his files and pulled out the Finkelstein folder. There was a note from five years ago. Vinny wanted a big diamond ring and Arthur agreed to make a trade. Arthur selected a mid-price range casket in oak with brass trim. Vinny had two of those in stock and one was already designated for Velma Gladwell.

"Tell Arthur I'll pick up Goldie and get right to work." Vinny checked his schedule for the next ten days. He had over thirty unclaimed bodies scheduled for cremation for the state and with the addition of Goldie Finkelstein he had four traditional funerals. Vinny knew Goldie would be a tough one. Art wanted her to look like a queen but he didn't want to pay for it. Vinny was anxious to get to work on Velma but he might need to put her on hold until Goldie was laid to rest. He decided to assign his hired help to prepare Alfonse and Fiori but Goldie and Velma were his.

Vinny unrolled his shirt sleeves and clipped the gold cuff links. He adjusted his tie and put on his Versace jacket. The black Lincoln hearse had just returned from the city morgue with Velma Gladwell in the back. As soon as she was unloaded, he was off to visit Arthur Finkelstein and offer his condolences.

It was a tough job but someone had to do it.

CHAPTER 26

In three words I can sum up everything
I've learned about life: it goes on.
– Robert Frost

"Here's the plan." Maggie sipped her Long Island iced tea and set the glass back on the coaster. She looked around the VFW. It was the middle of the afternoon and only one other table had guests. She opened a small spiral bound pocket calendar from her purse and held it for Mick to see.

"Vinny promised to have the body ready by this weekend. He said we can pick her up or they'll deliver. But it's an extra fifteen hundred if he does." She looked at Mick for his response.

"Pay the money. I'm not driving that U-Haul through Chicago again." Mick sat back and glanced at the golf tournament playing on the big screen television behind the bar. "When are you going to tell Father Muldoon?"

"I think he's on board but he hasn't given me a final yes." Maggie said. "Anyway, he won't have a choice. When I'm declared dead, everyone will expect him to do the funeral."

"I'm having second thoughts about this Maggie." Mick stuck his finger in his ear and adjusted his hearing aid. "It just doesn't seem right, tricking your family like that."

"It's too late to back out. I'll have the body delivered as soon as she's ready. We can keep her in your garage until I'm dead."

"You want me to just call your family and say you croaked? It won't be easy."

"Here." She slipped a brochure across the table. "There's a square dance convention in Mason City, Iowa this weekend. I made reservations for us at the Holiday Inn."

"But I don't know how to square dance." He said.

"That's not the point. We'll get to be friends with one or two other couples, that way we have witnesses. While we're square dancing I'm going to fake a heart attack and you can carry me out."

"What if someone calls 911?"

"I'm not going to fake it that much. I've been reading up on the signs of a heart attack. I'm practicing so it looks convincing but not bad enough to scare anyone."

"Then what?"

"Vinny Maldonado has someone working for him who is going to pretend to be the coroner. He'll call Mary and tell her the bad news. Vinny has the cause of death and a fake death certificate printed and ready to go. He's just waiting for the date and time."

"But someone from your family will need to identify the body."

"I got that figured out too." Maggie pulled another brochure from her purse. "My husband is going to identify me."

"Albert has been dead for seventeen years."

"We have an appointment with the judge in Mason City. We're getting married on Friday."

"Are you serious?"

"Don't get your undies in a bunch, after the funeral we're getting a divorce."

#

Patrick was a good cop. As soon as Maggie left the house in her car, he hit the speed dial to Mary.

"What was she wearing?" Mary asked.

"Long black coat. Fancy shoes. And a frilly hat."

"Good, that means she's going somewhere other than the grocery store. Thanks Patrick." Mary remembered one more thing. "I'm having an electrician stop by the house while mom is gone to fix a light switch. He'll be driving a black truck."

"No problem. I'll let you know when he leaves." Patrick closed his phone and scratched Pickles behind the ears. He wrote a quick note to himself and set his binoculars beside his sandwich on the couch. He was ready.

Within fifteen minutes a black Ford truck pulled up to the curb in front of Maggie's house. An average sized man with a baseball cap, sunglasses and a small backpack disappeared around the house. In less than ten minutes he was back in his truck and drove away.

#

Maggie ordered the fish sandwich and fries and another Long Island iced tea. Mick seemed to be thoroughly enjoying himself, now that they were engaged to be married. He ordered himself a microbrew with a fancy name and a steak sandwich.

Maggie hadn't thought about being married for many years. She had grown accustomed to quiet nights talking to no one, watching old movies and reading books in the corner of the sitting room with a bowl of popcorn and a ticking clock. She liked being alone but she hated it at the same time. Loneliness was a terrible thing. Maybe having lunch and going on long walks with someone wasn't a bad thing. Then she thought about dirty socks and underwear on the floor and mud tracked in from the yard. And snoring, she hated snoring.

Halfway through his steak sandwich Mick stopped. "Maggie I can't do it."

"What?"

"I won't marry you in the way you are planning." Mick looked away from her eyes.

"You can't do this to me. It's all planned out."

"We were both taught to marry for love. I'll marry you if you really want me to marry you but I won't do it for convenience or to trick your family."

Maggie was quiet. If Mick didn't marry her, they could still go through with the plans but what if Mary insisted on identifying the body. It could be trouble.

"Maggie think about the reason you're doing all this. All you want is to know if your family really cares or if they are using you or tolerating you until you die." Mick sat back in his chair and wiped some spit from the corner of his mouth. "I want the same thing."

"What do you mean?"

"I want to know if you really care or if you are just using me or tolerating me until you get what you want."

It was five minutes of quiet between them. Their food got cool and a napkin slipped off Maggie's lap and onto the floor. Just as she was about to speak, her phone buzzed.

She touched the screen and a message from Vinny's House of Eternal Rest appeared along with a series of photos. *Three wig options. Pick the one you like and make sure your hair is cut and dyed the same. Let me know ASAP.*

"How do you like my hair?" she asked Mick.

"Maggie you don't have to do anything fancy to please me. I like you just the way you are."

"Black hair or auburn? Wavy or straight?"

"I'm not going to answer unless you tell me what's in your heart."

"I'm not sure what's in my heart, but I need to give a reply to Vinny." She touched her phone and scrolled through the photos. "I think I like the wavy auburn. That's how my hair was when I was young. Do you like it?"

"Are you asking me as a co-conspirator or as a friend?"

Maggie was quiet. She extended her hand across the table. He took it.

CHAPTER 27

Get busy living or get busy dying.
-Stephen King

The crematorium was working overtime. When ashes of one body were retrieved and packaged into an economy urn for disposal, another body took its place. While his assistant was manning the fires, Vinny was in the prep room at the back of the mortuary. He was dressed in white coveralls and stood between two tables, each holding a body. They were cold, stiff and lifeless and it was his job to make them appear alive.

Vinny stretched a pair of blue latex gloves over his hands and turned on the bright overhead flood lights so he could see every detail. Goldie was a bit pudgy and had a double chin and fuller cheeks. Despite the sixty-pound difference between Goldie and Velma, they were surprisingly similar in size and shape. Goldie had a large, irregular mole on the right side of her neck and deep creases around her nose. Her thin, gray hair was lifeless but she had worn a wig for many years, changing color and style several times a day depending on her mood.

Velma was thin and pale from living her last years in an institution. Her skin was loose and hung off the back of her arms but that didn't matter because clothing would cover it. It was her face that mattered. That's what everyone looked at, her face and her folded hands across her front.

Vinny reviewed the notes he received from Goldie's family. They wanted the dark brown wig, the black dress and a simple wedding band on her finger. They had given him a thin gold chain with a Star of David pendant for her to wear as well. On the inside of the casket cover was to be an embroidered Star of David and "Shalom".

It took him three hours of prep to get Goldie ready for display. Her eyebrows were carefully trimmed and accented with a dark pencil. Opaque makeup covered the blotchiness of her skin He held the lipstick in his hand and checked the label. *Strawberry Milkshake*. The color complimented her wig. The pendant was clasped around her neck and with some final adjustments of her hair and clothing, he was satisfied. The casket, on its wheeled stand, was pushed into the viewing room, awaiting transport to the synagogue on Friday. It was time to face Velma.

Vinny warmed the mortician's putty in his hand and pinched off a small piece. He pressed it into her cheeks and temples, trying to erase the vestiges of disease and age. He filled the sunken areas at the base of her neck and under her jaw.

There was a large flat-screen television attached to the wall of the prep room used primarily for the entertainment of the preppers but he used it to his advantage. He projected the images from his laptop onto the television so he could better see the details of Maggie's photos. It took him more than an hour until he was satisfied with the shape of her face and neck. It was the shape of the face and the eyes which transformed the dead into the living in the eyes of the loved ones. He had to erase the hollows of skin stretched over a skull. Even though the eyes were shut, they had to have fullness as someone sleeping, not sunken and vacant. It was his job to give her flesh where none existed so the nuances of light and shadow would play their role in bringing someone to life. Makeup, jewelry and clothing were nothing more than camouflage to cover a dead body. But when the foundation was true, people saw what they wanted to see; a loved one asleep.

After two hours of sculpting, Vinny switched off the high intensity overhead lights and brought in lamps to cast a soft glow from the side and front. He studied Velma's face from several angles, shooting a dozen photos in the process. After uploading them onto his laptop for magnification he took a break for lunch to allow his mind a break. He knew he lacked objectivity about his own work unless he separated from it, for a time.

#

Mary felt her heart skip a beat when she realized she was spying on her own mother. She reviewed the instructions from the private investigator and downloaded the app onto her iPhone. It was much easier than when she spied on her ex-husband a few years ago. Now all she needed was her cell phone. The tiny listening device recorded up to three hours of conversation and was easily downloaded and archived. It was voice activated so it didn't transmit three hours of the cat purring in the background. Mary's finger trembled as she poked the icon. Within seconds she could easily hear the investigator's voice in the background. "Test, test from kitchen". There was a brief pause, "test, test from front room." He did a sound check from three more locations and every time it was clear enough to make it sound as if the speaker was within arms-length of the listener. The other nice thing was the ability to listen live. She received notification on her phone whenever the listening device was activated.

Mary was repulsed to think how simple it was to eavesdrop on someone. She hated herself for doing it, because she wouldn't want this done to her but if it saved her mother's life then maybe it was worth it.

After the listening device was activated, Mary looked up the number for the memory clinic provided to her from Dr. Smith. She dialed the number but just as the receptionist answered, Mary hung up. *Mom better be demented because if she isn't, she'll never forgive me for this.* Mary dialed the number again.

"I'm calling to make an appointment for my mother." Mary said.

"What seems to be the problem?"

"She thinks she's pregnant."

"Congratulations."

"She's seventy-seven."

"Oh...I'll need more information."

#

Father Muldoon sat alone in his office long after Bishop O'Connor left. He reviewed the recent events in his life. His concussion still bothered him but at least he could make sense of it, and he hadn't heard any more jokes at the Main Street Café since the week it happened. Despite Maggie's claim of planning to kill herself, she still seemed rational, albeit eccentric. Patrick Murphy was another story.

Shamus couldn't understand why everyone seemed to be focused on Maggie's sanity when Patrick appeared to be the one on the edge. The name "Jezebel" worried him. It wasn't a badge of honor. The last time he heard that name spoken was by a Pentecostal Preacher on television, and he wasn't talking about his wife. The accusations toward Maggie, *she did it,* didn't make much sense either, unless Patrick was referring to his meeting Maggie in the bathtub.

Father Shamus gently probed the margins of the laceration on the top of his head. He could feel the stitches bristling in his hair. Patrick's assault was sudden and unexpected. Shamus doubted he was the target of Patrick's outburst although he was the recipient but that didn't explain much.

Shamus pulled open the top drawer in his desk and pulled out the shiny brass .38 caliber pistol bullet which had fallen from Patrick's pocket during confession. If Patrick was dangerous with names and the crook of a cane, he feared the damage Patrick might inflict with a loaded gun.

Shamus adjusted his clerical collar and took a long drink of water. He was sent to shepherd the flock not bring accusations. It wasn't time to confront Patrick and it wasn't time to go to the police.

But it might be a good time to have a heart-to-heart talk with Maggie and find out the truth.

CHAPTER 28

Only put off until tomorrow
what you are willing to die having left undone."
-Pablo Picasso

Maggie pulled her big suitcase onto her front porch and waited. It was still dark in the early morning and she could see her breath in the pale blue glow of the street light. She had enough clothes packed for 5 days but she planned to be back home by Monday. She hated traveling during November because wild animals roamed the highways by night and if the weather turned sour, one could be trapped for days waiting for roads to be cleared. An extra change of clothes never did anyone harm.

Maggie picked up her phone. "Mick, where are you?"

"Just getting ready to leave my place."

"Don't waste any time. We have to be there by two o'clock to sign the marriage license. Make sure you bring your ID."

"I have it packed."

Fifteen minutes later he pulled into Maggie's driveway and loaded her suitcase. They drove out of Peterville and headed south before Main Street Café was open for breakfast.

Two blocks away Patrick clipped the leash on Pickles and they stepped out of the house in the predawn. Patrick checked his watch and scribbled something in his notebook.

#

Mary awoke to a drab gray November morning. There was a light rain, somewhere between a mist and a drizzle, a mizzle, and it didn't help her mood. The icon for her listening device blinked on her phone screen.

After listening for five hours yesterday she was crabby. She heard nothing but her mother's local AM radio station blabbing about the recent election results. If Maggie had said anything significant it was drowned out by the news and static. Mary was having second thoughts about eavesdropping. She felt guilty and she wasn't learning anything of value anyway. She checked the time of the notification, five o'clock in the morning, almost three hours ago.

Mary started the coffee maker and sat down to listen to her phone.

Heat turned down...stove off... passport...

Mary listened to the voice three times, not sure what she heard. It was her mother talking to herself at five in the morning. *Passport...*

Mary ran up the stairway, two steps at a time and rapped on the guest bedroom door. "David, get up. Mom's leaving."

David rubbed the sleep from his eyes and opened the door. "Leaving? How do you know?"

"Listen to this." Mary replayed the voice from her phone. "She's talking to herself."

"So? Don't you talk to yourself sometimes?"

"She's checking off a list. *Turn down the heat. Turn off the stove. Passport.* What does that mean to you?" Mary ran her fingers through her morning hair and pushed it out of her face, hooking a curl behind her ear.

"It sounds as if she was leaving. You don't need a passport unless you are leaving the country. She wouldn't do that would she? Alone?" David shrugged his shoulders and stepped back into his bedroom. He changed out of his pajamas and reappeared fully dressed.

"Who do you know that might travel with her?" David asked.

"She doesn't have many friends as far as I know. The church ladies and her old bridge club, but I don't think she's played in a couple years."

"What about that Mick guy?" David asked.

"Mick Torkelson? It's worth a check."

Mary went through her list of contacts and dialed Mick's number.

"This is Mick. Leave a message."

Mary said nothing and hung up. Next, she called Father Muldoon.

"This is Father Muldoon at St. Michael's Parish. I'm out of the office..." Mary hung up again and checked her watch.

"Let's go to the Main Street Café. Father Muldoon usually goes there for breakfast. Maybe we can catch him and see if he knows anything." Mary pulled her hair back into a ragged bunch and wrapped an elastic band around it. She pulled on a coat and was out the door before David could respond. He pulled the door shut and followed her into the garage.

#

Vinny Maldonado was in the prep room by 5:00 AM because it was Friday and his bodies weren't quite ready. Three traditional funerals today and Velma-Maggie was scheduled to be shipped before noon.

Goldie looked as good as he could get her and he doubted anyone would complain. Any more fussing probably wouldn't matter because Arthur was more concerned about the bill than Goldie's appearance.

Vinny held a thick makeup pencil in his right hand and leaned over Fiori's rigid mask. One eye stubbornly gapped open so he dabbed a small bit of superglue on the lid and went back to filling in the eyebrows. The superglue did its job and he switched to a thin eyeliner and outlined the margins of the lids and lashes and added a subtle shade of pink on the upper lids. Once the base makeup was applied, he used various flesh tones to highlight some features and minimize others. The visitation for Alfonse and Fiori was tonight but their actual funeral service was out of town, tomorrow. They were family and he was expected to attend.

"Mr. Maldonado, the delivery truck is here."

"The Jensen Furniture truck?"

"Yes. Do you want to talk to them?"

"I don't have time. It's the one on the right. Instructions are on my desk."

The assistant relayed the message to the two delivery men. She reviewed the cover letter and instructions with the driver. Maggie had insisted that Velma's body be delivered using a furniture truck so no one would suspect anything unusual. The destination was printed in bold letters, *Mick Torkelson, 93712 Five Mile Creek Road, Peterville, Minnesota. The key was on a nail behind the hanging flower pot on the side of the garage. Place the casket in the garage and cover with a blanket.*

Vinny returned to his task. Fiori was done. Alfonse had enough fat on his cheeks there were no hollows and his ample chin made it difficult to button the top button of his shirt and make the knot of his tie appear natural instead of a noose. All he needed was enough color to mask the pallor of death. If hair were a symbol of wealth, Alfonse was destitute but the little he had was highly treasured. The sparse strands started somewhere behind his ears and were carefully positioned over his expansive glistening scalp and tacked in place with a healthy dose of hairspray.

Vinny tidied the satin casket liner and brushed away some stray flakes of dandruff from the front of Alfonse's blue suit. He clicked the lid shut and checked his watch. The Lincoln Continental hearse was ready to give Alfonse and Fiori one last ride. Vinny and an assistant wheeled the caskets to the open back of the hearse and slid them both in headfirst. He had just enough time to shower and change. It was an hour drive to St. James Cathedral. There was no time to spare.

CHAPTER 29

*The No. 1 reason people fail in life is because
they listen to their friends, family, and neighbors.*
-Napoleon Hill

"Turn left...not this street, the next one." Maggie tried to orient the map with their direction of travel.

"Use my phone."

"Do you want me to call for directions?"

"Never mind." Mick pulled the car over to the curb and tapped the icon for Google maps. "It says we are five minutes away."

"How does your phone know that?"

"It just does." Mick turned into the parking area for the county courthouse and turned off the car. "Are you ready for this?"

Maggie pulled out a compact mirror from her purse and checked her lipstick. "How do I look?"

"Like a bride."

"Don't lie to me. I'm an old bag."

"Listen to yourself. You think everyone is lying to you. You wouldn't know the truth when you do hear it."

"You sound like my mother."

"You want to know the really sad part? You expect to hear the truth but you are the one lying to everyone. All of this is nothing but one big lie." Mick looked down the street.

"Are you finished? The judge is waiting." Maggie opened the passenger door and stepped out into the afternoon cold. Her heels clicked on the frozen pavement and Mick hurried to catch up.

Maggie stopped before the main reception desk near the entrance to the courthouse. "We're here to get a marriage license and get married."

"Congratulations." The round-faced receptionist smiled back at them.

"Don't congratulate us yet." Maggie rolled her eyes slightly and nodded her head toward Mick who was just coming through the main entrance. "We had to get married, if you know what I mean."

The receptionist's eyes widened and she looked slowly from Maggie to Mick and back. "The office you want is on the second floor, number 207." She pointed toward the elevators and stared at them until they were out of sight.

#

Mary and David pulled open the Main Street Café door and a wall of warm air tainted with the smell of burnt pancakes, rolled out of the restaurant and into the cold morning air. Father Muldoon was alone at a corner table drinking coffee and finishing the last of his corned-beef hash and poached eggs. He set aside the morning paper as they approached his table.

"May we sit down?"

"Of course." Father Muldoon said. He pushed his dirty dishes aside and motioned toward the empty chairs. "I thought you had returned to San Francisco," he said to David.

"That was my plan but you know how things change."

"Yes, I do." Shamus touched the top of his head where the stitches bristled up through his clipped hair. "I assume you are here because of your mother."

"How well do you know Maggie?" Mary asked.

"Fairly well. I've been at St. Michael's Parish for several years. She's very consistent with church attendance, as you know." He raised his coffee cup and motioned toward the waitress.

"Has she ever mentioned travel?" David asked.

Shamus thought for several moments while his coffee cup was being refilled. "Not that I can recall. She always seemed like a homebody."

David asked, "do you have any reason to believe she might not be stable. You know…going senile?"

"Judge not, lest you be judged."

"Are you talking to me or yourself?"

"Myself. Maggie has always been eccentric but I don't think she's crazy. Why are you asking this?"

"Five years ago, my daughter was planning a wedding in Cancun, Mexico," Mary said. "She wanted Maggie, her grandmother, to attend. It nearly took an act of congress to convince her to get a passport and agree to come to the wedding. Then at the last minute she backed out. She has never used her passport. Then this morning we overheard her talking about needing her passport. And now she's gone."

"I'm sorry. I can't help you," Father Muldoon said.

"She hasn't traveled a hundred miles in the past three years but recently she went to Chicago with Mick Torkelson to get an antique desk from a funeral home. It doesn't make sense."

"Have you talked with Mick?"

"He's gone too," David said.

"Dr. Smith thinks Mom is irrational and might have dementia. I'm concerned that Mick is manipulating her to get at her money. He needs to be stopped." Mary took the elastic band out of her unruly hair bunch and reassembled it with little improvement.

"What does your sister say?"

"Eliza went back to Portland. She doesn't want to be bothered with an aging parent." Mary leaned back in her chair and watched Father Muldoon gently scratch the top of his head. "How's your head?"

"I've had worse."

"Father Muldoon, thank you for your time. I'm sorry to involve you in family affairs." Mary stood up to leave. Her phone buzzed and the green listening device icon blinked.

#

"Do you have your identification?" the clerk asked Mick and Maggie. They handed their passports through the window to the clerk. "It will be a few minutes." They took seats in the waiting area and watched others coming in to pay traffic fines and apply for housing permits.

"Michael Torkelson and Margaret O'Reilly?" They turned toward the clerk in the window. "I have your marriage license and your passports. That will be sixty dollars. Don't sign it until you are formally married. It is good for ninety days. If you don't get married in that time you will need to reapply."

"No problem. We're meeting with the judge at two o'clock." Mick said.

"Today?" the clerk asked.

"Thirty minutes from now we'll be Mr. and Mrs. Torkelson." Mick smiled.

"I'm keeping my maiden name." Maggie said.

"You have plenty of time to discuss it." The clerk cleared her throat. "In Iowa there is a seventy-two-hour waiting period after you get your license. You can't get married until next week."

"But...what if I die this weekend?" Maggie asked.

"If you want to get married today you better go to Vegas."

#

Alfonse and Fiori were proudly displayed in the side room at St. James Cathedral as grieving family and friends wiped tears and laughed half-heartedly at old stories. Alfonse and Fiori were good Italians and their family made certain the best wine was served. Vinny was tired after several long days of tedious work. After tonight he could finally relax. Vinny checked the label as he poured himself a glass, it was a seven-year-old Barolo from the Piedmont area of northern Italy. Alfonse would have been proud. Their daughter, Anna, came up to Vinny and gave him a polite hug and a kiss on the cheek. "Thank you for your kind care of Mom and Dad. They look so natural, like they're sleeping."

"You're welcome." He swirled his glass of wine and took a sip. "I'm sorry for your loss."

Anna nodded and dabbed a stray tear. "How can you do this every day? Don't you get depressed being surrounded by death every day?"

"It's a job." His phone rang.

"Vinny, Arthur Finkelstein here."

"Arthur, I'm sorry about Goldie. I hope the service went well."

"Vinny, don't be sorry. We buried Goldie before sundown so it was all done before the Sabbath. Thanks to you and your staff, I don't know how you did it."

"Did what?"

"It was the best Goldie looked in years, and you even removed that hideous growth from the side of her neck."

CHAPTER 30

Love lasts forever but a tattoo lasts six months longer.
-Anonymous

Maggie was silent for a few minutes after the clerk cancelled the wedding plans. She knew Mick was feeling lucky but this way it eliminated the need for a divorce or annulment. She took a deep breath and turned to Mick.

"Alright sunshine. Plan B."

"You have a plan B?" Mick asked.

Maggie opened her iPhone and said, "Tattoo parlors near me."

Siri answered, "There are three tattoo parlors within 10 miles." Maggie checked directions and started toward the parking lot.

"Where are you going?" Mick chased after her.

"River City Ink. I've always wanted to get a tattoo before I die."

"Are you serious?"

"Serious as a heart attack."

"Why?"

"Identification. After it's done, I'll take a picture of it and send it to Mary."

"She'll think you're nuts."

"Then when the coroner calls her this weekend, he can forward the photo of the tattoo and she'll agree it's me."

"What are you getting?"

"My name and address and a little butterfly."

"Where?"

"On my butt. I don't want anyone to see it."

\#

When Mary and David returned to her Toyota, she checked her phone. "The listening device activated while we were in there. I didn't want to say anything while we were with Father Muldoon."

She touched the screen and turned the volume up. There was a faint voice in the background.

"I think I heard 'help' but I can't be sure." David said. "Play it again."

"It doesn't sound like Mom." Mary pushed the volume as far as it would go but the static increased and it picked up the sound of the furnace running.

There was a minute of quiet then in the background came a voice, "Pickles get help".

\#

Dr. Smith reviewed his notes and entered the phone number for Adult Protective Services into his phone. He went through three interoffice transfers until he found the person he wanted.

"Emily Kane."

"Ms. Kane, this is Dr. Smith from Baxter clinic. I'm calling about a patient of mine who may be at risk for exploitation and I'm not certain her family is taking this serious."

"Do you think the risk is imminent?"

"She has a health condition that needs immediate attention and she hasn't followed up for recommended testing and treatment."

"In your professional opinion has she made an informed decision to forego treatment?"

"Let me summarize her situation. She came in requesting a complete examination because she thinks she could be pregnant and she reported not knowing who the father might be."

"That sounds like half of the cases in social services."

"This is different. She's seventy-seven and she's coughing up blood."

"Have you talked with her family about this?"

"Yes. The daughter was going to arrange a consultation through a dementia clinic but they haven't followed through with it."

"What do you want me to do? We have a backlog of over sixty people who may be at risk and a staff of three. Unless you can show me real evidence of exploitation, we aren't going to do anything."

"She's worth plenty of money. She never travels but recently was taken to Chicago by an unrelated man without the family's knowledge. The family found a receipt for funeral expenses for an unknown person in the amount of nearly thirty-thousand dollars all paid by the person of concern"

"I'll run this by our district attorney and see if they want to initiate temporary custody until the details can be investigated."

#

Mary and David parked by the curb in front of Maggie's house. From the street the house looked dark. The windows are intact and the drapes were all closed.

"What should we do?"

"I'm certain it's Patrick Murphy but why is he in Mom's house?"

"He's an ex-cop and you're paying him to watch the place. Probably loves playing the part. I bet when mom left, he let himself in the back door," David said.

"I asked him to keep track of her activities, not break and enter."

"What do you make of his Jezebel comments in church?"

"Mom always said, Patrick was weird. He likes to read apocalyptic conspiracy theories. Once he said the airliner exhaust trails in the sky is the government trying to spread viruses for population control."

"But why call her Jezebel?"

"I think it's like jealousy in junior high school. If he can't have her then no one should."

"Should we go in or should we call the police?"

"Listen on your phone again."

Mary accessed the listening device. They waited five minutes but heard no voices. Then there was a dog bark twice.

"Let's go in. Patrick's harmless."

Mary led the way around the house. The back door was ajar. They pushed it open slowly and listened.

"Patrick?" Mary yelled. Pickles shuffled toward the back door and whined.

Patrick was in the hall crumpled on the floor. His right leg was twisted out at an awkward angle and there was a small pool of blood on the floor from a cut on the back of Patrick's head.

"Call 911," David rushed to Patrick's side and pushed his fingers against the side of his neck to feel for a pulse. Patrick's eyes were half open, staring straight ahead. He didn't blink.

"Is he dead?" Mary asked.

"I can feel a pulse." David gently slipped a pillow under his head. "His leg looks funny. I think he broke his hip."

It took the ambulance thirty-five minutes to get to Maggie's house. David was waiting by the picket fence gate and waved them around to the back door. The driver had turned off the siren but the flashing lights could be seen all over Peterville. The hardware store and Main Street Café emptied and three of Maggie's neighbors were on the street with canes and walkers, surveying the situation.

Father Muldoon sprinted four blocks to Maggie's house and rushed in the back door. "Maggie?"

"It's Patrick," David said as Father Muldoon walked into the house. "Mary and I stopped at the house to check on mom but she was gone. We found Patrick lying on the floor." Mary glanced over at them.

Patrick groaned and yelled as the paramedics splinted his hip as they rolled him onto a backboard. Despite his obvious pain, everyone seemed relieved that he was alive.

"On the count of three," one of paramedics said. He counted to three and they lifted Patrick straight up and onto the gurney. Wide belts were clicked into place over Patrick to prevent him from rolling off the gurney. Patrick flailed his right arm and struck the person nearest him. The EMT grabbed his wrist and tucked his arm next to his side as they guided him down the hall and through the kitchen and out the back door.

Once the ambulance was gone and the echoes of the sirens had faded, the locals dispersed, each muttering their own version of the story. Father Muldoon helped David and Mary clean the muddy wheel tracks and foot prints on the hardwood floor.

"Patrick lost his notebook." Father Muldoon bent and picked up the small pocket-sized notebook under the edge of the furniture. There were five pages of notes recording every time Maggie stepped foot outside her door. The time, weather and her appearance were documented in minute detail. Mick was also in the notes. The last entry was from 5:30 this morning.

Maggie, wearing black, leaving with a suitcase. Mick, driving blue Chevy Malibu.

"Why is Patrick recording this?" Father Muldoon wondered aloud.

"Because I asked him to do it," Mary said.

"I think he has his own reasons for doing it," David added. "Look at the next page."

Ethel has released me. Maggie, you're the sunshine of my heart. Next to his shaky penmanship was a tiny sketch of a flower.

CHAPTER 31

Every child is an artist,
the problem is staying an artist when you grow up."
-Pablo Picasso

River City Ink was clean and bright. On the reception counter were several books with idea sketches and photos of past work. Maggie was impressed. The quality of tattoos was lightyears beyond the smudged blue inkblots on Albert's old Army buddies. A girl young enough to be one of Maggie's grandchildren came from behind a curtain. She had a sleeve of ink extending from her neck to her fingers, brilliant flowers and vines woven through skulls and daggers and a serpent that seemed to writhe with each movement of her arm.

"Can I help you?" She extended her hand. The snake wriggled. "My name is Christine."

"Hi Christine. I need a tattoo today." Maggie said.

Christine raised her eyebrows slightly but said nothing.

"I used to think tattoos were the devil's notebook but I've changed my mind."

"Welcome to the River City Ink. Tattoos are very common now, even nice grandmothers like yourself."

"I'm from out of town so I was hoping to get one today, before I change my mind."

"I might be able to do something simple." She pointed toward the books on the counter. "Have you already decided on what you want?"

"Name and address and a small butterfly."

"That's all?" Christine asked. "Have you ever had a tattoo before?"

"Never."

"Why now?"

"Body identification. My funeral is next week."

"Nothing like waiting until the last minute. Anything for you, sir?"

Mick shook his head. "No thanks. I'll just watch."

"You won't be watching this one," Maggie said.

Once Maggie had signed the consent forms, Christine led her into the private back room where tattoos were applied on modest locations. Mick was left to peruse tattoo and biker magazines in the reception area.

"While I'm here can you add a small tattoo?" Maggie asked. "I want my name and address on my butt and "Do Not Resuscitate" between my breasts."

"Are you serious about this funeral thing?"

"Absolutely." She winked at Christine. "But I'm coming back to haunt my kids so don't tell anyone."

There was no one else in the shop. Christine and Maggie struck up a friendly exchange of ideas while the ink was being injected into her right buttock. Maggie winced with the first couple of pokes but she adjusted and the time passed quickly. She was glad she didn't have a long address. Christine seemed pleased with her work and offered to add yellow and red into the butterfly for free. When the zip code was finished Maggie handed Christine her phone.

"Snap a couple photos but don't use the wide angle. My butt is big enough without help."

Christine took a half-dozen from different angles, trying to preserve whatever modesty Maggie had.

#

The house was cleaned and furniture was rearranged to its original state before David, Father Muldoon and Mary left. The afternoon sun was anemic, casting long thin shadows from the bare trees. The corn fields west of town were picked and with nothing to impede the wind, it cut through town and whirled about in the eddies between houses.

"You guys hungry?" Father Muldoon asked.

"What do you have in mind?"

"Let's meet at Lars and Lena's Pizza. It's a good place to talk."

"Sounds good." David said.

They found a table in the corner and ordered two hand tossed pizzas, one with pepperoni and the other was the Lars and Lena special.

"Do you have an opinion on Maggie?" David asked the priest.

"Everyone has an opinion. It depends on what you're looking for."

"Are we looking for something?" Mary asked.

"We're all looking for something," Shamus said. "Mary, what are you looking for in your life?"

"I'm talking about Mom, not me," Mary said.

"You won't understand anyone else unless you understand yourself."

"You sound like a Buddhist monk."

"Does that make my observation less valid?"

"I guess not," she said. "but I didn't come here for counseling. I think Mom has flipped her lid and we're trying to minimize the damage."

"Why do you think she's 'flipped her lid' as you say?" Shamus sipped his lemonade and wiped the wet circle on the table with a napkin.

"Have you heard the doctor's story?" Mary spent the next ten minutes recreating their previous conversations with Dr. Smith.

"So?"

"So? That's all you can say about an old woman acting strange?" Mary asked.

"Just because you don't agree with her doesn't make it right or wrong. All you're hearing from the doctor is his perspective. Before you cast judgement don't you think you should talk to her?"

Mary sat back in her chair and was quiet. The pizzas arrived and they spent a few minutes pulling wedges of crust oozing with molten cheese and pepperoni onto their plates.

"David, I haven't heard anything from you," Shamus said. "What are you looking for?"

"I think it's my fault. She was as predictable as snow in winter until I left the church and moved to San Francisco." David took a bite of pizza and chewed for a minute. "Then she changed. She's hanging around this Lutheran Mick guy and she's dyeing her hair."

"You feel guilty but that doesn't explain what you're looking for."

"This is dumb." Mary said.

"What is your mother looking for?" he asked.

"What could she be looking for? She's at the end of her life. She has plenty of money. She doesn't need anything." Mary said.

"Really? Isn't she looking for the same thing we're searching for?"

"What's that?" Mary asked. Before Shamus could answer, Mary's phone vibrated. A text message appeared.

"It's from Mom." She said. She waited until the image downloaded.

"What is it?" David asked.

"Oh my gosh!" Mary held the screen so they could see the photo. The right side of Maggie's white butt was exposed with the bright letters and numbers of her name and address tattooed into her skin. There was a red and yellow butterfly next to her name. Under the photo was the text *Positive Identification*.

"What's that supposed to mean?" David asked.

Father Shamus started to laugh.

"What's so funny? That's my mother's butt you're looking at." Mary said.

"You might think she's going crazy but I think she's the most rational of any in my congregation."

"That's not saying much."

CHAPTER 32

Life is made of ever so many partings welded together.
-Charles Dickens

"We've had a change in plans. Do you have another room?" Maggie asked the Holiday Inn receptionist.

"I'm sorry we're all booked. It's the square dance conference."

"Is it a room with two beds?"

"No problem." The clerk tapped on her keyboard and stared at her computer screen for several minutes. Three sheets of paper came out of the laser printer. "If you would sign here...here...here and initial here... and here. Do you have any pets?"

"Just him." Maggie nodded toward Mick who was settling into the lobby with a complimentary newspaper.

"You're in room 214, between the elevators and the ice machine."

They took the stairs instead of waiting for the elevator and found their room. Maggie dropped her bag on the first bed. "Don't get any ideas," she said. "We aren't married."

"I've never had a bad thought toward you."

"You might be a washed-up golfer with a twenty-seven handicap, an artificial knee and a bent putter but you're a man."

"I want to be your friend." Mick took a step toward Maggie. "If I show you my tattoo, will you show me, yours?"

"I didn't know you had a tattoo," Maggie said.

Mick pulled off his shirt. On his right deltoid was an eagle with the words, 101st Airborne. He stepped back, smiling.

149

"What's so funny?"

"You're turn."

Maggie pulled her phone out and tapped the screen. Her name and address appeared, black letters etched on white skin with a yellow butterfly. "My tattoo is bigger."

#

Vinny Maldonado was pleased with Arthur Finkelstein's compliments but something bothered him. If Arthur thought Goldie looked the best ever, it could only mean two things; Arthur never looked at his wife or something went wrong. He had to find out soon.

He tried checking his calendar but every time he pulled out his phone another handful of relatives started offering condolences for Alfonse and Fiori. Finally, when he had a few minutes alone he looked ahead to the next week. Maggie was scheduled to die this weekend and the funeral was to be scheduled next week, Wednesday or Thursday.

He stepped outside and called his delivery man. "Wally, did you deliver the casket up to Peterville?"

"Yep, just like you asked. Why?"

"Which one did you take?"

"The one on the right. It had a tag that said O'Reilly."

"Good. Thanks."

"Is that all you wanted to know?"

"Where did you leave her?"

"It was the Torkelson place a few miles out of town. There was no one home as expected. We left her in the garage and locked the door."

"That's all I wanted to know. Thanks."

Vinny paced the floor trying his best to avoid well-wishers and mourners. He wandered back to the family reception area and had another glass of Barolo. *I can't call Arthur to ask what she looked like. I need someone to get inside the garage and see the body. I must call Maggie.*

Vinny called Maggie's number but it rang five times and went to her voice mail. *I better not leave a message. What if someone else listens.* He tried again ten minutes later. No answer.

#

"Let's go down to the bar. We've got work to do." Maggie said.

"Work? I thought we were here to learn square dancing?"

"I'm supposed to die this weekend. We need to meet someone and pretend to be friends."

Maggie was surprised at the noise in the Holiday Inn, hotel bar. Most of the tables were taken and the bar was full. Several televisions flashed golf tournaments and college football but the big screen behind the bar had a Texas square dancing competition. Women with gingham dresses and men with cowboy hats were stomping their heels and spinning one another as the liquored-up bar patrons clapped their hands to the rhythm. It differed little from an Irish pub, Albert and Maggie had visited on a trip to Ireland, many years ago. She felt herself moving to the clapping and music.

"Wanna join us?" A couple sitting alone in the corner offered them the empty chairs at their table. "I'm Carson and this is my wife, Angel. Where ya'll from?"

"Minnesota." Mick said as he pulled out one of the chairs for Maggie and they sat down.

"I love your accent." Angel said. "Can you say it again?"

"Minnesota?"

Angel laughed and turned to Carson. "Don't you just love it darlin'?"

Carson asked, "You like square dancing?"

"Never did it before," Maggie said. "I applied to Make-a-Wish for Disney World but all they had left was Mason City square dancing."

"Ha...that's funny," Carson said. "You're gonna love it, ain't that right, Angel?"

The waitress came around to their table. "Do you want to order?"

Angel ordered a wine cooler, Mick and Carson ordered light beers and Maggie ordered a double shot of eighteen-year-old Jameson whiskey, straight.

"How long you two been married?" Angel asked.

"We're not. We came to get married this afternoon but the judge made us wait seventy-two hours." Maggie said.

"Aww...that's so sad," Angel said. She blew her nose so hard it honked. "But you can get hitched on Tuesday."

"If I live that long," Maggie said.

"What do you mean?" Carson asked.

"Bad heart," Mick said. "Doctor told her it could be any minute."

"I don't want to scare you but have you ever seen anyone die?" Maggie asked.

"I watched my uncle die from a bad heart. He was all wheezin' and gurgling and turning blue." Carson said. He tipped back his beer and drained the bottle. He waved his hand at the waitress and pointed for another round at the table.

"You never told me that," Angel said. "What did your aunt Gladys do?"

"She turned up the volume on a Willie Nelson record and went outside to have a cigarette."

"And she left you alone?"

"No, I went with her. When we came back in the house, he was a goner." The second round of drinks arrived at the table. Carson ordered some appetizers, crab cakes and stuffed, deep fried jalapenos.

"Do you have family?" Angel asked.

"Mick has two kids and I have five."

"I bet it's hard on them, about your heart and all," Angel said.

"Haven't told them yet," Mick said. "Maggie has some bucket-list things to do first."

"Like what?"

"I got a tattoo."

"Really?" Carson asked. "I've always wanted one but Angel thinks tattoos are from the Devil."

Angel blushed. Maggie wasn't sure if the pink wine cooler was too much or if she was embarrassed. "I used to think that too," Maggie said. "But this one was for utilitarian purposes only."

"What do you mean?"

Maggie reached into her purse and pulled out her phone. She showed off the photos of the tattoos. Her name, address and butterfly on the right buttock and *Do Not Resuscitate* between her breasts.

"This way if I croak on the dance floor, I don't want anyone crushing my chest with CPR. They can look at my butt, put me in a box and ship me home."

Maggie noticed her phone blinking. She had two missed calls but no voice mail.

"Is that your family calling to check on you?" Angel asked.

"No, it's my mortician. I have him on speed dial."

CHAPTER 33

And hand in hand, on the edge of the sand,
They danced by the light of the moon.
— Edward Lear, The Owl and the Pussycat

"Therese, you can't keep doing this." Freddy unfolded the credit card statement and held it in front of her face.

"Doing what?" She dipped the brush and applied a thin layer of pink flamingo nail polish to her left index finger. She waved her hand and ignored the paper.

"Buying stuff. We can't afford it." Freddy dropped the statement onto the table. "Whether you want to believe this or not, we are nearly bankrupt."

"It's not my fault we don't have money." She blew a bubble with her gum. "Daddy warned me."

"He warned you about what?"

"About marrying you."

"Why didn't you listen to your father?"

"You told me you loved me so I assumed you could afford me. And don't blame my father for your incompetence."

"My incompetence? Your father was the stupid one."

"His company went broke in the stock market crash. That's why he jumped off the bridge."

"He jumped off the bridge because the police were chasing him. Besides the bridge was only six feet off the water and it was a drainage ditch." Freddy went to the refrigerator and pulled out a beer.

3

"That's your answer to life," Therese said.

"What?"

"Alcohol. You're just like your mother."

"Don't criticize my mother. She's a good Catholic woman." Freddy tipped his bottle back and chugged half of it. "And she warned me about you because you were a Baptist, a Southern Baptist no less."

"Is that why she wore black to the wedding?"

"I'm done talking." Freddy went to the hall closet and slipped on a heavy jacket.

"While you're out, can you stop by the post office. I'm expecting a package from Amazon."

#

Larry Torkelson pulled his old hunting coat from the storage room and hung it outside on a hook. He set his heavy winter boots and gloves alongside the coat on the back porch.

"Going somewhere?" his wife asked.

"Last spring Dad and I talked about going deer hunting together. We haven't done that in years."

"Does he know you're coming?"

"No. I think I'll surprise him."

"What if he's got something planned?"

"Dad? He's old and alone. He doesn't do anything anymore. I'll leave early on Saturday and be up there before lunch."

#

Maggie slept fitfully. The tattoo on her butt was tender and the one on her chest itched. She tried lying on her back and her left side and her stomach but nothing was comfortable. It didn't help that Mick snored like a diesel truck in the other bed. Midway through the night she threw a shoe at him but she missed.

Before Mick was awake, Maggie grabbed a change of clothes and went into the bathroom. The shower felt good on the needle work but she was gentle when toweling off. She applied some lotion to her skin and got dressed.

Mick was still sleeping so she went down to the motel lobby for coffee. She was hoping to get some time to think before the giddy square dance crowd arrived. She found a small table next to the window and sat down. Using a free motel pen and pad of paper from the reception desk she started a check list.

Confirm the body is delivered.

Make sure the coroner has Mary's phone number.

List of funeral requests to Father Shamus.

Motel reservations out of town with Mick's credit card.

Fake heart attack during evening square dance.

Give Angel and Carson Mary's phone number and address.

Leave Mason City tonight.

"Good morning darlin'."

Maggie jerked her head up and laid her hand over the list. Angel was bubbly at finding an empty chair next to Maggie.

"Is Micky joining you?" she asked.

"Sleeping in," Maggie said. She took a quick slurp from her coffee cup and set it to the side as Angel sat down.

"I was so touched by your words last night, I had trouble sleeping." Angels false eyelashes fluttered and her eyes grew moist.

"My words?"

"About dying and all." Angel glanced around the room and lowered her voice. "Aren't you scared?"

"Dying's easy. It's the funeral that gives me fits."

"Do you know if your heart is right with God?" Angel asked.

"I just live my life and I leave the judgement part up to him. I don't drink beer on Sunday and I confess my sins every Friday whether I need to or not." Maggie glanced at the clock on the wall. "Now if you'll excuse me, I need to wake up lover-boy."

"Don't forget the first session is at two o'clock this afternoon."

"My toes are tapping already," Maggie said. She stood up and walked away.

#

Larry Torkelson stopped at a drive-through fast food place in Maple Grove before heading north. He slopped coffee onto his hand and dropped his potato cakes in the crack between the front seats on his Ford F-150. He pulled into one of the parking spots to organize his breakfast and tried calling his father.

"This is Mick. Leave a message." Larry figured Mick was at the Main Street Café with the locals catching up on local gossip over a plate of scrambled eggs and greasy hash browns. He clicked his phone off without leaving a message and merged into traffic.

After two hours of listening to the morning farm report and the latest political bruhaha, he flipped his blinker for the Baxter exit. Peterville was another ten miles of country highway from Baxter marked by farmhouses and windbreaks and idle corn fields awaiting another season. The tall brown stemmed grasses lining the road, quivered in the November wind, refusing to bow or bend to the early winter wind. A lone deer hesitated in the shadows, then leapt across the highway in front of him. Larry jammed his foot against the brake and he felt the truck shudder as the anti-lock brakes worked against the icy pavement and slid toward the ditch. No more deer followed and he eased back into the right lane and continued toward Peterville.

Two miles out of Peterville he turned left onto Swensen Road and then into his dad's driveway. There was a skiff of fresh snow in front of the garage and he saw no recent car tracks in or out. Larry went to the front door and knocked. He waited. He knocked again and tried to look through the window but the curtains were pulled.

Larry went around the side of the house and checked the back door. Locked. No foot prints in or out of the house this morning. Larry began to worry. He knew there was a nail under the eaves of the small outbuilding where Mick kept the extra house key. Larry retrieved it and let himself into the house.

The house was dark and the thermostat was turned down to sixty-five degrees. There were a couple pieces of mail on the kitchen table from three days ago, nothing recent. Larry checked his watch. It was eighteen minutes past noon. It became obvious to

Larry, Mick had been gone overnight or he was somewhere in the house…dead.

"Dad?" he yelled as he picked up the pace. Larry walked quickly between rooms. "Dad?"

The bed was made. Larry checked in the bathroom, his toothbrush was gone. He called his wife.

"Did you recall if dad mentioned going somewhere? He isn't home." Larry leaned back against the wall and closed his eyes as he spoke.

"I don't recall anything. Maybe he's just downtown having lunch?"

"No, he's gone. This isn't like him to go overnight without telling me."

"Why don't you ask around town. If you don't find out anything let me know."

"Okay." Larry buttoned his coat and went to the mailbox. Inside was two days-worth of mail, Friday and Saturday. Nothing from Thursday. He carried it into the house and dropped it with the other unopened mail and headed toward the garage. *I hope he isn't dead in the garage.*

Larry took a deep breath clenched his teeth. He pushed the garage door open and stepped inside. He fumbled for the light switch on the wall to the right. The pale blue overhead florescent lights flickered in the cold.

Mick's car was gone. In its place was a mahogany and brass casket.

CHAPTER 34

Life is what happens to us while we are making other plans.
— Allen Saunders

"Mick, we need to get this right the first time. I won't get a second chance."

"Square dancing is easy, you just do what the caller says."

"I'm talking about dying."

The music had a Willie Nelson feel to it and Maggie found it comforting but she didn't know why. She didn't care for country music and she didn't view Willie Nelson as a role model, but he lived life with a chip on his shoulder and she admired that. Women in pleated skirts whirled and twirled as they hooked arms with men around the circle. The man on the stage stomped his cowboy boots and called out the cadence "...allemande left and do-si-do...right hand turn and bend the line..."

Mick and Maggie observed the others before venturing onto the dance floor. Maggie was certain this was going to be her first and last square dance and the most important part wasn't getting the steps right, it was dying on the floor without causing too much ruckus. She knew it wouldn't be easy.

"Let's go through it again," Maggie said.

"On your signal, you faint into my arms and I lower you to the floor...then what?"

"Check a pulse. Didn't you read the CPR manual I gave you?"

"I looked it over."

"What comes after that?" Maggie asked.

"I yell for help."

"Good. But don't yell too loud, you'll make me jump."

"Then I'll help you to the side of the room and when everyone has gone back to square dancing, we are going to slip out the side door."

"Mick, it's simple, even my ex-husband could have done it."

Maggie checked her phone. There was poor cell service inside the dance hall. She checked for missed calls and saw that Vinny had called twice but didn't leave any voice mail. *Everything must be ready.* She took out a small card with her name and address. Maggie printed Mary's name and phone number on the bottom with a note...*oldest daughter.*

The dancers all cheered and clapped as the dance came to an end. Angel and Carson separated from the group and picked their way through the crowd.

"Wasn't that wonderful?" Angel asked. She wiped the sweat from her forehead and checked her mascara in her small compact mirror.

"You guys are great dancers," Mick said.

"It's easy. We've been going to these shin-digs for years." Carson came from the cash bar in the corner carrying a handful of drinks for their table. "You just do what the caller says."

"Angel, I want you to have this," Maggie said. She handed her the address card with Mary's phone number written on the back.

"Thank you. Now we can exchange Christmas cards." She reached into her purse and pulled out a home printed business card with Angel and Carson King in bold print. Underneath their names was printed, *Amway Distributer.* She handed it to Maggie. "I think this is the start of something wonderful and if you ever need some soap, just call."

"Listen up folks," the dance caller waved his left hand in the air to get their attention. "We're going to start the evening session in fifteen minutes, so grab a drink and lace up your shoes." There was a sudden buzz of activity with people running to the bar for last minute sustenance.

Mick looked at Maggie across the table. He raised his eyebrows at her, she winked back. Angel chatted incessantly about the benefits of being an Amway distributer and Carson made another trip to the bar.

Then it was time.

#

Patrick blinked his eyes and groaned. He tried to raise his right arm but it was strapped to the side of the bed. He twisted his neck so he could see around him. The IV pole stood near his left side with three bags of fluid and tubes looped through a pump attached to the pole. He heard the soft irregular beeping coming from the heart monitor and wondered if it was his own heart or someone else.

The oxygen tubing tugged at the corners of his nostrils. He struggled with his left hand but discovered that was restrained as well. His hip and leg throbbed and his toes felt numb.

"Mr. Murphy?"

"Anngaahh."

"Mr. Murphy, I'm Janice your nurse. Do you know what happened?"

Patrick tried shaking his head but he felt strangled by the heart monitor wires and oxygen tubing. "Water."

She held a big plastic container with a bent straw to his mouth and he took a long suck. When he nodded, she set the water back on the bedside stand.

"Do you know where you are?"

He nodded no.

"You're at the hospital. You fell and broke your hip." The nurse adjusted all of his tubing and punched some buttons on the IV pump. "The surgeon fixed your hip with a pin."

He was quiet for a few minutes, then his eyes widened. "Pickles?"

"The doctor doesn't want you eating anything yet."

"No. Pickles my dog."

"There's a note here that says Mabel Feely is watching him. Is she a friend?" Nurse Janice held out a tiny paper medicine cup with three different colored pills. He opened his mouth like a small bird at feeding time and she dumped them. He sucked on the straw again and relaxed his head back into his pillow. His eyebrows furrowed and he stared at the spots on the ceiling of his hospital room. *Pickles was okay. What happened? How did I fall? Jezebel. It must have been her fault.*

#

Maggie reached out and took Mick's hand as they waded into the sea of dancers. They tried to join a circle near their corner of the room but Angel led them toward the center. When they came to their circle Maggie realized they were near the front left of the stage, just below the caller.

The music started. The fiddler played a modified version of *Turkey in the Straw* as a lead-in for the main dance number.

"Bow to your partner...bow to your corner...circle left...promenade..."

Maggie hesitated with each call but before she could think someone grabbed her arm. She was pushed and pulled around the circle doing her best to skip and step in time. She laughed aloud when she turned the wrong way and ran face first into the man next to her. He was quick to catch her and turn her around before they crashed to the floor. And then it was done, her first square dance since she was in junior high school. Everyone clapped and cheered as the dance ended. Maggie smiled at Mick as they were both breathing hard as the music stopped.

Maggie felt her heart pound then it fluttered, just a bit but it was enough to make her feel light headed. She coughed and felt better.

"Mick..." She started to speak and felt as if her breath was gone and she couldn't get the words out.

"Mick," she said again and she stepped in his direction and leaned on his shoulder.

"I thought you said you were going to wait until the third dance?" Mick asked.

Maggie didn't answer. She leaned on his shoulder. Mick stepped back with one leg to stabilize himself and keep from getting pushed into the path of the other dancers.

"You're making this look real," he said. "Maggie?"

Mick wrapped one arm around her waist and another caught her under the arm. He lowered her to the ground. "Can someone get help?" Mick yelled. Maggie didn't jump. "Somebody?"

"I know CPR!" Angel lunged toward Maggie, knocking Mick backwards onto the floor. Without checking for a pulse, Angel ripped the front of Maggie's dress open. She clenched both hands into a club. Raising both arms above her head she walloped the middle of Maggie's chest, directly over the fresh *Do Not Resuscitate* tattoo.

There was a dull thud and the air rushed out of Maggie's nose and mouth. Angel bent forward and planted her ruby-red lips directly over Maggie's mouth and gave a ferocious blow. Maggie's stomach and chest swelled and then as suddenly as it started, Maggie vomited and took a big gasp of air.

"Turn her head to the side," someone yelled.

"I called 911."

"Give her some air."

"Raise her legs. I heard that helps when you're in shock." One onlooker took a chair and propped up both legs.

"Is she diabetic? I've got some sugar."

"Here's a pillow." Someone stuffed a thick pillow under her head so she was bent like an Irish banana with her butt on the floor and her head and feet in the air. Someone else took a napkin from the bar and wiped the vomit and red lipstick away from her face.

Mick sat back stunned as a hundred square dancers gathered around them, pointing and praying and offering advice.

"The paramedics are here." A person from the hotel lobby announced over the crowd noise. The emergency responders parted the crowd as they pulled a loaded stretcher on wheels to the front of the dance floor.

"What happened?" one of the paramedics asked.

"We were dancing and she fainted." Mick tried to piece the events together. He told the story as best as he could remember it but he wondered what was real and what was his rehearsed script. But this time Maggie wasn't pretending. "Angel started CPR as soon as Maggie was unconscious."

"You probably saved her life," the first paramedic said. He took out his stethoscope and pressed it to Maggie's chest. Her heart was beating fast and irregular. She was taking shallow breaths on her own. He pushed her eyelids up and flashed a light into her pupils. They both responded.

"Are you her husband?" the second paramedic asked.

"They were supposed to get married on Monday." Angel started to cry. "You can't let her die."

Five or six others started to sob. One large man with a leather vest and a full beard, wiped his own tears and wrapped his arms around Mick. "We're here for you brother."

"Can you tell me about this tattoo?" Paramedic number two asked Mick as he pointed to the tattoo on her chest. "Is this for real?"

"She just got the tattoo yesterday."

The heart monitor beeped loud enough for most of the dancers to hear. Many in the crowd whispered to one another, "She's going to be fine. I just know it."

Maggie was loaded and whisked away to the waiting ambulance sitting outside the hotel entrance. Mick was left standing on the dance floor surrounding by sobbing well-wishers. Some reached out their arms and touched him on the shoulder as they quietly turned away.

He returned to the table in the corner and gathered their things. As he picked up his things, his phone rang. Mick glanced at the screen.

"Larry?"

"Dad, where are you?"

"Mason City, Iowa. Where are you?"

"At your house. Did you know there's a dead person in your garage?"

CHAPTER 35

I'm not afraid of death;
I just don't want to be there when it happens.
− Woody Allen

"Is she okay?" Mary ran her fingers through her hair and shook her head in disbelief. "Where is she now?"

"The hospital in Mason City, Iowa." Mick said.

"What are you doing in Mason City."

"Square dancing." This wasn't on the script, Mick was on his own. They had planned to sneak out the side of the dance hall and leave Mason City. Vinny was supposed to be the one to call Mary and give the false notification of death. Maggie was booked at a hotel in Alexandria under an assumed name until the visitation and funeral, when she would reappear wearing a disguise. Now he was stuck telling Mary the truth or at least enough of the truth to make everything sound reasonable. He was struggling to remember where the lies ended and the truth began.

"Square dancing?"

"Mary, I know you have questions but it's best if you come down...soon. Your mother is in the ICU." Mick felt his voice catch as he blinked away the tears.

"Is she going to die?"

"The doctors think she might have had a stroke but they are running some tests." Mick felt a tear run down his cheek. He sniffed and wiped his eyes with the back of his hand. "Call your brothers and sister and bring Father Muldoon."

#

"How long will you be gone?"

"As long as it takes." Freddie threw some shirts, socks, pants and a few changes of underwear into a small suitcase. "And you can have Thanksgiving dinner at your mother's place without me. I'm not coming."

"But mother is expecting you. If Maggie had a stroke, she won't know if you're there or not."

"But I'll know."

Freddie clicked the suitcase shut and slammed the door to the garage behind him. He checked his watch. Mary was going to meet him at Maggie's house in Peterville. He had forty minutes to get there.

Just before he backed out of the garage there was a shadow across the driver's side window. He fumbled with the switch and lowered it.

"What?"

"Let me know how she's doing."

"Why?"

"If she's not doing well, I might drive down on Friday. I could do some Christmas shopping at the Mall of America on the way."

#

Eliza ended the call and set her phone on the table. *First dementia and now a stroke. Maybe she won't linger.* She checked her schedule for the next week. There was a rally in downtown Portland for global warming awareness and then she was scheduled as a panelist at a weekend conference for discussions about marine mammals ingesting plastic garbage. *What's the difference? She isn't aware of what's going on. But I would know.*

Eliza spent the next twenty minutes sending out emails with regrets about not attending. She checked three online discount travel sites and booked a red-eye flight from Portland, through Denver to Minneapolis at 11:57 PM, pacific time, tonight.

I hope I make it in time.

#

David sobbed for ten minutes after Mary delivered the news. Steven sat next to him and said nothing. He reached out and rested his hand on David's shoulder but there was no move to acknowledge it.

They sat in silence until David spoke. "Will you come with me?"

"Of course."

"I was the favorite one."

"What do you mean?"

"I was the youngest. My parents doted on me. The others hated me because I was treated differently. They broke my crayons and scribbled on the walls so I would get blamed."

"People can change," Steven said.

"When I was thirteen, I told my mother I hated her."

"Did you mean it?"

"Maybe at the time but not really. I loved my mother but the more she expressed her love for me, the more abuse I received from my brothers and sisters." David blew his nose. "I can still see her eyes when I said it."

"That was a long time ago."

"Like yesterday to me. I never said I was sorry."

"It's never too late."

"I might be too late this time," David said.

He glanced at his watch and looked out the window toward San Francisco Bay. The late afternoon light was fading and fog was collecting in the low areas.

"Why is it always foggy here? I hate fog."

#

Like a bicycle tire with a nail puncture, Father Shamus exhaled slowly and forgot to breathe. He lowered himself to his chair and folded his hands in front of his chest.

"Mick wants you to come. It's serious." Mary had an ample supply of tissues in her pocket and she went through several in the first few minutes after meeting Father Shamus.

"Do you want me to come?"

"Please. She would want her last rites, even if she can't ask." Mary dabbed her eyes again.

"I'd be honored. Give me a few minutes to pack an overnight bag and I'll be ready to go." He wrote in large letters on a sheet of paper and taped it to the church door:
SUNDAY MASS CANCELLED DUE TO ILLNESS.

#

Sunday afternoon.

"I'm assuming you are all family?" Doctor Jenkins sat on a gray upholstered chair in the small family meeting room. The walls were a pleasant shade of ruddy-gray like the color of someone's face five minutes after they quit breathing. The others pulled chairs into a semi-circle and faced the doctor.

"I'm Mary, the oldest." She introduced Freddie, Eliza, David, his friend Steven and Father Muldoon. "And you've already met Mr. Torkelson."

"I'm Dr. Jenkins." He began, "We aren't completely sure what happened to Margaret."

"She didn't have a stroke?" Freddie asked.

"She's acting like she had a stroke but the MRI on her head doesn't show it. There's no bleeding in the brain and we didn't find any aneurysms."

"That's good isn't it?" Mary asked.

"Of course, that's good. She responds to pain and she's breathing on her own but otherwise she's comatose."

"Then tell us what happened."

"Based on the report Mick gave us, we suspect she had a cardiac event."

"What's that?"

"A rhythm disturbance of the heart. She may have brain damage due to lack of oxygen. I'm hopeful she will recover but there is no guarantee."

"What can be done?"

"At this time, just supportive care and see if she responds."

"And prayer," Father Muldoon added. Everyone murmured and nodded in agreement.

"Before I go there are a couple things I need to clarify." Doctor Jenkins looked toward Mary as he spoke. "Does she have a living will?"

"A what?"

"I noticed the tattoo on her chest. It looks nice but I can't accept a Do Not Resuscitate tattoo as a legal document."

"She got the tattoo on Friday." Mick said. "And she got her name and address tattooed on her butt, for identification purposes."

"Was she anticipating this?" Doctor Jenkins asked. He looked around the room. No one answered. "One more thing. She can't make decisions on her own. I have asked our social services department to initiate a temporary health care power of attorney. That allows one of you to make health care decisions on her behalf until she is able to assume those duties."

"This means she's incompetent?" Freddie asked.

"Until further notice." Dr. Jenkins nodded at the group and stepped out of the room.

CHAPTER 36

Inconceivable!
-Vizzini, William Goldman, The Princess Bride

"Are you still in Mason City?" Larry asked.

"I can't talk right now."

"You have a body in your garage with no explanation and you can't talk to me?"

"I'll call you back in ten minutes." Mick tucked his phone into his pocket and stayed in the periphery of the O'Reilly clan. *This is a disaster. I almost hope Maggie doesn't wake up.*

"Mick, can you tell us what's happening with Mom?" Eliza asked. "Do you think she's been acting strange?"

Mick rubbed his eyes and looked toward the door. "Have you ever heard how elephants go home to die?"

"Is this a bedtime story?" Eliza asked.

"Forget I said that." Mick paced the floor. "Maggie is a very special person to me and I know she's very special to each of you as well." He stopped and pulled a folded sheet of paper from his shirt pocket. "Here," he said and handed the paper to Mary. "I think you should see this."

"This is a marriage license."

"That's right. We were going to be married on Friday."

"You were going to get married and not tell us?" Mary asked.

"But you're a Lutheran." David said. "Mom would have never married outside the church."

"It was her idea, she arranged everything," Mick said. "But sometimes you do funny things if you love someone or if you want to know if that someone loves you back."

"Why didn't you do it?" Eliza asked.

"Seventy-two hour waiting period. Since we couldn't get married, she wanted to get a tattoo."

"Do you think she's playing with a full deck?" Freddie asked.

"More than any of us," he said. "Maggie always plays with a full deck and an ace up her sleeve."

"You don't think she was developing dementia?" Mary asked.

"You can ask her yourself when she wakes up."

Mick excused himself from the family and headed down the hospital corridor. His shoes squeaked on the tile floors as he stepped around wheelchairs and patients clinging to IV poles and walkers. He took the elevator down two floors until he found a quiet spot in the main lobby and checked his phone for signal strength. He called Larry.

"Dad, you're freaking me out." Larry said as he answered his phone.

"What's wrong?"

"What's wrong? I came home to go deer hunting and you were gone. No explanation, no phone calls, nothing, just gone. Then I find a casket in the garage with a blanket over the top. What's going on?"

"Calm down Larry. It isn't what you think."

"Is this normal for you?"

"I'll explain when I get home."

"Why don't you try explaining a little bit now so I can sleep tonight. Are you selling body parts?"

"I said I can explain." Mick looked up to see several people staring at him. He smiled and gave them a thumbs-up. They backed away slowly.

"What are you doing in Mason City?"

"You wouldn't believe me."

"Try me."

"We bought a marriage license, got a tattoo and went to a square dance convention."

"Who's we?"

"Maggie O'Reilly and me. The marriage thing didn't work out but we were going to get a divorce next week anyway."

"They have medications for things like this." There was a long pause then he added, "Is she the one you got all worked up about when your putter got bent?"

"That's the one. I think she had a stroke. She's in the Mason City hospital now."

"I'm sorry to hear that. I hope she's okay."

"Larry don't worry, everything's fine. Before you go, I need a favor. Check on the casket and see if there's an envelope or phone number for Vinny Maldonado."

"I'll look and send you a text, one way or another."

Tonight, was the night and visions of the plan replayed in Mick's mind like a Mel Brooks movie. Vinny had instructions to call Mary at 10 PM and deliver the false death report. Maggie had Vinny's personal cell phone number on her list of contacts but if someone didn't call him to cancel the deal, the whole thing would blow up. Maggie's family would probably accuse Mick of fraud and abuse of a vulnerable adult. He was the one who took Maggie to get married, he paid for the hotel with his credit card. He took her to the tattoo parlor and the square dance contest. And he had a body in his garage.

Mick checked his watch. It was 9:23 PM. He had two options, either stop Mary from getting the phone call or call Vinny. *I hope there's a number on the casket.*

His phone buzzed, it was a text from Larry. The words appeared on the screen. *Maldonado's House of Eternal Rest 1-800-276-2533, 1-800-CROAKED.*

Mick punched in the numbers and crossed his fingers. "This is Maldonado's House of Eternal Rest. Our office hours are 9 AM to 5 PM." He ended the call. *I have to find Maggie's phone.* His watch read 9:29.

#

"I think David should be the person." Eliza said. "He's a priest, or he was one and Mom loved him best."

"David's a sap. He can't decide what to eat for breakfast." Mary said, "and you think he can make health care decisions for someone else?"

"That's not true. Every morning I have avocado slices on free-range organic poached eggs. Steven makes them for me."

"See what I mean?" Mary said, "I should be the one. I've been home with Mom when each of you left. After dad died, I was the one to visit her every week and make sure she didn't drink herself to death."

"Does anyone here think Tommy should have a say in this?" Father Shamus asked.

"He's in prison and he isn't eligible for parole until spring," Eliza said.

"That's true, but he is your mother's son and your brother." Shamus added.

"You're right. I would trust him more than Freddie." Mary said.

"You prefer a felon to me?"

Eliza grabbed Freddie by the shirt and looked straight into his eyes. "Freddie if you were chosen to be Mom's health care advocate, you'd pull the plug and Therese would have her shopping list done before Mom quit twitching." Freddie pulled back and looked away.

"At least Tommy was honest. He killed someone but he didn't steal." Mary said. "Father Shamus, you probably know Mom as good as any one of us. Why don't you do it?"

Shamus thought about Maggie's Last Will and Testament in his desk at home. He had a guaranteed life income if she died. And if she lingered?

"I can't," he said. "It isn't right."

"Then you decide who should be the health care power of attorney. It's obvious we can't." David looked at Steven for approval. He nodded.

Mary stood on a chair like a peeved school teacher trying to address an unruly class. "Listen up everyone. Dr. Jenkins wanted us to make a decision by 10 PM. He was going to have the social worker stop by with paperwork. It's 9:45 now."

"Mary should be the one." Father Shamus said. "She's the oldest and she has spent the most time with Maggie over the past few years. I know some of you may not agree but this is the best decision at the moment."

There was a moment of quiet followed by muttering but the decision was obvious to everyone. Mary was an extension of Maggie and as Shamus had a habit of saying; *the nut doesn't fall far from the tree.*

#

Mick retraced his steps to the family waiting room outside of the ICU. The door was still shut on his arrival and he could hear yelling from within, chairs were being pushed about then a period of quiet. He slowly pushed the door open and stepped inside. Freddie was standing alone in the corner, staring at his shoes. David and Steven were chatting and waving their arms as if telling some great adventure. Eliza leaned back against the wall talking with Father Muldoon. Mary sat alone in the corner tapping the screen on her iPhone.

"Are they letting visitors back into Maggie's room yet?" Mick asked.

"The nurse said we can go in to see her, two people at a time, but not until after ten o'clock."

"Do you have her cell phone?" Mick asked Mary.

"No, it must be with her stuff in her room. Why?"

"I wanted to show you some square-dancing photos."

"Maybe tomorrow." Mary started to say something else as the social worker came into the room.

"Have you decided on anything? Dr. Jenkins asked me to check with the family." Her name tag said Ellen. Mick thought she looked like a chubby grandmotherly type with a forced smile from dealing with impossible situations all day.

"I'm the one." Mary raised her hand. There was no vocal opposition from the rest. She signed her name on five different pages and Father Muldoon signed as an independent witness to Mary's identity and authority for making decisions on behalf of Maggie.

When it was completed, the social worker said, "Dr. Jenkins has certified that Maggie is incompetent and you now have the authority to make health care decisions on her behalf. The first thing Dr. Jenkins wants you to decide is whether Maggie should be resuscitated if her heart should stop."

"Absolutely, we want her to be resuscitated." David said.

"Shut up David," Eliza said. "You got voted out, remember?"

"But you can't let her die." he said.

"Remember the tattoo?" Mary turned away from David and spoke directly to Ellen. "No resuscitation." She signed and dated the form. It was official.

Mary walked toward the door. "Can I go see her now?" Ellen nodded.

Mick checked his watch. 9:57 PM. "Mary do you mind if I go with you? I just want to take a minute and say goodbye, then I'll leave for the night."

Mary glanced at the others. Seeing no argument, she motioned for Mick to follow her. The family waiting room was at the end of the corridor fifty feet from the ICU entrance. The custodian was cleaning one side of the hallway as they passed. Bright yellow caution cones stood along the midline of the hallway to caution passersby about the wet floor.

As they neared the yellow mop bucket on wheels Mary's phone rang. She looked at the screen.

"Illinois? Must be a scam call."

Mick checked his watch, 10 PM.

CHAPTER 37

It's easier for a rich man to ride that camel
through the eye of a needle directly into the Kingdom of Heaven,
than for some of us to give up our cell phone."
— Vera Nazarian, The Perpetual Calendar of Inspiration

Vinny Maldonado rechecked his records three times but he couldn't be certain. Something bothered him about the message Arthur left for him. *Goldie never looked better.* It was bad form to call Arthur Finkelstein and ask him to describe his wife in detail especially since the last memory was her lying in the casket with her eyelids superglued shut. *You even removed the growth on her neck.* He called his assistant a second time.

"Jimmy, do you remember the Gladwell case a few days ago?"

"Do you mean last week?"

"Yeah, the one you delivered to Peterville."

"Sure. I did it myself."

"Which casket did you take?"

"The one on the right, just like you said. The tag said O'Reilly." Jimmy looked puzzled. "You asked me the same thing a couple days ago."

"Thanks, I just wanted to confirm it."

"Is there a problem?"

"No everything's fine." *Everything isn't fine.*

He checked his watch. He was supposed to call Mary at 10PM and set everything in motion but he wasn't sure and if something was wrong it would be his fault. He had to talk to Maggie first.

Vinny called her phone five times in the next three hours but Maggie never answered. He knew he had to leave a message but if it was heard by others it could lead to trouble. He called her phone again.

"This is Maggie. I'm not available right now. Please leave a message."

"Vinny calling. Package delivered. Possible wrong contents in the box. Please confirm." He ended the call and poured a double shot of grappa. *Why did I agree to this? If this gets out, it could ruin me.*

#

Mary walked toward the entrance to the ICU alongside Mick. She was quiet, staring at the floor as they walked. Mick checked his watch and then checked it again. 10:03 PM.

Mary's phone rang.

She pulled it from her pocket and checked her screen. She tapped the phone icon.

Mick felt his heart pound. *It must be Vinny. He can't tell Mary anything. Do something.* Mick stepped slightly to the left around the yellow warning sign in the hall, around the custodian wiping the floor with the mop.

He let his foot slip on the wet floor. *Get the phone.* He pitched himself forward grabbing at Mary as if to catch himself. His left arm came down like a karate chop on her right forearm. Her iPhone tumbled end over end like a perfectly kicked football, bouncing once off the wall, directly into the pail of steaming, soapy, antiseptic solution just as the janitor was about to dip the mop one more time.

"Are you okay?" Mary asked as she gripped his arms with both hands.

Mick replayed the iPhone dunk shot in his mind. "I'm fine now. Thanks for catching me." The janitor and two nurses rushed to his side but he was already back on his feet.

"Did you see where my phone went?" Mary asked.

"No, I'm sorry. Did I knock it out of your hand?" *A couple more minutes in the bucket should be enough.* Mick stared down the hall each way looking for a cell phone. He took a deep breath and asked the janitor. "Did you see her cell phone fall?"

He pointed to the pail.

"Mary, I'm so sorry," Mick said. "I'll get you a new phone, I promise."

The janitor pulled on some blue rubber gloves and stirred around in the pail. A dripping phone came up. The images on the screen were already distorted. Mary shook the water off and the phone went black. "As long as you're not hurt," she said. "That's the main thing."

Now I need to get Vinny's number from Maggie's phone. "Thank goodness I wasn't hurt. I can't thank you enough Mary." Mick stared at the floor as they continued toward Maggie's room in the ICU.

Maggie appeared peaceful. There were two IV's running, one in each arm and she had an oxygen sensor on the index finger of her left hand. Clear tubing was looped around her ears and two plastic prongs delivered pulses of oxygen into her nostrils. A monitor was mounted to the wall beside the head of the bed. Her pulse was 88 but it skipped and danced on the screen and the beeping noise was anything but regular. Her oxygen level was 96%.

"Are you family?" the nurse finished adjusting Maggie's pillow and turned toward them.

"I'm her daughter and this is a friend, Mick." Maggie said.

"She's a fighter," the nurse said. "The doctor can't find anything wrong"

"If there's nothing wrong, then why is she in a coma?"

"She's being sedated. The doctor is concerned about brain swelling. A CT scan of her brain is scheduled in the morning. If everything looks okay, they might stop some of the medications."

"Can we all come in the room together. The priest is here to give Mom her last rites in case she doesn't make it." At the end of her words Mary's voice cracked and she started to cry. Her shoulders shook and the tears ran down her face and dripped from her chin and she made no effort to stop them. Mick felt a lump in his throat and swallowed hard. He put his arms around Mary and they sobbed together, two people who loved the same person in very different ways, and the pain was real. Finding Maggie's phone was suddenly unimportant. All that mattered was right before him.

BEEEEEEP-BEEEEEEP. The monitor flashed and the heart beat tracing jumped around like a salsa dancer. BEEEEEEP-BEEEEEEP. The noise was piercing. Mick stuck his finger in his ear to adjust his hearing aids. He and Mary were pushed into the corner by people rushing into Maggie's room.

"CODE BLUE-ICU. CODE BLUE-ICU." The announcement through the overhead speakers drowned out the normal hospital noise in the hallway.

"V-FIB" the doctor said. "Charge 300 joules." He grabbed the handles on the defibrillator beside the bed as the nurse ripped Maggie's hospital gown open. He put some gel on the paddles and reached across the bed to push them against Maggie's chest.

"Is this for real?" he said, pointing with his elbow at Maggie's *Do Not Resuscitate* tattoo over the middle of her chest. BEEEEEEP-BEEEEEEP.

"It says DNR on her chart." The nurse said.

The doctor hesitated and looked at the nurse.

"She's dying!" Mary jumped forward and slammed her hands over the tattoo and started pushing.

"Stop." The nurse said. "She didn't want to be resuscitated." She pulled back on Mary's arm.

The heart line on the monitor went from a scribbled line to a wavy line. BEEEEEEP-BEEEEEEP.

"Do it." She yelled. "I changed my mind. You can't let her die." Mary pulled away from the nurse and pressed again on Mary's chest. There was a cracking sound and Mary hesitated. She jerked her hand back as Maggie's ribs broke from the CPR.

The on-call doctor stepped forward and put the paddles onto Maggie's chest, one near the top of her sternum and the other beneath her left breast. "CLEAR." He looked around. No one was touching Maggie or the bed. He pushed the buttons.

Maggie's body jerked as if she was struck by lightning. There was a faint smell of burnt hair and skin. The heart line on the monitor went flat. BEEEEEEEEEEEP. Then it started scribbling again, up and down in jagged lines.

"Charge to 360." The doctor held the paddles up as the nurse cranked the dial on the defibrillator. "CLEAR."

Maggie's body jumped again. Mick turned away. Mary wept. No one spoke. The line on the monitor was just a line, nothing more. The skipping and dancing were over.

"Do you want me to try again?" The doctor turned to Mary.

"No," she said. "Let her go." Mary leaned into Mick and cried. "She's gone. I need to tell the others."

The nurse gently pulled Maggie's hospital gown into place to cover her nakedness. She reached to unclip the wires from pads on her chest. BEEP...BEEP...BEEP... There was a gasping noise from Maggie's throat.

"Doctor, she's back."

CHAPTER 38

May you live to be a hundred years,
With one extra year to repent!
-Irish Blessing

They took turns standing vigil at Maggie's bedside through-out the night. Her heart beat dutifully for several hours until 3 AM when there was another flutter. It was felt by everyone watching but she didn't need to be shocked again. A third IV dripped into her right arm and the nurse checked the flow every fifteen minutes.

Immediately after her resuscitation and three times over the next few hours a lab tech came into her room. Maggie never flinched when the tourniquet was applied and the large bore nee-dle was jammed into her arm. A bandage was wrapped around her arm at the crease of her elbow but overnight the bruising spread up and down her arm.

After the 3 AM flutter, Father Muldoon was summoned and the hospital chaplain joined them. The family dared not wait.

"In the name of the Father, the Son and the Holy Ghost. Amen."

"Amen" they said in unison.

Father Muldoon took a bowl of water and blessed it. He dipped his right thumb into the water and touched it to Maggie's forehead. "Our Father we pray on behalf of our sister Margaret, who is unable to speak, to ask for forgiveness of her sins and rec-onciliation with you. Amen."

"Amen."

Father Muldoon took the communion wafers from the chaplain. He broke a small piece and held it up and blessed it. "The Body of Christ." He took the piece in his own mouth and prayed. Then he took another tiny piece and put it into Maggie's mouth. "The Body of Christ, broken for you. Amen."

"Amen."

The chaplain offered communion wine from the chapel. Father Muldoon poured a small amount into a paper cup and blessed it. He raised his right hand and made the motion of the cross. He took a small sip, then dipped his finger into the wine and touched it to Maggie's lip. "The Blood of Christ," he said.

Everyone said, "Amen."

It was over. All they could do is wait.

#

By midmorning little had changed. Maggie was still sleeping but she was breathing on her own and her heart wasn't doing the cha-cha. Mick extended his stay at the Holiday Inn and offered his room to the others if they wanted to sleep or shower. One by one they took advantage of his offer.

Maggie was wheeled away for the CT scan and the family huddled sullenly around the waiting room coffee pot.

"We should have let her go," Eliza said. "She didn't want to be resuscitated."

"She would have died if we didn't do something," Mary said.

"Isn't that the idea? There are some things worse than dying. She didn't want to live anymore," Freddie added. "Now look at her. She's going to be a turnip in a nursing home, drooling on her pillow for the next ten years."

"You don't know that."

"How long can the brain go without oxygen?" Eliza said, "her heart wasn't beating for minutes, add that to her square-dancing fiasco, and..." She paused to catch her breath, "...and, she was short a few brain cells before all this started. Isn't that why Mary got us all excited?" She opened Google on her phone and announced her findings. "Six minutes without oxygen and the brain starts to die."

She looked from face to face. No one argued with her. What little hope remained in the room was leaking under the door.

#

Mick excused himself from the family argument and slipped back into Maggie's room. The room was empty. He found the cabinet containing Maggie's personal belongings. Everything was in a large plastic bag with her name and room number written in large black letters on the front. He popped open the bag and found her purse. Inside was her cell phone. The battery was dead. He slipped it into his pocket, pushed the bag back into the cabinet and left her room.

Back in his own motel room, he plugged Maggie's phone into the charger and turned it on. Seven missed calls flashed on her screen, five of them from the same caller. One voice message. Mick dialed to retrieve her voice messages.

"Please enter your password."

Mick ended the call. He didn't know her password and he wasn't going to waste time guessing. He could try a hundred times and not be right. *Just call the number.*

Mick found the last number from Chicago.

"Vinny Maldonado."

"Mr. Maldonado, this is Mick Torkelson, the friend of Maggie's."

"Did you get my message?"

"No. Something happened to Maggie. She's in the hospital."

"What happened?"

"She's in a coma. Maybe a stroke."

"I'm sorry to hear that. Mick, there might be a problem. I need you to look at the body in your garage."

"I can't. I'm in Mason City, Iowa."

"Find someone you trust to look at the body."

"Am I going to jail for this?" I have a body in my garage and it might be the wrong one?

"You didn't do anything illegal."

"Okay, what should I do?" Mick hunched over his phone and lowered his voice as if someone was listening.

They spent the next ten minutes discussing options. With Maggie in a coma, the plan was dead but they still had a body. Now he needed to convince Larry to open the casket and take a picture. *We're all going to need a psychiatrist when this is over.*

Mick left Maggie's phone plugged in and called Larry with his own phone.

"I need a favor," Mick said.

"Does it have anything to do with the person in your garage?"

"Bingo. I need you to open the casket and tell me what she looks like."

"Are you crazy? This is creeping me out." Larry was quiet for a moment. "Do you want me to take a photo and put it on Face-book too?"

"Very funny."

"Dad, if you go to prison for the criminally insane, I'll never visit." Larry opened the door between the house and the garage.

"Vinny said we're not doing anything illegal."

"Someone named Vinny says it's okay? I feel so much better now." Larry walked into the garage and stood beside the casket with his jacket open at the front and his boots unlaced. "How do you open this thing?"

"There should be a latch near the foot."

"I found it. Now what?"

"Open it."

"I don't want to. I don't like dead people."

"Oh, for Pete's sake, Larry get over it. You're forty-seven years old."

"It's your fault. You rented the casket for the Halloween party when I was seven. I'll never forgive you for jumping out of it when I had to go to the bathroom."

"Just open the lid and tell me what or who you see."

Larry took a deep breath and lifted the casket lid slightly. Satin fabric was neatly folded over the sides of the body obscuring his full view. It smelled funny, not bad but not what you wanted from a prom date. Finally, the lid was fully open. He went to the side of the garage and turned on the bright overhead lights.

"I'm waiting," Mick said into the phone. "What do you see?"

"I'm not sure what you were expecting."

"Why?"

"I think she's Jewish."

CHAPTER 39

Grief is the price we pay for love.
– Queen Elizabeth II

The radiology department was dimly lit and cool. It took four people to slide Maggie from the gurney to the table of the CT scanner. Two of the IV lines had been capped but one was still running and the tubing was heavily taped to her arm. One person lifted from each side, one guided her head and neck and the third kept the oxygen and IV tubing from tangling.

Once she was positioned on the table, two foam blocks were anchored, one on each side of her head and a wide Velcro strap went across her forehead. A lighted grid appeared from the scanner and projected on her head to aim the machine. Once that was completed the table moved smoothly and automatically as the CT scanner took thin sliced photos of Maggie's brain. The radiologist stood behind the tech watching the successive images appear on the screen.

"Reposition her," the radiologist said. "She's tilted and I want to get a better angle."

The tech put the scanner on hold and stepped into the imaging room to adjust the position of Maggie's head. The foam blocks were moved and the forehead strap tightened. They started the scan again.

"Still not right," the radiologist said. This time he went into the scanning room with the tech. They moved the table and Maggie's head passed under the lighted grid.

She blinked.

"At least she's responding to light." He said. He loosened the foam bricks one more time.

Maggie opened her eyes again and looked directly at the doctor. "What are you doing?" she asked.

"Do you know where you are?" he asked.

She moved her eyes around staring up at a blank sterile appearing ceiling. "I guess I'm not in Kansas anymore."

When the scan was finished, she was moved back to her room. Mary and Eliza were waiting along with Dr. Jenkins in the hallway.

"Margaret, I'm Dr. Jenkins. Do you know where you are?"

"Why is everyone asking me that. And don't call me Margaret."

"Because you collapsed. Do you remember what happened?"

"Where's Angel?"

"Mom, did you see an angel?" Mary asked. She folded her hands together and blinked back tears.

"No, the ditzy blond square dancer who smacked me on the chest and smeared red lipstick on my face. That's the last thing I remember." Maggie reached up with her free arm and lifted her hospital gown. "I got this tattoo for a reason." She winced with pain as she moved her arm.

"Does she seem normal to either of you?" he asked Eliza and Mary.

"Unfortunately, yes," Eliza said.

News spread quickly. Within an hour, the family, including Mick and Father Shamus, had reassembled in the family waiting room, but instead of slurping lukewarm coffee in silence they gulped it down and chatted about the weather and the latest football games.

Dr. Jenkins performed a thorough examination and asked numerous questions testing Maggie's recall and reasoning capacity. She had to copy diagrams, draw clocks and write sentences.

For the sentence she wrote: *There's always some madness in love. But there's always some reason in madness. Nietzsche.*

The doctor reviewed everything and raised his eyebrows as he read the sentence. "Maggie, I'm not sure what happened to you but everything seems to be normal."

"Can I go home?"

"Not yet. Last night you had a potentially fatal heart rhythm and we had to shock your heart."

"I feel fine now, except for sore ribs."

"That's wonderful but something triggered the event. I suspect you have a blocked artery in your heart. That's probably what happened at the square dance."

"Won't a pill take care of that?"

"Nope. You need to stop smoking, stop drinking alcohol, you will need some medications and you are scheduled for an angiogram this afternoon, so nothing to eat or drink for the rest of the day."

"I didn't authorize this." Maggie clenched her jaw and looked toward the door.

"You were in a coma. Your daughter, Mary has been given authority to make health care decisions on your behalf for thirty days or until you are determined to be back to normal."

"Here I am, back to normal."

"Look Maggie...you really need this test. Without it you could die suddenly."

"Is that bad?"

"Think it over. I'll be back at 1:30." He left the ICU and walked down the hall.

#

The ICU was the center of frenetic activity. Nurses, doctors, interns, lab techs and chaplains buzzed in and out, extending lives, cheating death and offering condolences when efforts were futile. Mary and her siblings counted their blessings at Maggie's near miraculous recovery but it also left Mary in a quandary. As health care power of attorney, she was responsible for decision making until it was determined Maggie was fit. She seemed fit. She was bright, articulate and even witty in some of her responses but Dr. Jenkins privately questioned her judgement. An angiogram wasn't difficult and could easily prevent another cardiac episode.

"I'm not ready to declare her mentally stable. Not yet," he stated before he left them to figure it out.

It was clear to Mary, the doctor thought this was medically necessary and she was not capable of making the right decision. He was willing to treat Maggie as a child and force treatment upon her, for her own good. At least the doctor thought it was for her own good.

But Mary struggled with her role. If you truly love someone do you force them to do things or do you let them go? I can't force her to quit smoking. I can't force her to stop drinking. God knows I've tried. But if I don't force this and she dies, then what? I couldn't live with the guilt. I can't ask Eliza. She's ready to nail the coffin shut now. Freddie's own life is desperate. He can't buy a pair of shoes without getting his wife's permission. David's a limp rag. He would do everything to save her because he thinks it is all his fault. It's for her own good. That's what the doctor said. It's for her own good.

#

Mick returned to the hospital to the delightful news of Maggie's awakening. His steps felt twenty pounds lighter as he walked down the corridor to the ICU family waiting area. Small groups of people huddled in corners of the waiting areas, hoping and praying for miracles for their loved ones. Maggie's children wore faces of exhausted relief. Father Shamus clutched his rosary and pointed toward heaven.

"She's having an angiogram this afternoon," Freddie said as he took Mick aside. "She doesn't want it but Mary is forcing the issue."

"What do you want me to do?"

"I don't know. Talk to Mary, I guess. Maybe you can change her mind."

"I need to talk to Maggie first. When is the angiogram scheduled?"

"In twenty minutes. The doctor is in the room with her now."

Mick wasted no time. He marched down the hall and into Maggie's private room. Her heart was still beating like a bass drum in a high school marching band with a couple jazz notes thrown in. The doctor paused as Mick walked in.

"Sorry to interrupt but I have some important news."

Dr. Jenkins and Maggie both turned to face Mick.

"I have some news about your sister." Mick said.

"My sister?"

He looked at the doctor and back to Maggie. "You remember your homeless sister, Velma Gladwell?"

"Sister Velma...how is she?"

"Unfortunately, she's changed since you last saw her."

"Oh?"

"She gained forty pounds, she's living in a box in my garage and she converted to Judaism."

Maggie was quiet for several minutes. The doctor shifted his weight from foot to foot and fidgeted with his hands. Mick stood still with a blank face. The heart monitor fluttered slightly and skipped a beat.

"Doctor Jenkins?" Maggie asked. "Did you say I could die during the angiogram?

"That's always a potential risk."

"Okay, I'll do it."

CHAPTER 40

My Mama always said, 'Life was like a box of chocolates;
you never know what you're gonna get.'
-Tom Hanks, Forrest Gump

It was a week before Maggie was released from the hospital but by then everyone else had dispersed, trying to resume a normal schedule. Eliza, David and Steven returned to Baxter and were staying at Mary's house until Maggie was safe and settled, whatever that meant. Mary stayed in Mason City until Maggie was ready to go home. She didn't want Maggie to stay alone but Maggie would have none of it. Rather than starting World War III, Mary consented to Maggie's living alone as long as Mary could visit every day.

Mick had some explaining to do with Larry and made him swear on a stack of Bibles, never to tell anyone about the body in Mick's garage. Larry reluctantly agreed but called his father every other day, checking for signs of confusion or dementia. Mick was grateful for the sudden interest but was careful not to reveal anything about Maggie's plan. Mick explained that Maggie felt sorry for the homeless lady, abandoned by her family and decided to pay for a funeral because Jews were vehemently opposed to cremation and if no one claimed her that's what would happen. He wasn't sure Larry believed him but it sounded plausible and was the best explanation he could conjure on short notice.

Maggie had one stent in the main artery of her heart. The doctor called it a widow maker which didn't make much sense to

Maggie. She was already a widow. *Maybe in women it's called a widower maker.* She wasn't sure and didn't want to ask.

She glanced over her hospital discharge information. She went into the hospital without any medications, smoking a pack a day and drinking whatever and whenever she chose. She went home to a life without Guinness or Jameson; her cigarettes went into the dumpster; and she had five new prescriptions if you count aspirin. She was told she had a spot on her lung but she couldn't have a biopsy for a year because of the new blood thinner. She had a follow up appointment with Dr. Smith, or as she called him, the OB doctor.

The five-hour trip north from Mason City to Peterville was tedious. Mary drove her Toyota minivan and Maggie sat in the front passenger seat praying they would run into a beer truck so she could have a drink. After two hours she hinted to Mary about stopping for a Big-Mac and fries. Mary kept driving. After three hours she was restless and begged for a cigarette. After four hours she hated Mary more than any other person in the world, except maybe Albert, a few times, but that was long ago.

"Mom, do you want to get your prescriptions filled at Walgreen's or do you want to get them at Olson Pharmacy when you get home?" Without waiting for Maggie's answer, she turned on highway 65 heading north toward Baxter.

"Why don't you decide, you're the one in charge."

"What do you want from me? I'm trying to keep you alive."

"Do you really care or did your siblings put you up to this because you lost a bet."

"Lost what bet?"

"Eliza probably had a pool going for people to bet when the old lady was going to tip over."

"Aren't you a piece of work. While you were in la-la land we left our families and homes to be with you around the clock."

"The only reason David came was his guilty conscience. And Freddie..."

"What about Freddie?" Mary asked.

"I'm the lesser of two evils. Poor Freddie. The only choice he has in life is whatever Therese gives him. They're bankrupt and he doesn't have the guts to say no."

Mary turned on the radio and raised the volume. She picked country music because Maggie usually complained about it. It didn't work. Maggie talked louder.

"At least Tommy doesn't complain," she said.

"Tommy's in prison." Mary reminded her.

"He's happy to see me when I visit." Maggie looked out the dirty car window at a passing farm in the distance. A handful of black cattle were pulling grass from a large round bale. Then they were gone from sight, replaced by another farm and forest and marshland. Everything was a blur, speeding past and she sat on the sidelines wondering at the meaning of it all.

"Mary, I need a cigarette."

"You heard what the doctor said."

"I don't care what the doctor said. I need a cigarette. Just one."

"You made it a week in the hospital without one, don't give up now."

"I was on drugs in the hospital." Maggie closed her eyes and laid her head back against the seat. "You wouldn't understand."

"I used to smoke. I know how hard it is to quit."

"You were younger."

"And that makes it easier?"

Maggie felt her hands shaking. She crossed her arms and held them tight against her body. Her rib hurt. She coughed as gently as she could. "I need to use the bathroom."

Mary took the next exit and pulled to a stop next to the gas pumps. "Go ahead. I need gas." She slipped her credit card into the card reader and pulled out the gas pump nozzle. Mary filled the gas tank and printed the receipt while she waited. Other cars were lining up behind her so she drove her car into a parking spot next to the store and went in to check on her mother.

"Did you see an older woman come in here with short black dyed hair?"

"Bathroom." The attendant pointed toward the sign hanging the back. Mary stepped aside and waited.

A few more minutes passed then a high-pitched alarm sounded from above the beverage cooler. "Oh my gosh. Mom needs help." She stepped around three customers and raced to the back of the store. The sound grew louder as she approached the bathroom.

As Mary rounded the corner, Maggie stepped from the bathroom and walked past Mary, directly to the check-out counter. "There's something wrong with your smoke alarm," she said and exited the front door.

"You're going to die, you know." Mary said as they drove away.

"We all have to die from something."

They drove in silence for the remaining seventy-three and a half miles.

#

Father Shamus was the first to visit Maggie but by evening Sally McTavish had dropped off a loaf of pumpkin bread, Mabel Feely left a green-bean casserole without salt and another neighbor brought a pot of homemade chicken soup in a crockpot. Maggie was enjoying the attention but she had important things to discuss with Father Shamus. Finally, after Maggie had recited the square dance story three times and the neighbors had departed, she had Father Shamus alone.

"Have you ever buried a Jewish person before?"

"What are you talking about?"

Maggie leaned forward and lowered her voice. "Remember when you jumped in the bathtub with me?"

"How could I forget." He involuntarily touched his right cheek. "What does that have to do with a Jewish funeral?"

"It's a long story." Maggie reviewed the plan with Father Shamus and reminded him of the Last Will and Testament

195

guaranteeing him a lifetime annuity. He appeared uncomfortable and shifted his position several times. "So anyway…I claimed this body from the Chicago morgue for two-hundred bucks and Vinny made her up to look just like me."

"So…what happened?"

"There was an accidental switch. Velma, who looked like me, got buried as Arthur Finkelstein's wife and he doesn't know it. His wife, Goldie is lying in Mick Torkelson's garage. Inside the casket is a big blue Star of David and *Shalom*."

"I could get kicked out of the church for this."

"It's the compassionate thing to do. Just have a respectable funeral and no one will know."

"I'll know."

"You're Catholic. Confess your sins and move on."

"Who is she again?"

"She's Goldie Finkelstein but she's supposed to be Velma Gladwell. I have her death certificate. It's already filed with the State of Illinois. She's legally dead and accounted for. She died homeless and penniless and alone and spent the last three months lying in a freezer until I rescued her from the fiery furnace."

"I can't lie to people."

"Let me do the talking."

CHAPTER 41

*The best way to find out
if you can trust somebody is to trust them.*
-Ernest Hemingway

Prior to her square-dancing collapse, Maggie spent evenings with her old friend Jameson but he didn't visit anymore. The first week after her return home she popped open a bottle of Guinness and poured the glass full until the foam ran over the side. She was half-way done with the beer when Mary showed up at her door. Maggie tried to hide the evidence but Mary knew. It was as if she were listening to everything Maggie did. Mary confiscated the beer and walked around sniffing for tobacco smoke. The pleasure she received from drinking waned and by the end of the first week the craving was gone.

Freddie called daily for the first three days and then it ended. Maggie thought she recognized disappointment in his voice when she told him how well she felt. Therese never called or stopped by to visit, but she sent a get-well card. It was signed *Your son, Freddie* but it was Therese's handwriting. Maggie used the card as a hot pad under her microwaved, low salt, low flavor, single serving dinner and tossed it when she was done eating.

David returned to San Francisco but called Maggie every other day. Twice she had to hang up because he always sounded weepy. He said he was sorry about fourteen times. Maggie told him to "suck it up" and "get over it" but she wasn't sure he got the message.

Eliza emailed because it was efficient and didn't kill any trees or use petrochemicals in the delivery process. The emails were always cordial but brief; *How are you, I am fine...* messages. Maggie wrote back the first couple times but after that she hit *delete*.

Maggie and Mary didn't talk much anymore. Mary dutifully visited every other day but it wasn't the same. She was more of a policewoman than a daughter. The roles of protective parent and sulking adolescent were switched but Maggie harbored a secret enjoyment from the game. She remembered when Mary first got her driver's license. Maggie sat in the back seat and kicked the driver's seat for ten miles while asking repeatedly, "Are we there yet?"

#

Rabbi Benjamin Abramovitz stuck his fingers deep within his beard and scratched his chin. "You want me to perform a funeral for your homeless half-sister who converted to Judaism and died penniless in Chicago?" He sipped his tea. "Did I miss anything?"

"No, I think that's everything." Maggie said.

"And you want her buried in a Catholic cemetery in northern Minnesota in the middle of December?"

"Is that a problem?"

"This is most unorthodox," he said. "When did your sister pass?"

"Three months ago. We're keeping her in Mick Torkelson's garage until arrangements can be made."

"And is Mr. Torkelson Jewish?"

"Lutheran."

"Mrs. O'Reilly, you intrigue me. I've never been asked to do anything like this before. If you have no other options, I'll do it."

"Wonderful," Maggie said. "How about Wednesday."

"Wednesday it is." He cleared his throat. "I will require $500 paid in advance and overnight arrangements on Tuesday."

"Thank you so much." Maggie wrote a check and shook hands with Rabbi Abramovich. "There are no motels in Peterville. You can stay at my house."

"It seems funerals always come in groups. My cousin's wife died a few weeks ago."

"I'm sorry," Maggie said. "Did she live around here?"

"No. Chicago just like your half-sister. Her name was Goldie Finkelstein. Perhaps they knew each other."

#

After the visit with the Rabbi, her return drive from Minneapolis to Peterville went quickly despite the light snow. Mary and the doctor hadn't approved of her driving yet, but they weren't around and she wouldn't have obeyed anyway. There was one accident, a minor one, where someone tried to negotiate a corner too quickly and slid into the ditch. The flashing lights from the tow-truck and the deputy sheriff warned other travelers and the pre-holiday traffic came to a stand-still until the car was back on the shoulder of the road. It gave Maggie a chance to think.

What if the Rabbi recognizes Goldie? What if he calls cousin Arthur? I'm going to jail for this. Forget jail, I'm probably going to purgatory or hell. I need to call Vinny.

It was dark by the time Maggie turned into her driveway in Peterville. Roger the cat was purring at the door and followed her around the house until his bowl of cat food was refilled. Maggie opened a can of soup and dumped it into a bowl. While it was warming in the microwave, she called Mick and explained the dilemma.

"Can you get another Rabbi?" he asked.

"Are you kidding me? He was the third one I called. I didn't know about Conservative, Orthodox and Reformed. There's even Jews for Jesus. They're as bad as you Lutherans."

"What do you have against the Lutherans?"

"Don't get me started." The microwave beeped. Maggie set her phone on the table and pushed the speaker phone. "Can you still hear me? I have the radio playing."

"I'm fine."

"I can't get a new Rabbi, it's too late. Maybe he doesn't know Goldie very well but I can't take that chance." Maggie blew on her soup and took a quick slurp. "We have to change Goldie's appearance."

"I'm not touching her." Maggie thought she heard Mick shudder.

"I already called Vinny. He can't help. It's cremation week and he needs to finish fifty-three bodies before year-end."

"What are you going to do? Tomorrow is Tuesday."

"Vinny gave me some ideas. I need a candle and a sharp knife."

"I've got that."

Maggie took the last bite of soup and drank the remaining broth in the bottom of the bowl. She looked at her watch. She reached over and turned off the radio on her countertop. "I'll be at your house in fifteen minutes."

#

Mary pulled off her winter boots and coat and collapsed into her living room chair. It felt good to get off her feet after a long day of Christmas shopping. She mentally checked off her list. She had gifts for children, friends, neighbors, the mail carrier and even her mother, but the best gift was for herself, a new iPhone X. Mick was overly apologetic about knocking her phone into the wash bucket and agreed to pay for a new phone. She accepted his offer.

The Verizon carrier activated the phone at the store and she synched her contact list with her Google account. The only thing left to do was download the app to access the listening devices at her mother's house.

Since Maggie's return home their relationship was strained. More than once Mary felt like giving up but she wanted the best for her mother, at least her opinion of what was best. Visiting every other day was tiresome for both of them. Mary checked Maggie's weekly pill box to make sure everything was organized. Maggie insisted she was taking her medications as prescribed but Mary had no way of confirming it.

When the app was downloaded and activated, Mary entered the access code. A small green light appeared on one corner of the icon. Six hours of recorded conversation was available which was the maximum and any new recordings replaced the oldest audio files. She also had the option of listening live. Mary didn't expect much but hit the *listen now* button.

There was interference from background noise and the microwave caused static but she was able to piece together some words and phrases. What she heard gave her concern.

I can't get a new Rabbi...too late...have to change Goldie's appearance...candle and a knife...cremation week...fifty-three bodies...fifteen minutes...

Mary checked her watch. It was only 6:20 PM but she was tired. Mary pulled on her boots. *Mick lives three miles out of Peterville. Time for a surprise visit.*

CHAPTER 42

Ven dos ferd volt gehat vos tsu zogn, volt es geredt.
-Yiddish Proverb

The wind whipped out of the northeast, rattling the shrubs against Mick's house; moaning as it whirled in the corners between the buildings. Maggie parked behind the house out of the wind and out of sight from the road. She let herself in without knocking and slammed the door behind her.

"Did you get the truck?" Maggie asked.

"The black panel truck wasn't available so I called Dexter. He said we could borrow his."

"Mick, you can't deliver Goldie in a meat truck. She's Jewish. The truck has a massive photo of smoked bacon on the side."

"Why didn't you just have the funeral home take her."

"I paid Vinny to deliver her. This wasn't part of the deal. If I pay for another undertaker someone will get suspicious. Maybe the grave-digger can haul her in his dump truck."

"You should call Vinny. This whole screw-up is his fault." Mick said. "He owes you."

"I guess it doesn't hurt to ask." She picked up her phone and checked the time. It was still early. She dialed his number. When he answered, Maggie explained the situation and was surprised when Vinny agreed to make everything right. He was even willing to refund some of the money and he was going to drive the hearse himself. The funeral was scheduled for 11:00 AM on Wednesday.

He would leave Chicago in the early morning and pick up Goldie from Mick's garage and take her to the church.

"And Maggie..." Vinny said, "I know she's really Goldie but you have to remember to call her Velma Gladwell, that's what the death certificate says." Vinny sounded apologetic for the mess.

"Velma it is. Thanks Vinny. I'll see you Wednesday morning." Maggie ended the call. "At least she doesn't have to ride in the dump truck."

After a few minutes of thought Mick asked, "what about the grave?"

"Before Albert died, we bought three extra cemetery plots. Don't ask me why. He thought they would be a good investment if the church was running out of land." Maggie took off her winter coat and hung it on the hook in Mick's closet. "Ross said he'll get everything dug tomorrow."

"Don't we have to file something with the state?" Mick said. "This whole thing seems wrong."

"Why? Everything's filed and done except the burial." Maggie pulled out a kitchen chair and sat down. "Got any tea?"

"No Jameson?" Mick was already reaching for his liquor stash.

"I gave it up. It nearly killed me but I came this far, I'm not going back."

Mick had his hand on the kitchen cabinet when the lights went out. It was completely black in the house except for the twilight filtering through the windows.

"Powerline's probably down from the wind." Mick walked to the kitchen window and looked out. Tree branches flailed like giant arthritic hands in the night casting moonlit shadows across his face. "Let me find some candles and a flashlight."

He opened and closed three different drawers, fumbling around with his hands trying to feel the contents. "Here it is," he said. He flipped the switch on the flashlight and there was a faint yellow glow which couldn't outcompete the moonlight.

"Battery's dead."

"Just light the candle." Maggie said. "Let's get to work."

Mick lit one more candle and took out his sharpest kitchen knife. "What are you planning?" he asked as he offered the handle to Maggie.

"You'll see."

It was cold and dark in the garage. Maggie's breath condensed into a frozen fog around the flickering candle light. The wind whistled around the garage and shook the doors. In the two-car garage, one stall contained Mick's car and the other had a casket with an Amish pattern quilt covering the top. Maggie raised the quilt and hesitated.

"Have you ever touched a dead person?" she asked Mick.

"Just you at the square dance."

"That doesn't count. I was still warm."

The top was closed but not latched. Maggie handed her candle to Mick. She lifted with both hands and the lid opened easily and quietly not creaking as she expected. There in the dark was a cold waxen face with a grim half-smile. Her hands were crossed above her stomach and frozen in place. On the inside back of the cover was a blue Star of David and embroidered words, *Shalom*.

"I'm almost glad it isn't Velma. It would have been weird seeing myself in a casket." Maggie leaned toward the body and held the candle so she could see better. "There, on her neck. Do you see it?"

"What is it?"

"Vinny said she had a big growth on her neck that everybody knew about. He suggested cutting it off and dripping some wax over the wound to make it look like a skin condition or blisters."

"What if she bleeds?" Mick said. He hung back behind Maggie and tried to hold his candle high enough so she could see.

"She's dead. There's no blood flowing through her veins." Maggie took the big kitchen knife and pointed it toward Goldie's throat. She pushed the blade against the ugly brown growth. Nothing happened.

"Help me. She's frozen."

"Not me. This is your idea." Mick wavered in the background. "I'll hold the candle."

"Get me a hammer, then."

"You're gonna bust it off?"

"I'll chisel it off." She pressed the butcher knife against the growth and tapped the back of the blade with Mick's carpenter hammer. Tap-tap-tap.

"She's tougher than I thought." Tap-tap-tap.

"Hit it harder."

Maggie raised hammer above her head and gave it a robust swing. Whack!

"Oh shoot."

"What?"

"I missed the knife and hit her jaw."

"Here, let me try." Mick handed the candles to Maggie and took the knife and hammer. He lined up the blade with the thing growing out of her neck and gave it a firm thump with the hammer. The blade went in at an angle but the lump remained intact. He swung again. Whap!

"It's off."

"Where did it go?"

"I don't know. It flew somewhere but I can't see without any lights."

"Let me see." Maggie leaned over the casket with both candles. "Mick...there's a big chunk out of her neck. We're just doing a bit of surgery, not chopping down a tree."

Maggie held the candle over the deep scar on Goldie's neck and also over her dented chin. Goldie's mouth was half open from the hammer blow. The jaw was frozen and try as she could, Maggie couldn't quite close the mouth so her teeth weren't showing. The wax dripped slowly onto the wounds and gradually filled in the defect. It wasn't going fast enough for Maggie and she held the candles together. A big gust of wind caused enough of a draft in the garage that both candles blew out. Maggie jerked her hand as some of the hot wax burned the bare skin of her wrist.

Maggie closed the lid without surveying their handiwork and pulled the quilt over the top. "Good enough. Rabbi Abramovitz wouldn't recognize her if she was his own sister."

They closed the garage door and went into the house.

#

Mary parked her car a hundred yards from the old Torkelson place in a spot that was sheltered from the wind and more importantly sheltered from the sight of Mick's house. Based on the words she overheard, Maggie should be here and she didn't expect they were discussing politics or the price of aged cheddar.

Mary locked her car door and started walking against the wind along the shoulder of the road. She saw headlights approaching and crouched in some tall weeds alongside the road to avoid detection. The last thing she wanted was for someone to offer assistance and reveal that she was spying on her mother. As the car passed it slowed slightly when it came to her Toyota parked around the corner but kept going. Mary climbed back onto the road and resumed her reconnaissance. The quarter moon offered enough light for walking but an occasional cloud passed over and deepened the murkiness. She knew Mick's place was just a short distance but everything was dark. Looking down the road and across the bare cornfield, the other homes were also lost in darkness.

When she was close enough to see the outline of Mick's home and outbuildings silhouetted against the night sky, she left the road and walked around the grove of trees planted as windbreak. From the edge of the trees looking into the backyard, she saw nothing and heard only the wind. The house windows were black. Her foot was wet after breaking through the ice in the ditch. With each step her sock squished and she stumbled trying to feel the ground as she rapidly lost sensation in her toes. She tripped on a tree branch in the yard and fell onto her chest and face. Mary spit crumbles of frozen dirt from her mouth and felt her cheek start to swell.

She gathered herself into a crouch and leaned against a tree. In the window she saw a flicker of light. A candle stood on a table and then another. Mary crawled closer until she was ten feet from the window. She stood and peeked over the window sill. Mick and Maggie sat by candle light, at the kitchen table lifting mugs of hot beverages. *What am I doing? Leave them and go home.*

#

When they returned from the garage into the house, Maggie felt nauseous at what they had just done. Never in her life had she imagined herself chipping at a dead body to change their appearance. *What have I become? Get over it. You've come this far. See it through.*

"Want some tea to warm up?" Mick asked. "There still plenty of hot water left from before the power went out."

"Thanks. Green tea and honey if you have it."

Mick poured two mugs and they sat together at the table with two candles between them. Maggie clutched the mug of tea with both hands trying to warm her fingers. No one spoke for several minutes. The wind howled, the candles flickered and the old wind-up clock on the wall ticked.

Maggie turned toward the window and looked out. "Mick, don't make any sudden moves. I think there's a person in your yard looking in the window."

Mick raised his mug and turned to look. The tail end of a cloud passed the moon and the landscape became a hint brighter. There in the yard, crouched in the frozen grass, was a person.

"Should I get my gun?" he asked.

"I think it's a woman." Maggie's hand trembled. She took a sip of her tea, trying to remain calm and natural. "She's trying to see us. Blow out the candles." The room went dark.

The figure in the dark crawled toward the house and ten feet from the window got to her feet behind a small shrub. Maggie leaned toward the window as the figure crept closer.

"Mary?" she whispered.

CHAPTER 43

Of all the haunting moments of motherhood, few rank with hearing your own words come out of your daughter's mouth.
-Victoria Secunda

Neither Mick nor Maggie moved as the shadowy figure lurked outside their window. Maggie second guessed her initial thoughts, not wanting to believe it was her oldest daughter.

"Why would Mary be sneaking around in the dark?" Mick whispered back.

"Why would I know?" Mary sipped her tea. "I made up my mind to come over here fifteen minutes before I left. Either she's here spying on you or she knew what I was doing."

There was a sudden surge of air as the furnace clicked on. The lights blinded Mick and Maggie momentarily. In the bright room they could no longer see clearly into the backyard. When Maggie's eyes adjusted, she looked through the window into the darkness but there was nothing to see.

"What are you going to do?" Mick asked.

"I'm going to act as if nothing happened." Maggie drained the last of her tea and wrapped a scarf around her neck. "I'm too busy to worry about her, besides, the Rabbi's coming tomorrow and I have to clean my house."

#

Mary jumped back when the lights went on. She was thankful there were no outside lights. She retreated backwards into the grove of trees around the house and cut across the cornfield toward her car. Twice she tripped on clods of frozen dirt and fell onto her face. Her wet foot was nearly frozen and she couldn't feel her fingers. The first time she fell, two buttons on the front of her coat ripped off and the cold wind cut through the gap, freezing the cold sweat running down her back. Before she was back to her car she was shivering uncontrollably.

Mary fumbled with her car keys, dropping them twice before jamming them into the ignition. She pushed the heater fan as high as it would go but for the first mile and a half it blasted out frigid air. Within five miles the shivering subsided and the numbness of the skin on her face went away, replaced by a throbbing pain from contact with a dirt clod. She adjusted her mirror and took a quick look. A smear of coagulated blood above her eyebrow was caked with dirt and chaff. Her eye was half-closed and she had a bruise on her chin. *What if she saw me? She didn't act like she saw anything. How can I explain this one?*

Once home, Mary took a steaming shower and weighed her options. She was convinced her mother was on a path of self-destruction and the Rabbi comments didn't make sense. *Fifty-three bodies...cremation...too late?*

After her shower, she put some antibiotic ointment on her forehead and laid on the couch with an ice pack over her bruises. *This spy business is too risky.*

#

The next morning Maggie was out of bed earlier than usual. She mentally checked off her to-do list and started cleaning the guest room. It hadn't been dusted in months. She had never hosted a Rabbi before and she wanted to make a good impression. From there, she did the second bathroom, the hallway and the front sitting room pausing only for a mid-morning cup of black coffee. After her coffee she attacked the lamps with her feather duster. She pushed the button to turn on the lamp and the bulb made a quick flash and popped.

Maggie reached into the shade and unscrewed the bulb. As she did, a small black disk fell from the lamp onto her floor. She picked it up but couldn't figure out if it was part of the lamp or something else. It was magnetic and without giving it much thought she stuck it back on the lamp and continued cleaning.

When she was done vacuuming the floor, Maggie sat down in the easy chair and put her feet on the ottoman. Thoughts of Velma's funeral occupied her morning but as she rested, she looked again at the lamp. The small black disk was attached to the post holding the shade. Maggie reached over and took the disc in her hand. Using a magnifying glass tried to read the fine print on the side. It was some type of model or serial number, she couldn't be certain. There was a small indentation along the side. She took a fingernail file and pressed it into the slot. The cover popped off and inside was a tiny electronic circuit and a battery like Mick's hearing aids.

Last night at Mick's house. Mary was listening.

Maggie pressed the cover back into place and set the microphone transmitter on the side of the lamp. She stepped outside and called Mick. "Can you pick me up in your car in fifteen minutes. I need to do something."

"Is there something wrong with your car?"

"Maybe. I'll tell you later."

Maggie went back into the front room and pretended to speak to Mick on the phone. She sat next to the lamp and said, "Mick I'm sick and tired of playing these games. Let's get drunk and eat greasy food until we throw up." She paused a few minutes as if Mick were responding. Then she said, "I'm going to Willie's liquor store in Baxter and I'll be over to your place in an hour." She turned off her phone, put on a winter coat and hat and waited by the back door.

Mick picked up Maggie and they drove off.

"Where to?"

"Willie's Bait and Booze."

"I thought you gave up drinking."

"I did. I'm expecting to meet someone there."

As they entered Baxter, Maggie directed Mick to park across the street at the auto repair shop. He pulled into a spot between two pickup trucks that hadn't been driven in weeks. It gave them a clear view of Willie's across the street. He kept the car running and they waited.

"Who are you meeting?"

"You'll see." Maggie reached up with her gloved hand and wiped the condensation from the window. Cars came and went. Three different trucks stopped at Willie's. Patrons came out with 12 packs of beer, bottles of peppermint schnapps and bait for ice fishing. Then around the corner a Toyota minivan came. It slowly circled the parking area but never stopped. Then it made one more circle and parked near the back. Maggie took a small pair of binoculars from her purse and steadied herself against the window.

"It's her. And she's got a bruise on her forehead and a bandage on her cheek." Maggie handed the binoculars to Mick. "I wonder what she was doing last night?"

Mick handed the binoculars back and looked at Maggie. "What do you want me to do?"

"Nothing. Wait until she leaves then take me home. I'm going to teach them a lesson they'll never forget."

"What are you planning now?"

"I'll think of something."

CHAPTER 44

*There are more people who wish to be loved
than there are who are willing to love.*
-Nicolas Chamfort

Mary sat in her minivan for fifteen minutes but Maggie never showed. She wondered if she misheard the words but they sounded clear and direct. It was Willie's Bait and Booze and there wasn't a second location. She was somewhat relieved that Maggie didn't show. If she had appeared, then Mary would have had to deal with a confrontation she would rather avoid and she didn't want to expose her surveillance plan.

It was also possible that Maggie changed her mind, or... went somewhere else for a pint of Jameson, or...she was joking around with Mick, or... Mary hatched several scenarios in her mind but none of them were logical.

She still had a headache and her knee throbbed from last night's reconnaissance patrol across the frozen landscape. If Maggie was going to resume drinking, Mary probably had little control to stop it anyway. *Who am I fooling?* She went home and propped an ice pack on her head and took a nap.

#

Rabbi Benjamin Abramovitz arrived Tuesday evening and Maggie welcomed him with tea and shortbread cookies.

"I have never done something like this before. I hope you'll forgive me if I seem anxious."

"I'm so grateful that you are willing to give Velma her final rest." Maggie caught herself before she mentioned Goldie's name.

"Can I ask why she converted to Judaism?" the Rabbi asked.

"It was a rather sudden conversion."

"Sudden?"

"Don't ask me how it happened. She was Catholic the last time I saw her in Chicago but when she came up here, she was Jewish."

"Most unusual."

"Rabbi Abramovitz, I don't want to offend you but I've never been to a Jewish funeral. Is it different?"

"Please call me Ben. Other than the obvious difference between Judaism and Christianity we have many traditions. At the end, the mourners take a handful of dirt and sprinkle it on the top of the casket as a symbol to help them on their way to heaven."

"That isn't much different."

"I don't know what you were planning but we don't usually have an open casket." Ben took another cookie and brushed a crumb from his beard.

Maggie sighed. "I would prefer that."

"But...could I?"

"What?"

"See her."

"Of course. Anytime."

"She's at the funeral home?"

"Mick Torkelson's garage."

When they had finished their tea, Rabbi Benjamin unpacked his overnight bag in the guest room. He reappeared in the kitchen wearing a long black woolen coat with a warm cap and gloves. Maggie considered faking a heart attack again but her rib was still tender.

"We're on our way." Maggie said into her phone. She hung up, not waiting for Mick's answer.

Mick was waiting at the door. "Welcome Rabbi," he said and shook his hand with vigor. "May the peace of Almighty God be with thee."

Mick turned toward the garage door. "And if thou wouldst follow me."

"Are you reading Shakespeare again?" Maggie whispered to him as they walked toward the garage.

"He's a Rabbi. Don't they talk differently?"

"He understands English."

The casket sat exactly as it had last night. Maggie noticed small spots of wax on the floor and the side of the casket. She nodded to Mick and he lifted the lid.

The harsh overhead lights revealed all her faults. Mick reached into the casket and unfolded the satin liner. He stepped back to allow Rabbi Ben access. Ben took a half step in the direction of Velma but no closer. Maggie watched him move his hand up to his throat and rub the side of his neck.

"Her neck?" he asked.

"Surgery gone wrong." Maggie said.

"And her skin?"

"Leprosy."

"And the growth on her arm?" Maggie followed his gaze. The prodigal lump returned.

"She's been losing body parts." Maggie asked, "do you think your cousin in Chicago knew her?"

"Not a chance." Rabbi Benjamin took two steps back. In the glare of the overhead florescent lighting his face was ashen. "Thank you, I've seen enough."

#

Wednesday morning was cold and gray but there were clearing skies in the west. Vinny left Chicago at 4 AM and headed north on interstate 94. He didn't want to do it but he owed Maggie. Somehow the bodies got mixed up and he was ultimately responsible. He made it to Peterville with an hour to spare. Vinny adjusted his black coat and tucked his scarf tight around his neck. He turned up his collar to block the wind.

"Have you arranged for pallbearers?" Rabbi Benjamin asked Maggie.

"Never entered my mind." She said. "Can't we do it?"

"Jewish tradition doesn't allow for mourners to do the heavy lifting. Do you know anyone?"

"No problem. Up here, everyone is neighborly." She called Father Shamus.

His phone rang just as he was finishing his pancakes and sausage at the Main Street Café. Maggie explained her situation. Father Shamus long ago gave up questioning Maggie's eccentricity. If she needed six pallbearers at Mick's garage now, he'd find them.

He stood on a chair in the restaurant and announced Maggie's predicament. Six hands shot up. They stuffed themselves into the back of Bert Griffin's Ford pickup and headed to Mick Torkelson's place.

"Maggie I'm so sorry." Bert wiped a tear from the corner of his eye. "I didn't know you had a sister."

Maggie looked at the line of burly men standing outside Mick's garage. There was Elmer Swensen, Bert Griffin, Rick Miller, Lars Larsen, Eno Toivola, and Gus Rasmussen. Three of them had red and black plaid caps with the ear flaps down. Two of them were wearing canvas work coats with holes in the sleeves and frayed hems. Lars had his barn boots on. Maggie didn't dare tell the Rabbi he was a hog farmer. No one said a word. They took turns giving Maggie a warm hug to soften her loss.

They solemnly loaded Velma into the back of Vinny's hearse and went directly to the cemetery. Ross had the grave all dug and the platform to hold the casket was in place with a perimeter of dark red carpet surrounding the grave. Three rows of cold metal folding chairs were placed on the side, awaiting mourners.

Bert called his cousin at the Ace Hardware and he called five others. Before the hearse arrived in town, thirty people were waiting at the grave side. Three of them had casseroles ready for lunch and Lena Larsen had a green Jell-O salad with shredded carrots and miracle whip on top.

The six volunteer farmers, carpenters, plumbers and truck drivers reverently carried Velma and placed her over the open grave.

"*Baruch Atah Adonai, Dayan Ha-Emet* - Blessed are You, *Adonai*." Rabbi Benjamin began. Everyone bowed their heads and removed their plaid woolen caps. "*Adonai natan, Adonai lakach, yehi shem Adonai m'vorach* - God has given, God has taken away, blessed be the name of God."

Rabbi Ben read from the Psalms. Bert Griffin's shoulders shook. Betty, his wife, hooked her arm in his and leaned against his shoulder.

The Rabbi nodded toward Maggie to follow his lead. Without speaking he reached down and took a handful of crumbled frozen dirt. He reached his hand over the casket and sprinkled it gently on the polished wood cover. As Maggie did the same, she leaned forward and rested her hand on the casket. Tears welled up in her eyes and ran down her cheeks. She made no effort to stop them.

This was supposed to be her funeral. It was supposed to be her in the box. If she wanted to know who loved her, she needed to look no further than the weather lined faces standing around the casket.

"You're all invited to lunch at the café." Bert announced as the service ended.

Lars Larsen walked up to Maggie. He reached out his hand and softly touched her on the shoulder. In a low quiet voice, he asked, "How's your car runnin'?"

She nodded.

He understood.

CHAPTER 45

We can know only that we know nothing.
And that is the highest degree of human wisdom.
-Leo Tolstoy

In the days following Velma Gladwell's interment, Maggie stayed home. She started reading a book but lost interest in the second chapter. She started another but set that one aside as well. Three times a day she went to the lamp and stared at the black magnetic button. She considered saying something into the microphone to see if Mary was still listening but changed her mind. Once Maggie got over the shock of being secretly monitored, like a bit of grit forming a pearl in an oyster, her thoughts turned from anger and hurt to revenge. She wanted one last chance to teach her children a life changing lesson.

She coughed into a napkin and saw a faint streak of blood. It was the first time since her heart attack. She went to her floor lamp and wrapped the magnetic listening device in the bloody phlegm and dropped it into the garbage.

She remained deeply touched by the compassion of her neighbors and wondered how to repay their kindness, but she knew they would accept nothing and any attempts to repay them would only cause embarrassment. She found herself viewing people differently and began to visit the Main Street Café once or twice weekly to participate in the rumor mill. If the townspeople were curious about Velma Gladwell, they never asked.

#

Mary feigned illness for several days after knocking her head on Mick's dirt clod. It was easier to stay home and tell people she had malaria or cholera or some other life-threatening contagious disease, than to explain the knot on her forehead. She was certain, Mick or Maggie discovered her outside the window but Mary never heard them say anything about it.

She waited until dark to retrieve her mail from the mailbox on the corner of the street. All the mailboxes were clustered together so the mail carrier made one stop rather than tripping over everyone's sidewalk and doorstep. After dark, the bruises and scratches were less visible and she wasn't likely to meet anyone. She picked up her mail and sorted through the junk and the maybe-junk, tossing most of it into the trash before entering her house.

She unfolded the Peterville Press weekly newspaper which was printed every Thursday evening and delivered on Friday. In the middle of the front page, two-thirds of the way down was a picture of a woman dropping a handful of dirt onto a casket. Her head was downcast and her face shaded but there was no mistaking her identity. The caption read: Peterville Matriarch Loses Sister to Leprosy.

Mary felt the strength go out of her legs. She lowered herself into a chair and searched the newspaper article for insight. *Mom was an only child. Converted to Judaism? And no one told me?*

Mary checked her watch and called Eliza. It was two hours earlier in Portland, she should be off work by now.

"Liz, did you know Mom had a half-sister?" Mary asked.

"I thought she was an only child."

"That's what I thought, but it's not what the paper said." Mary flipped through the paper searching for more clues. "Go to the Peterville Press website and check the headlines." Mary tried to slow her breathing.

Mary could hear Eliza punching the keys of her laptop. "Look at all the people attending the funeral and she never said anything to you or Freddie?"

"Nothing. Not a word."

"There's only three possibilities." Eliza cleared her throat. "She either has a secret life, or she's divorced us as a family or she's finally lost her marbles. And none of these options are good. Remember the invoice from Maldonado's House of Eternal Rest? Velma Gladwell...it's starting to make sense."

"But the newspaper said she was Jewish. The article mentioned Rabbi Benjamin Abramovitz."

"I thought we were Irish." Eliza said.

"We are, but Mom kept this quiet for years. You know what this means don't you?"

"What?"

"Grandpa must have been a Nazi spy and that's why she never said a word."

"Are you crazy?" Eliza asked.

"His name was Kurt. His father was Irish but his mother was a Claudia Klinkenheimer from Berlin. Have you ever heard of anyone else of Irish descent named Kurt? If you put his picture next to Kaiser Wilhelm, there's a resemblance." Mary pulled some old family photo albums from her shelf as she talked.

"What should we do?"

"We need to get control of her assets and the simplest way is to get her declared incompetent as soon as possible."

"Don't you think we should just talk to her?"

"If she buried a secret sister and never told her family anything, do you really think she'll tell the truth?"

"Is there anything you want me to do from this end?" Eliza asked.

"Don't tell anyone especially not David. I'll try to be friendly with her and suggest changing to joint bank accounts and do some estate planning."

"What if that doesn't work?"

"Then we file a lawsuit to have her declared incompetent."

#

Since Velma's funeral, Mary acted extra friendly to Maggie. Instead of visiting on Fridays only, Mary started dropping by her mother's home unannounced, often two or three times a week. Twice Maggie saw Mary inspecting the floor lamp in the front room but said nothing about it. Mary dropped a few hints to her mother about estate planning and what to do with the house if she had another heart attack but Maggie never took the bait and the conversation died.

Christmas came and went with little fanfare. Maggie dutifully attended the Advent services at the church alongside Mabel and Sally. Patrick was still recovering in the nursing home after his hip surgery. He was expected to return home in the spring if he did well with his physical therapy. Pickles went to live with Patrick's daughter in St. Paul.

The midnight mass on Christmas Eve was as well attended as any Maggie could remember in recent years. Mary invited Maggie and Freddie for Christmas dinner. David stayed in San Francisco and Eliza was more concerned about the effect of global warming on sea slugs than spending Christmas with her mother. But she did send a Christmas card printed on recycled paper.

Maggie gave up Christmas shopping years ago but decided to give each of her children something this year. She hated fighting crowds and the concept of Cyber-Tuesday didn't sound any more appealing. She gave each family $1000 cash and a $250 Visa gift card. Therese had the gift card spent before Freddie was done flossing his teeth after Christmas at the dinner table.

"Mom, I know this was a tough year for you," Mary said. "You never want anything for Christmas but we have a gift for you, anyway." She handed Maggie a small gift-wrapped box with a red bow.

"Thank you," Maggie said. "You didn't need to get me anything."

"Open it."

Maggie untied the ribbon and carefully undid the taped edges of the paper. She folded it and set the paper aside. She removed the lid on the shoebox and lifted the figurine from beneath the tissue paper. It was wax figurine of the Virgin Mary. Unfortunately, it had sat too close to the heat register and her right side drooped slightly. It reminded Maggie of Velma's leprosy. She started to laugh.

"What's so funny?" Mary asked.

"You've given me a thoughtful gift. Thank you." Maggie said. She continued to giggle quietly.

"It wasn't that great," Freddie said. "She picked it up from the bargain bin at Walmart."

"Memories are more important than stuff," Maggie said. "You've given me a great idea."

"What's that?" Freddie asked.

"I'm going to have a surprise party for the whole family."

#

The first Sunday in January was cold even by Minnesota standards. The Wells Fargo Bank thermometer quit working and Maggie's free Ace Hardware thermometer registered as a red smudge in the bottom of the bulb. The only positive thing anyone would say about the weather was the lack of wind and the sun was shining. It was so cold the frozen tree trunks popped like gun shots in the night. The water main in Baxter burst and flooded the streets for three quarters of a mile out of town. School was cancelled for the week and kids played hockey between Walnut street and 3rd avenue.

Maggie was the only person to attend mass that morning. Mabel and Sally stayed home and Patrick was still in the nursing home. If Father Shamus had a prepared message, he never delivered it. They spent the morning drinking tea in his office where he had a small electric space heater running on high.

"How's your family?" Shamus asked.

"The same. Mary's trying to cozy up to me because she wants to get her name on my checking account. Nothing has changed."

"Did you ever think, the reason you don't get along with your kids is partly your fault?"

"I suppose that's true."

"Did you learn any lessons from Velma's funeral?" Shamus poured himself more hot water and dropped in a fresh tea bag. He offered the tea pot to Maggie. She added a bit of hot water to her own cup.

"Yes, I did."

"And what might that be?"

"Next time I'm going to do it right."

"Maggie, you can't be serious about this fake funeral thing." He stood up from his desk and paced. "What can you possibly gain from this charade?"

"I've moved beyond trying to understand my children."

"Why? Do you really believe they don't love you? When you were in a coma, they sat by your side day and night."

"And they treated me as if I was crazy. They want to get me declared incompetent so they can get my money."

"And how do you know that?"

"They bugged my house to listen to everything I said."

"That can't be true."

"I found it."

"Aren't you acting a bit paranoid? Look at the past few months. You bought a dead homeless woman and spent a fortune making her look like you. You got tattoos all over your body and you went square dancing. Then your twilight-zone plan failed because you had a heart attack and nearly died." Father Shamus lowered his eyes. "Maybe they are right. Maybe you should have your head examined."

"I have an appointment to do just that."

"Then you agree with them?"

She pulled out two airline tickets and pushed them across his desk. "I'm leaving on Wednesday. I want you to come with me."

CHAPTER 46

You can't see the world through a mirror.
-Avril Lavigne

The Delta Airlines flight 967 touched down at McCarren International airport in Las Vegas and taxied to the terminal. Maggie and Father Muldoon took their carryon luggage and headed to the taxi stand.

"Where to?" The well-dressed driver took their bags and placed them in the trunk of the car. He opened the side door and assisted Maggie.

"The Venetian," she said.

He negotiated heavy traffic and turned from E. Flamingo onto the strip. Father Muldoon gawked at the garish lights as the taxi slowed for pedestrians.

"First time in Vegas?"

"Yes." Father Muldoon said.

"Here to gamble?"

"Business," Maggie said. The driver said nothing more.

At the Venetian, he stopped the meter. It read $15.75. Maggie handed him a twenty. "Keep the change." She said.

They checked in at the desk and each were given keys for their rooms. A porter took their bags and led them to the elevator.

"When are you going to tell me what we are doing?" Father Muldoon asked as the porter punched the button for the seventh floor.

"We have a meeting with Clark Burgess at the Hangover Bar at 3 PM. After that it's dinner and high stakes bingo."

"What does this have to do with getting your head examined?"

"You'll see." Maggie stepped from the elevator and followed the signs to her room. She tipped the porter five bucks a bag and said to Father Shamus, "I'll call you in twenty minutes."

#

A short round man with soft hands greeted them in the Hangover Bar. "Clark Burgess," he said as he extended his hand.

"Maggie O'Reilly and this is Father Shamus Muldoon."

He led them through a maze of tables into a quiet side room designed for small informal business meetings and private parties. He asked the waiter for three champagne flutes, a bottle of sparkling wine, a plate of calamari and a side of stuffed mushrooms with gorgonzola.

"Please sit down." Clark pulled out a chair for Maggie and motioned for Father Shamus to have a seat. "When you called me last week, I was skeptical about your request but we discussed it and I think it would be fun."

"What are we talking about?" Father Muldoon asked.

"You haven't explained anything?" he asked Maggie.

"Clark is the senior development director for Madame Tussauds." Maggie explained.

"Which is...?"

Clark put his hand over his mouth and sat back in his chair. "You haven't heard of Madame Tussauds?"

"Is it what I think it is?" Shamus asked.

"It's a world-famous wax museum. We have over a hundred wax celebrities on display." Clark opened a photo portfolio and pushed it in front of Father Shamus. The sparkling wine and appetizers arrived as Shamus reviewed images.

"Here's a photo of Julia Roberts beside her wax replica. Most people can't tell which one is the real person from the photo. Can you?"

Father Shamus and Maggie studied the photo as Clark poured them each a glass of sparkling wine. "I think it is this one." Maggie said and pointed to the person on the right.

"You're correct but more than half of the people who see this, get it wrong."

Clark raised his glass, "To your project." They clinked glasses.

"The price for what you requested will only be $23,000." Clark opened the folder containing notes from a previous conversation with Maggie. Father Shamus choked on a bite of calamari and coughed into a napkin. "Since you don't need to be standing, you don't need legs and no one will see the back of the figure."

"What are you talking about?" Shamus asked.

"Clark, will you explain this to Father Shamus?"

"Miss Maggie has requested a replica of herself for display in a casket."

"You're willing to pay $23,000 for the top half of a wax model that looks like you? Are you nuts?" No one spoke for several minutes. Clark interrupted the tension.

"A full standing figure could cost as much as a quarter of a million dollars, sometimes more." He popped a stuffed mushroom into his mouth and swallowed. "This is a good deal."

Father Muldoon drained his wine glass and leaned back in his chair. "I can't be part of this anymore."

"Would you rather be saying the rosary in Sweetgrass, Montana?" Maggie asked.

"Don't threaten me Maggie. I've done nothing but support you through this."

"Do you need more time to think about this?" Clark asked.

"No. I've made up my mind. I need her before Valentine's Day." Maggie poured another glass.

"That's five weeks away." Clark said as he checked his calendar. "Why then?"

"My son is getting out of prison February 1st. Everyone will be home for the family reunion."

#

The physical therapist held onto the wide nylon belt around the waist of Patrick Murphy as he limped down the hall of Happy Valley Nursing Home. He gripped the handles of the walker, sliding it ahead of his steps as he made progress toward his room.

"Mr. Murphy, you're doing wonderful. Keep this up and you'll be home by February 1st."

"That's good news," he said. "I miss my dog, Pickles."

He turned from the hallway into his room and eased himself onto a chair. "Did you hear that Ethel?" he said to the framed photo beside his bed. "I'm going home in a few weeks. I bet Maggie will be surprised."

#

Mary sat in the waiting room until Dr. Smith was done seeing patients for the day. It gave her time to read old magazines and think about her mother. It was 5:50 PM before he plodded down the hall toward the reception area.

"Mary, nice to see you again." Dr. Smith shook her hand. "How's your mother?"

"That's what I came to discuss. Thank you again for seeing me on short notice."

He ushered her into his office and leaned back in his swivel office chair. "Did you ever get her to the memory clinic?"

"I had good intentions but never did." Maggie leaned forward. "Did you get her records from the Mason City hospital?"

"I don't recall. What happened?"

Mary spent the next ten minutes describing the tattoos, the square dance competition and the heart attack. "She was comatose for several days and we didn't know what to expect."

Dr. Smith checked Maggie's records. "It looks like I did receive some information. How's she doing now?"

"There are more issues. She just buried her half-sister before Christmas."

He glanced at Maggie's family history information in the medical record. "It says here she has no siblings. I should update this so it's accurate." He moved the keyboard to a comfortable position.

"Don't change anything. We didn't know she had a half-sister either. It was all hush-hush and sudden. There may be more going on than we thought."

"Such as...?"

"I did a background search for Velma Gladwell, the name of my mother's supposed half-sister. She died in a nursing home in Chicago four months ago. She was a ward of the state. The record says she was cremated by Maldonado's House of Eternal Rest in Chicago, but how did she end up in Peterville, Minnesota having a Jewish funeral by Rabbi Benjamin Abramovitz?" Mary squeezed her hands together. Two knuckles popped. "Something's fishy."

"How do you know this?"

"It's in the public record. Read it yourself."

"This is an interesting story but what does it have to do with your mother's mental health?"

"She isn't just demented, she's hiding something from us."

"What would she be hiding?"

"Look at these photos. The one on the right is my grandfather." She laid two printed photos side by side on his desk.

"And who is this?"

"Kaiser Wilhelm." Mary raised her voice and her hands trembled slightly. "Can't you see the similarities?"

"I'm not sure if I'm following you." Dr. Smith scrunched his eyebrows and rubbed his chin.

"Forget the memory clinic. If we do anything it needs to be quick and decisive before she destroys any evidence."

"What do you want me to do?"

"If I claimed she was suicidal could we get an emergency forty-eight-hour detention in a locked unit?"

"If she's deemed to be an immediate threat to herself."

"When I call you, I want you to call the police to have her detained."

"I can't do that unless it's true. I could lose my license for this." He stood up and stared into the darkness through his office window.

"It's our word against hers, and she's crazier than a bag of nuts. You said it yourself."

"When?"

"The first part of February. We're getting together for a reunion when my brother is released from prison. I want this to be a family decision."

CHAPTER 47

Wisdom begins at the end.
-Daniel Webster

Vinny smiled when he opened the letter. Repeat customers were a sign of a good business and now Maldonado's House of Eternal Rest had their first, Maggie O'Reilly.

Dear Vinny,

Thank you for your kind service. Velma or Goldie had the nicest funeral I've attended in years. I hope you weren't offended about the fake leprosy. I hated to cover up your good work.

I'm sorry the original plan didn't work out. I've made some modifications and I need a new casket by the first week of February. Give me something cheaper this time and disable the latch.

As we discussed during our recent phone conversation, the figure will be shipped from Las Vegas directly to you. Get her tucked in and ship to Mick Torkelson, same as before.

Happy New Year,

Regards, Maggie

He checked his inventory and picked out the perfect casket. The bright green casket with a shamrock symbol on the ends had been in his inventory for several years. He tore up Maggie's check. She was a good customer, this one was on him. He opened the calendar on his phone and entered Maggie's information.

\#

Bishop O'Connor flipped through a travel magazine daydreaming of a tropical getaway. He hated the cold. It weighed him down and made his bones creak. It had been two years since he breathed warm salty air in the winter. He pressed the intercom button for his personal assistant.

"You called sir?" The young man appeared in the doorway of his office.

"Can you print out my winter schedule. I want to find a couple weeks where I can get away."

"Certainly." He disappeared into his own office and within minutes he reappeared with printed months of January, February and March containing detailed side notes about people and places.

"Thank you, Robert." He studied the calendars and considered his options. It was already January but there might be some last-minute travel deals. Easter was early this year and he was expected to be at the Vatican because this was the first year with the new Pope. That eliminated March. February was his best option and there was a Princess Cruise special offer for two weeks in the Caribbean.

"Robert, what's this note you have here during the last half of February? Performance review?"

"Father Muldoon. You scheduled a follow up visit and review."

"Have you heard any complaints?"

"Nothing sir."

"Cancel it," he said. "Better yet...let's make an unannounced visit the first week of February. I'll go straight from there to the airport."

#

Mick sat alone on the bench in Miller Hill Mall watching shoppers come and go. Even though he drove two hours to get to the mall he hesitated the last fifty feet. He stood at the entrance to the store but turned and went to the food court. After eating a massive cinnamon roll and downing two cups of coffee he was back on his bench.

I don't belong here, I'm too old. Look at these people, I'm not like them. I should have asked her first. What if she says no?

When the store was empty of customers, Mick took two deep breaths and walked into Kline Jewelers.

"Are you looking for something special?" The perky young woman behind the glass case smiled.

"I'm not sure."

"Are you looking for a Valentine's gift? We have many nice pendants and earrings over here." She pointed toward another case glittering with gold, silver and diamonds.

"No...forget it." He turned and walked out of the store and sat on the bench again.

Two more customers entered the jewelry store. A man and a woman gawked at the gem stones and held up diamond rings, admiring the glint and flash in the bright lights. They smiled and leaned closer, touching their foreheads together. They kissed, alone in a sea of people, oblivious to the clerk and a thousand shoppers passing by.

When the transaction was done, Mick walked back into the store and gave a half-baked grin to the sales person.

"I want what they got." He pointed at the couple holding hands, walking slowly toward the exit.

"Do you know what they have?" she asked.

"It doesn't matter."

The clerk pulled out a tray of sparkling engagement rings. "This is what the couple before you bought." She held up a diamond solitaire.

"How much?"

"This one is $2500."

"I'll take it and earrings to match."

CHAPTER 48

Saying nothing sometimes says the most.
-Emily Dickinson

"I don't feel like going to Minnesota. Not in February." David poured some fresh squeezed orange juice into a glass and offered it to Steven. "But Mary's being a real jerk about this."

"What's the event?"

"Tommy is getting out of prison. Mary claims Mom wants us all together. It's been years since we had any type of reunion."

"It's your family. If you don't want to go, that's up to you." Steven swirled his juice to loosen the pulp from the edge of the glass and gulped it down.

"I don't know. I still feel bad about Mom. In her Christmas card she hinted at something happening this winter." David walked to the window of their apartment and looked toward San Francisco Bay. The fog was dispersing in the late morning sun. "Mom probably doesn't have much time left."

"So, now you're going?"

"When we were kids, Tommy was a bully." David's voice trailed off. He moved slower than the bay area fog.

"You're staying?"

"Do you remember the first thing Mom said when she came out of her coma?"

Steven looked toward David and shrugged his shoulders.

"I don't remember either. I need to go home."

#

They huddled together in the February chill, like a band of misfit cheerleaders outside the gate at Waupun prison. The sky was a heavy gray and snow was in the air. Promptly at noon the gates opened and Tommy O'Reilly was ushered through the locked doors and into the waiting arms of his family.

Maggie was the first to give him a welcome home hug and she kissed him on the cheek. Tears ran down their cheeks and froze onto their coat collars. Mary, Eliza, Freddie and David closed the gap around them forming a big group hug. Steven stood awkwardly to the side letting the family get reunited.

They piled into a rented eleven passenger van and started the six-hour drive back to Peterville. The first fifteen minutes were filled with excited chatter, updating Tommy on all the local news. He nodded and tried to laugh at jokes but most of the time he was quiet. Seven years of being quiet does that to a person.

Maggie asked, "Are you hungry? We can stop at Culver's if you want."

"I'm fine."

Mary asked, "Did you get along with the other prisoners?"

Tommy glanced down at the scars on the back of his right hand and slipped it into his pocket.

Freddie spoke up. "Remember Bootsie, your old girlfriend from high school? She got busted for selling meth."

"Knock it off, Freddie. You just ruined his homecoming." Eliza shook her head and glared out the car window at piles of frozen cow manure stacked next to faded red barns.

For the next five and a half hours they listened to country music on the AM radio.

#

The next couple days Tommy arose early and made coffee for his mother. Much of the time they sat together in silence, broken by trivial chatter and comments about the weather.

"I'm glad you're home."

"It's good to be here."

"You can stay here as long as you need." Maggie said.

"Mary said the same. Freddie too, but Therese wants to charge rent."

"You decide."

"Mary invited me for pizza tonight."

"Oh..."

"Reconnecting."

"Yes."

#

"Pizza is here." Mary tipped the driver and slid two large pizzas onto the kitchen counter. "There's cold drinks in the refrigerator if you want some."

Freddie jumped in line first and took a slice of each and a cold Miller Lite.

"Fred, why didn't you let Tommy go first?" Eliza slapped him on the arm and motioned for Tommy to go next. David and Steven remained seated in the front room.

"It's okay," Tommy said. "I don't mind."

"I'm glad you're here." Mary gave him quick hug and popped open a diet coke.

"What's the agenda, Mary?" Freddie asked. "The last time we were together like this was when Dad died, seventeen years ago."

"Why do you think there's an agenda?"

Freddie rolled his eyes and took three gulps of his beer. Eliza and Mary's eyes met as if each was waiting for the other to speak.

"Is Mom's heart acting up again?" David asked.

"I wish," Freddie said.

"What would you say if I told you we might be Jewish?" Mary said.

"I thought we were Irish? Didn't great-grandpa O'Reilly's family come from Dingle?" David asked.

"He did," Eliza said. "But what about Mom's side of the family?"

"What about it?" Freddie asked.

"Look at this." She opened the Peterville Press weekly newspaper and spread it out for everyone to see. Maggie O'Reilly, dressed in black was sprinkling dirt on a shiny wood casket with brass trim.

She waited until everyone had enough time to digest the contents of the article. "I don't think we have much time."

"Time for what?" David asked.

"I believe Mom has borderline dementia and is suicidal."

"You can't be serious," David said. "I've heard her say some crazy things but I would never guess her to be suicidal."

"Look at the evidence. She's doing strange things. She got tattoos on her butt and chest. We saw them when she was in the hospital."

"So, what? You have tattoos, does that make you suicidal?" Freddie asked. Freddie crunched his Miller Lite can and popped open another one.

"But she said hers was for positive identification. You don't need to identify anyone if they're alive."

"But any of us could identify her." David said.

"Don't you see? She's going to do it when we aren't around." Eliza said.

"But...weren't you claiming dementia before this?" Freddie asked.

"We can't prove it unless she goes to a memory clinic and has some tests and then we need two doctors to agree, which is almost impossible and then the judge will sign the paper."

"Why do you keep saying we don't have time? What's the rush?" David asked. He took another slice of pizza and sat down in the corner of the room.

"Eliza's the only one who knows this, but I hired a private investigator to bug Mom's house."

"Wait a minute. This is going too far. Would you like to have your house bugged?" Freddie belched and took another gulp. "What else have you done?"

"I've been tracking her phone calls too."

"I don't want any part of this," David stood up and reached for his coat.

"Don't go yet. Hear me out. In the past week she's made six phone calls to Maldonado's House of Eternal Rest, in Chicago. The same funeral home which handled Aunt Velma's funeral. You don't call a funeral home six times in the same week unless someone died...or is going to die."

David hung his coat back on the hook by the door and returned to his seat. The room had a dull silence like the seconds after a bomb goes off and no one knows which way to run.

"Tommy, do you have anything to say?" Mary asked.

"You can't make this stuff up."

Everyone remained quiet expecting more out of Tommy. Nothing came. He reached for a slice of pepperoni and took a bite.

"What's next?" Freddie asked.

"Tuesday I'm calling Dr. Smith to report Mom being suicidal. He's prepared to call the police and have her placed under an emergency forty-eight-hour detention in a locked psychiatric ward."

"Other than completely destroying your relationship with her, what do you hope to accomplish?" David asked.

"It could save her life and force the issue of competence."

"Why are you doing this Mary?" David asked.

"Because I love her."

"You have a funny way of showing it."

CHAPTER 49

He who flees at the right time can fight again.
-Marcus Trentius Varro (c.116-27 BC)

Monday night.

"Is someone there? Tommy is that you?" Maggie sat up in bed and bunched a pillow in front of her. "Is someone there? Tommy?"

There was no answer. The wind had picked up again and branches from the big oak tree raked against the siding. The wind whispered and moaned around the corners of the house. Snow pelted against her window. Maggie climbed out of bed and looked out. In the distance she could see the headlights of the county snow plow spreading salt on the highway. Snow whipped through the cones of light under the street lamps.

She climbed back into bed and pulled the old heavy quilt up close to her chin. She began to feel the warmth when she heard it again. This time it was no mistake. The eighty-year-old floor boards groaned again.

"Tommy?" she asked. She sat up again in bed. "Is that you?"

Her bedroom doorknob rattled slightly and in the faint light she saw it turn.

"Who's there?" she asked again.

The door swung open slowly and she could see the outline of the shape of a man. He moved slowly into the room toward her bed.

"Stop or I'll shoot." Maggie backed up against the headboard. Her heart bounded.

"Shhh...It's me, David."

"David? What are you doing? You're going to give me a heart attack."

"Shhh...I don't want Tommy to know I'm here."

"Why?"

"They're coming tomorrow."

"Who?"

"The guys in the white coats and the police."

"David are you sleep walking? What are you talking about?"

David stepped forward and sat on the edge of the bed. He reached out and took his mother by the shoulders. "Mom, you need to listen to me. Mary is calling the doctor tomorrow to get you committed. She made us all sign a paper to agree that you're crazy and suicidal. She said if we didn't agree, Tommy would take care of us."

"What does that mean?"

"You need to go now."

Maggie looked at the clock on her bedside stand. "It's after midnight. What am I supposed to do?"

"Get dressed and go out the back door. Don't take anything. Steven is waiting in the car two blocks to the south. He'll take you to Mick's place."

"Then what?"

"Mick knows. He has a plan."

Maggie felt her heart pounding again. She tiptoed across her bedroom and into her walk-in closet. She quietly clicked the door shut behind her and turned on the light. She blinked and tried to shield her eyes from the sudden brightness. Maggie stripped off her flannel pajamas and dressed as quickly as possible. *They're coming after me. I knew it. I knew it all along. They think I'm crazy.*

She turned off her closet light and worked her way through the bedroom by feeling along her bed. She came to her dresser and opened the top right drawer. She felt in the drawer and grabbed two pairs of underwear and extra socks and stuffed them into her pockets.

"David?" There was no answer. The wind moaned and she heard ice pelts ticking against the window.

Maggie pushed the button on her bedroom doorknob and carefully pulled it shut. It clicked when the latch snapped into place. She tried the knob. It was locked. *They'll think I'm still inside.*

Maggie ran her hand along the wall until she came to the kitchen and then the back door. Without turning on a light, she took her long woolen coat from the hook behind the door and her warm winter boots and stepped into the night.

I forgot my phone. Maggie tried the door. It locked behind her. She walked into the night. A pair of dark eyes watched her from the upstairs bedroom window.

#

Mary got out of bed around seven and felt miserable. Eliza was still in bed. David and Steven were staying at Freddie's place and Tommy was at home with Maggie. There was a knot in her stomach and she didn't know if she should eat or vomit. She tried eating but shouldn't have. Her coffee tasted sour and she felt restless.

Her phone rang. "Tommy?"

She listened for a minute. It was the most Tommy had said since he got out of prison.

"Sounds good," she said. "If Mom isn't out of bed by nine, I'll come over."

Eliza blinked when she came out of the bedroom and walked into the kitchen. "I couldn't sleep last night. I'm having second thoughts on this whole thing."

"We're doing this because we care. If we didn't care we would just let her go."

"I still don't know if this is the right way." Eliza poured some coffee. "When are you going to make the call?"

"I'm waiting to hear from Tommy."

They sat in silence for the next thirty minutes. Eliza drummed her fingers on the kitchen table and Mary never quit biting her nails. When the phone rang, they both jumped.

"Her bedroom door is locked?" Mary asked. "Did you knock?"

"Call Freddie. We'll be there in fifteen minutes." Mary put her phone into her pocket. "We need to go. Mom's not responding."

"What?"

"Tommy knocked on her door. She didn't answer."

"I hope it isn't her heart again." Eliza said.

"What if it isn't her heart? What if she did something?" She slipped her feet into her winter boots but left them untied.

Her car tires spun when she turned onto the snow-covered street. The minivan skidded half way around before she regained control. "I hate winter," she muttered.

#

David, Steven, and Freddie converged on Maggie's house minutes before Mary arrived. Mary drove down the street too fast and locked up her brakes. She skidded out of control and her front bumper slammed into Freddie's fender. There was a sudden explosion in her car and the airbags erupted, blowing out the steering wheel, smashing into Mary and Eliza.

Freddie's car was pushed into Maggie's mailbox creasing his front fender. His car sagged as the air rushed out of the right front tire.

"Mary?" Freddie jumped out his car and rushed back to Mary's Toyota.

He pulled on the door handle but her door was still locked. Mary fumbled around and opened the door. Mary rolled out from under the airbags and slumped into the snow-covered street.

"We're okay," She said.

Leaving the wrecked cars beside the curb they entered the house.

"Mom?" Mary yelled as she walked down the hallway to her bedroom. "Mom?" Mary rapped her knuckles on the bedroom door. There was no answer. She tried the doorknob. It was locked.

"Tommy can you unlock this?"

He quietly walked up to the door and tested the knob again. Then he backed up and smashed his foot into the door next to the door frame. Wood splintered and the door swung open.

There was a curved lump under the heavy quilt. Mary pulled back the covers. Two pillows were rested end to end in the depression where Maggie had laid.

Mary pulled out her cell phone and called her mother. She heard a buzzing in the bedside stand. Mary jerked the drawer open. Maggie's iPhone lay in the top drawer, blinking, next to a box of tissues.

"We're too late," she said. Mary punched 911 into her phone.

"How do you know?" Eliza asked.

"If you're going to kill yourself, you don't take your cell phone."

CHAPTER 50

Lost time is never found again.
-Ben Franklin

Tuesday morning.

Mick glanced at the clock in the dash of his car as he took the first exit in Iowa. It was 6:12 AM. The eastern sky was a gray line between the horizon and the retreating blackness. Mick could finally see where the cornfields ended and the sky began. Maggie had her seat back and her coat was draped over her like a blanket. She appeared to be sleeping well and he hated to stop but he couldn't drive any further. He needed coffee.

Maggie stirred and stretched as the car came to a stop. "Where are we?" Maggie pressed the seat button and brought the passenger seat upright.

"Just crossed the border into Iowa." Mick turned the car off. "Time for breakfast."

They entered the truck stop and spied a vacant booth in the corner. Five truckers sat at the counter, chugging dishwater coffee and eating platter sized pancakes. One was a short muscular woman with a big wallet in her back pocket attached to a hanging chain, looping somewhere out of sight. No one spoke as Mick and Maggie tiptoed behind them.

A waitress with a rusty-red bouffant and a tattoo on her neck followed them with a pot of coffee and a small order pad in her pocket.

"Mornin' hon. Coffee?" She didn't wait for Mick's answer but poured two steaming cups. "We got specials on the board otherwise you can order from the menu." She slapped two clear vinyl covered menus on the table and left.

Mick studied the menu briefly then set it aside. Maggie didn't bother to look. She slurped her coffee and leaned forward. "What did David say to you?"

"Mary has a plan to get you."

"Get me? Why?"

"She thinks you're losing your mind or suicidal. At least that's what David said."

"She thinks I'm going to kill myself?"

"That's what she said."

"She's the one losing her mind." Maggie took another sip.

"David said the plan was to call Dr. Smith and report you as being suicidal. He was going to call the police and get you locked up until she could get you declared incompetent."

"Locked up? Like jail?"

"Psychiatric hospital."

"Am I crazy, Mick?"

"I don't' think you're crazy but I'm crazy about you." He reached into his coat pocket and pulled out a small box.

"Maggie, I planned to do this on Valentine's day but I don't want to wait that long." He opened the little black box and slid it across the table.

"They're beautiful." She pulled one of the earrings out of the box and held it up to the light.

"And I have this to go with it." He opened another box and pulled out the diamond ring. "Maggie will you marry me?"

Maggie took the napkin from under her coffee cup and pressed it to her eyes. She made no move to touch the ring. "Mick, I'm an old woman. I have nothing to offer you."

"I want nothing but to spend our final days together."

"My days are numbered."

"One day with you is better than a thousand without you." Mick pulled the ring out of the box and held it for her. "We can get married today."

"How?"

"Our Mason City marriage license expires on Friday. We can see the judge today."

Maggie extended her hand. The ring fit perfectly.

#

Vinny wanted to sleep late and catch up on his beauty rest. January was a busy month and the Chicago morgue was cleaning house, getting ready for the next wave of unclaimed bodies. But there was a special delivery from Las Vegas which came in last evening and Vinny was anxious to get a look. He knew what it was but he didn't want to open it until this morning. He checked his clock, it was 6:30 AM.

After coffee he entered the work area of the mortuary and pulled on his coveralls. The package was a wooden crate inside a double walled cardboard box. Inside the crate was enough bubble wrap and foam padding to stuff an elephant. Vinny carefully re-moved each layer of protection until he was left staring at Maggie O'Reilly without legs, asleep in the packing peanuts.

The details were exquisite. Each hair was individual and per-fectly arranged. Her skin was delicate with fine creases around her eyes and at the corners of her mouth. Her eyes were shut and there was a half-smile on her face. Her hands were carefully arranged with her fingers intertwined as if she were saying her bedtime prayers. Even the polished fingernails were finely detailed and col-ored to match the tint of her hair.

The wax manikin was heavy even without legs. Vinny used a special hoist to lift Maggie's figure out of the crate and gently place her into the emerald casket. She came already wearing the dress Maggie supplied to Madam Tussauds during her visit. He added a delicate string of pearls. Vinny adjusted the satin fabric around the manikin. He smiled at Maggie's determination as he closed the lid on a masterpiece. She was ready for delivery.

244

#

The dispatcher asked Mary more questions than she was prepared to answer.

"Do you think she's an imminent risk to herself or someone else?"

"Probably."

"Why?"

"Because she's on the edge of senility."

"Ma'am, thousands of people are going senile, that doesn't mean they are jumping off bridges."

"But...you don't know my mother."

"I'm sorry but it sounds like you don't know her either."

"But she's missing. We don't know where she is."

"I see you filed a missing person report on her earlier. I assume everything worked out fine?"

"Yes, she was moving furniture."

"I see... I'll file this report but until forty-eight hours have passed, this will be a low priority unless you have other urgent information you haven't shared."

"Thank you, officer." Mary put her phone down and looked at the others.

"I don't have a good feeling," she said. "Why would an old woman leave home in the middle of the night and not tell anyone."

No one answered. David glanced around the room and his eyes met Tommy's. Tommy folded his hands together as if praying and raised them to his chin. He extended his index finger and pressed it gently to his lips.

CHAPTER 51

When a man opens a car door for his wife,
it's either a new car or a new wife.
-Prince Phillip

"Nothing like waiting to the last minute." The county judge held the marriage license under his desk lamp and studied it through his bifocals. "Did you have second thoughts?"

"No sir," Mick said. "Just waiting for the right time."

"And this is it?"

Maggie and Mick nodded together. The ceremony was quick and painless, like getting a flu shot at Walgreens. No sappy speeches, no dilly-dally, just "I do" and they were out the door.

Mick found the nicest hotel in Mason City and checked in for one night. They had dinner at the Quarry restaurant but after driving most of the night, Mick nearly fell asleep in his martini. They made it back to their hotel room and both fell asleep during the evening news.

At 5 AM Maggie sat upright and looked around. She shook Mick awake.

"Do you know what day it is?"

"The first day of our lives together?" Mick sat on the edge of the bed and rubbed his sleepy eyes.

"It's Wednesday."

"What's so special about Wednesday?"

"This is the day I'm supposed to die."

"Well...good morning to you too." Mick groaned as he stretched his back. "Why do you want to die on a Wednesday?"

"It doesn't ruin the weekend."

Maggie made a miniature pot of coffee and brushed her teeth. When she was done, she took a sheet of hotel stationary and made a detailed list.

"Can you lie and cry at the same time?"

"I'm Norwegian."

"What's that got to do with the price of beans?"

"Irish people are emotional. You yell and swear and stomp around when you don't get your way. Norwegians are stoic. When my mother died, my father blew his nose twice and went back to work."

"When you get gout, what foot is the worst?" Maggie asked.

"The right one."

She threw her boot and struck him on the bunion. Mick howled and danced around until tears ran down his cheeks. He limped to the bathroom and wiped his eyes.

"How does it feel?" she asked.

"Like my first kiss from Lena Holmquist, when I was twelve."

"See...you can lie and cry, but you need more practice."

"Don't hit me again."

"Get dressed. We need to get going. Vinny is still five hours away."

"Slow down. We're on our honeymoon."

"We can honeymoon later. I don't want to be late for my funeral."

#

The sign hung crooked on the front door. *Welcome Home.* He was thrilled at being home after weeks of rehab. Patrick smiled all the way up the sidewalk as he limped along, behind his two-wheeled walker. Pickles barked and danced alongside, her entire sausage shaped body jiggling with ecstasy.

"Dad, I'm staying with you for a couple days," his daughter said. "Why don't you rest now and I'll go shopping so you have some food. Is there anything special you want at the store?"

"Just treats for Pickles."

Patrick settled into his easy chair and looked out the window. The curtains were open and the late winter sun glared off the snow. He lifted his bad leg and rested it on the ottoman. Pickles snuggled against him.

Through the window he could look down the street at the house on the rise, Maggie's house appeared the same except cars were parked in the driveway. While he waited for his groceries, Patrick took his binoculars, still on the end table next to the chair and looked out between the drapes. He adjusted the focus knob and counted six people. He recognized Father Muldoon and Mary but wasn't certain on the others.

It's good to be home.

#

Maggie sucked in a quick breath when she saw herself with folded hands lying in the shamrock casket. Suddenly life was short and time stood still. She reached out toward her manikin's arm but brought her hand back without touching.

Mick held back, hesitating on the edge of the room. It was Maggie...his Maggie in the box. He felt a lump in his throat and swallowed hard.

"Are you absolutely certain you want to do this?" he said as he stood alongside Maggie. "This will destroy your family."

"They're trying to destroy me. I'm beyond wondering if they care. It's time to make a point."

"It's your call Maggie, but when this is done, we might have to move to South America."

"It's time."

Maggie handed out the printed schedule of events. Mick and Vinny read through the script and Vinny faxed a copy to Sal at the Chicago Medical Examiner's office.

"Mick, you're first. Time to make the call." Maggie nodded toward his cell phone. "If you're having trouble crying, I'll hit your bunion."

Mick's finger wavered as he poked the screen of his phone. Mary's phone number was on speed-dial. He couldn't get it wrong.

"Hello?"

"Mary, this is Mick."

"Where are you? We're worried sick about Mom."

"She's gone." Mick sniffled twice and looked away from Maggie.

"Where did she go?"

"She's gone...gone."

Mary was quiet. Mick could hear her sniffling back. "Was it her heart?"

"We got married yesterday. It was her final wish. Last night in a fit of passion her eyes rolled back and..." Maggie aimed her heel at his bunion and gave a quick stomp. "AHHH...Maggie...."

"Mick I'm so sorry..." Mary wept along with him. "Where is she?"

"The coroner picked her up. I gave him your number." Mick sniffled again. "He should be calling you soon."

"Mick, what do you need us to do?"

"Please tell the others and give everyone a hug from me."

"What about services? Did you want us to arrange anything?"

"Maggie had everything prearranged. She knew her time was short and she didn't want to burden you." Maggie glared at him and made a motion with her hand across her neck. "I need to go; the police are here to ask some questions."

"Before you go, did she say anything about us...her children?"

"Just before her eyes rolled back, she said 'Mary...Mary...' and then it was over." Maggie whacked his foot again. "AHHH...Maggie."

"Don't torture yourself Mick. Memories can be painful."

"I need to go. I'll see you soon." Mick ended the call.

"When did you go to acting school?" Maggie turned away from Mick. "Short and sweet, isn't that what I told you? Short and sweet."

"Does this mean the honeymoon's over?" Mick limped toward the bathroom.

CHAPTER 52

A two-year-old is kind of like having a blender,
but you don't have a top for it.
-Jerry Seinfeld

Father Muldoon was the first one over to the house. David sat in the corner of the room. His eyes were puffy and red. Eliza stood in the kitchen checking messages on her phone. Freddie seemed mildly upbeat and Tommy was quiet. Mary rushed about in the kitchen making lunch for everyone. She barked out orders and started making a list of people to call. Father Muldoon walked over to Mary and gently touched her arm with his hand. She looked up at him and started to cry.

"What happened?" He asked.

"Too much whoopee..."

"Oh..."

"Thank you for coming," she said. "Mom thought the world of you."

He went from person to person, offering hugs and condolences. *Did she really do it? Is this for real? What about the wax manikin? Do I say anything?* Father Muldoon sat in the kitchen and nibbled at the sandwiches Mary made. *This is it. It isn't going to be the same without Maggie. There's almost no one left.*

"Have you made arrangements?" he asked.

"Mick said she had everything planned out," Mary said. "Typical for her. She never let any of us make our own decisions."

"When do you want the funeral?"

"The mortuary will bring her home tomorrow. We can have the wake tomorrow night at the church and the service Friday morning. Will that work for you Father?"

He nodded his head slowly. *This will be a tough one.*

#

A woman with mid-length blonde hair and Gucci reading glasses hanging from a chain around her neck, glanced around and stepped through the door to her room at the Huckleberry B&B. She paid cash and cancelled breakfast for the morning. She arranged to have a private driver pick her up with the destination being St. Michael's Parish in Peterville, about fifteen miles away.

She pulled a prosthetic latex nose from her handbag and a chin extension along with a wart for her right cheek. She reviewed the instructions from the professional make-up artist in Las Vegas.

Maggie applied a clear adhesive to the inside of the nose and turned on the bright light over the bathroom mirror. She wiped her skin with an alcohol pad and fanned her face until it was dry. She took the blunt, bulbus nose and pressed it into place, holding it until it felt secure. Repeating the process, she applied a latex chin and a flesh-colored growth to her right cheek. Then she applied a base filler to blend the margin of the fake chin and nose. Thick unruly eyebrows framed the picture. She leaned forward admiring the three long white bristles coming from the end of the nose. Maggie took a small, tight roll of gauze and stuffed it inside her cheek and did the same on the other side. It added a subtle jowly look and changed her voice.

Maggie removed the blonde wig and replaced it with a tangled short gray wig and held it secure with a black scarf tied in a simple knot under her chin

When the face was done, she put on a fat suit with gel filled pads over the chest, butt and hips that giggled with the slightest movement. It also had a hump on the back that made her look stooped and fragile. The size 22 dress fit over the fat suit with just enough tension to reveal the jiggles. She pulled on bulky black leggings and black utilitarian diabetic shoes. Maggie unfolded her wheeled-walker and tied a handmade apron with pockets between the handles. In the pockets she put a box of tissues and two adult diapers sticking halfway out of the opening.

She didn't recognize the reflection in the full-length mirror. Not even Mick knew what she was wearing. She could have been George Washington's mother.

Showtime.

#

Maggie checked the time in her room before leaving. It was nearly 6 PM. The wake was scheduled from 5 to 7 PM. It would take her fifteen minutes to get there and leave enough time for her to mingle but not engage in conversation. She glanced out the window. The driver was ready.

There was no parking available in front of St. Michael's and both side streets were full as well. Elmer Swensen and Bert Griffin were impromptu valets assisting mourners to find adequate parking without walking long distances. The driver pulled to a stop and Elmer reached for the rear door handle.

"Good evening." Elmer extended his hand and helped her out of the car. "Are you from around here?"

"Olga Benson from Brainard." She grunted as she tried to pitch herself forward and out of the back seat of the car. Bert opened the trunk and unfolded her walker. One of the adult diapers fell onto the ground. He retrieved it and stuffed it back into the apron.

"Thank you, young man." Olga reached out and patted Bert on the stomach. She leaned on the walker and started toward the front door of the church. Eno Toivola and Gus Rasmussen held the doors open. She nodded as she passed them, trying to avoid eye contact. She entered the back of the church and limped past the table of candles lit in memory of loved ones. The table seemed ablaze.

There was a small sea of people milling around and waves parted as she approached the front of the church. Patrick Murphy was in his usual pew, row number seven. Mabel and Sally sat in the third row on the right. There was a vacant spot next to them where Maggie usually sat on Sunday mornings. The bridge club milled about whispering and sniffing into crumpled tissues. Neighbors, friends and townspeople spoke in reverent whispers, nodding and hugging one another. Another wave of people parted and then she saw it. The glossy emerald green shamrock casket, shimmering under the display lights, lay open in the front with her children smartly dressed standing in a greeting line along the wall. She counted thirty people in line, hugging, laughing, crying and comforting her children and grandchildren.

Mary was the first in line, strong and confident with the well-wishers and mourners. Olga watched her laugh and cry with each person who approached her. Everyone had a story to tell and she nodded politely as if it was the first time, she heard it.

Tommy was next in line. He was quiet and avoided conversation but his eyes were red and swollen. He shook hands with people quickly and they moved down the line to Freddie and Eliza. Compared to Tommy, Freddie looked sharp in a new three-piece suit and seemed outright bubbly. He laughed and chatted with each person but looked toward the exit doors of the church whenever the line stagnated. Olga followed his gaze and saw Therese in a classy new dress, wearing a double string of pearls.

Eliza appeared pleasant and amiable but Olga noticed no discernable swings of emotion. Her eyes were clear either from eyedrops or lack of emotion. She received the people from Freddie and passed them onward to David at the end of the line without spending any critical emotional energy.

David's eyes were puffy but he managed a polite smile with each new person he faced. He stood nearest to the open casket and whenever he had a break from forced socialization, he averted his eyes from the body in the shamrock box.

Olga waited until the line was dwindling before getting up from her chair near the wall. She bypassed the line and stood before the casket, leaning on the walker with trembling arms. She felt her heart flutter just enough to give her a surge of anxiety but it quickly subsided.

The body in the casket was a sharp reminder of her own mortality. She saw herself in the box but she had strange sense of indifference as one looking at an old coat dropped into a lost and found bin.

"I'm sorry. Do I know you?"

Olga Benson turned stiffly, moving her walker inches at a time until she faced the voice. She felt the hump on her back shift slightly and prayed it wasn't too obvious to onlookers. "I'm Olga," she croaked and nearly swallowed the wad of soggy gauze tucked inside her cheek. Olga extended her gloved hand toward Mary.

"Are you a friend of my mother?"

"We were Siamese twins separated at birth."

Mary stepped back and took a long look at Olga. "Did you really grow up with my mother?"

"I know her better than I know my own children." Olga straightened her hump back and leaned on her walker as she turned to face Mary. "Was it peaceful or did she go kicking and screaming?"

"I'm sorry?" Mary asked.

"Maggie, how did she die?"

"It was her wedding night..."

"Poor thing."

"She didn't suffer."

"No...I meant her husband."

"Oh..."

"I can't remember the last time we talked. We always hope for just a little bit more, but it ends doesn't it?" Olga cleared her throat. "If you could ask her one more thing what would it be?"

"I have many questions. Do you have regrets? What would you do over? Who's your favorite child? Of course, we know it's David. I'm not sure what I would ask."

"Only one."

"Can I think about it for a minute? I'll let you know before you leave."

"You should tell me now. I could die in the next minute." Olga limped closer to the casket. She reached out her gloved hand and touched the satin alongside Maggie's face.

Mary stepped closer. She reached her hand and touched Olga's arm. "I know what I would ask."

Olga turned to face her.

"Her potato soup recipe."

"That's your question?" Olga shook her head. *Potato soup?* "I have her recipe, I'll send it to you."

"It wouldn't be the same,"

"Why not?"

Mary said, "When I was nine years old my best friend got mad at me and ripped off the arm of my doll and threw it into the street. I cried for two days. Mom said all the usual things mom's say and nothing helped, but then she made potato soup. It was rich and creamy with bits of corn and bacon and she shredded a little bit of cheese and took a small piece of fresh parsley to float on the top. I'm not sure why but, we were home alone, that day. We dressed up fancy. She picked a flower and put it into a small vase and set it by my bowl of soup."

They stood side by side looking at Maggie surrounded by house plants and flowers. Mary dabbed at her tears. Olga felt a tickle in her nose. She pulled two tissues from the box as she sneezed. The latex nose let loose as she released a powerful AHH-CHOO. The nose bounced off the back of the casket and fell into the folds of fabric around Maggie. Olga held the tissues to her face and jerked her head around to see if any was watching. Mary was still blotting her eyes.

"God bless you." Someone said.

Olga nodded. She picked up her walker with one hand and headed for the exit.

CHAPTER 53

Don't worry about the world coming to an end today.
It is already tomorrow in Australia.
– Charles M. Schulz

Maggie the manikin spent the night inside the emerald casket near the altar at the front of St. Michael's Parish. Father Muldoon turned off the lights but the table with memorial candles burned bright until the last wick flickered out.

Olga Benson returned to the Huckleberry B&B and stripped off the latex disguise. She was disgusted with herself because her nose fell off before she could talk with the other children. All she could do was seek shelter from prying eyes until the funeral tomorrow morning.

Potato soup. Maggie couldn't get it out of her mind. If I had one question to ask my mother before she died, what would I ask? Potato soup recipe? I can think of a hundred better things to ask. She had her chance.

#

Mick struggled through the afternoon and evening watching friends and family mourn while he knew she was alive and well. He wanted to shake her children and grandchildren and tell them the truth but Maggie made him swear to secrecy. She threatened dismemberment and divorce if he, as much as hinted to anyone.

The morning of the funeral was clear and cold and the wind was calm. It was Friday, confession day. He knew the truth would be revealed. *It isn't going to end well.*

He pulled out the list of details. He had things to do before the funeral. Vinny wasn't able to stay because people were dying to see him back home. Maggie knew this in advance and arranged for the Ding-Dong ice cream truck to transport the casket from the church to the gravesite which was only a quarter mile by road and barely a hundred yards from the front of the church.

Before the service, people began gathering in the church to console the family. Mick tried to avoid people but he was surrounded by mourners when they discovered, he and Maggie were just married and she died on their wedding night.

Bishop O'Connor and his assistant stepped through the double doors of the church to a crowded sanctuary. He glanced around at the activity and nodded his approval. They found some vacant seats near the back and blended in with the local mourners.

The pipe organ began to play mournful hymns, quietly at first but the volume gradually increased. People stirred about, jockeying for seating near the exit. David, Tommy, Eliza, Freddie and Mary along with their spouses and children clustered together near the back of the church. Mick joined them wearing a new black suit and an emerald silk tie to match the casket.

Father Muldoon slowly walked to the front of the church and lit a candle on a pedestal standing at each end of the casket. Without saying a word, he raised his hands, signaling for the guests to stand as the family was ushered in.

They walked single file down the aisle between the pews and took their places near the front of the church, on the right. Some coughed, some cried, some wiped their noses and blotted tears. Therese snapped her gum and walked behind Freddie. Her hair was tinted and feathered in a Farah Fawcett style and fluttered as she clumped along in her high heels.

"In the name of the Father, the Son and the Holy Ghost." Father Muldoon formed the cross.

"Amen."

"We are gathered together to honor a matriarch of our community, Margaret Rose O'Reilly-Torkelson who has passed on to glory." Father Muldoon paused to swallow and wipe his own tears. "I believe I knew Maggie well but if I were pressed to describe her in a word or two, I couldn't do it. Unique perhaps…eccentric…certainly one of a kind. When God made Maggie, he broke the mold." There was a soft murmuring of chuckles and whispers across the congregation.

Mick felt his phone vibrate. He pulled his phone from his inside breast pocket but didn't look at the screen until they were requested by the priest to stand for a hymn. He glanced at the text message. "All set."

#

Maggie checked her watch every five minutes. As the funeral service gradually tapered to an end, her anxiety increased. Her heart skipped and she felt a tightness in her throat. Her palms were clammy. There was a long empty cabinet on the inside of the Ding-Dong ice cream truck large enough to fit Maggie lying down. She stuffed herself into the side cabinet in the back of the Ding-Dong ice cream truck and pulled the panel shut. It was tight and squeezed her on all sides. She felt claustrophobic and struggled to breathe. She pulled at the neck of her shirt, trying to get more air. She closed her eyes and counted her breaths, trying to slow them. She remembered the time she hyperventilated and someone made her sit with her head between her knees and breathe into a bag. But she couldn't put her head between her knees since she was in her twenties and she didn't have a bag. Maggie squirmed trying to get more comfortable. She pushed her fingers against her neck trying to feel her pounding pulse. She counted 124 beats per minute. She checked her watch. Fifteen minutes left, maybe less.

Maggie pushed the panel open and dug through her handbag. *Valium 2 mg.* She found the bottle of tranquilizers left over from her heart attack. There was no water in the truck. She took out a pill and threw it into the back of her throat and tried to swallow. She felt it go down like a dry lump of shredded wheat.

The cargo area in the back of the ice cream truck was separate from the cab but visible through a small window. She cracked open the window and studied the church entrance, waiting for the pallbearers to appear.

Then it happened. The front door to St. Michael's Parish flung open and two men held the doors as Bert Griffin and Eno Toivola led the other pallbearers toward the Ding-Dong ice cream truck. Maggie scrambled to squeeze herself back into the cabinet and pull the panel shut behind her. *Breath slow. Don't make a noise. Don't move.*

The back doors to the truck opened and the six men slid the shamrock casket inside and closed the doors. Maggie counted to ten and listened. *Nothing.*

She pushed the panel open and latched the double back doors from the inside. Once they were secure, she opened the casket and took one more look at the manikin. She looked good for an old woman with no legs.

Maggie grunted as she tugged on the wax manikin. It was too heavy for her to lift straight out of the casket. *Hurry. You don't have much time.* She hooked her hands around the right arm of the manikin and pulled. The wax arm broke off and Maggie fell backward against the opposite wall. She felt a lump on the back of her head and her butt was sore over the tattoo. She opened the cabinet where she hid and tossed in the wax arm. She rolled the remainder of the wax figure out of the shamrock casket and pushed it into the side cabinet and shut the door. *Now it's your turn.*

Her heart raced. Her breathing got faster and she was light headed. *You can do it. Breathe easy. I can't wait to see their faces when I push the lid open and jump out. Resurrection time.*

Maggie took off her boots and tossed them into the side cabinet with the manikin. She climbed into the open end of the casket and slid her feet under the silk liner and squeezed into the space. She felt the driver's side door slam shut and the engine started. The Ding-Dong ice cream truck was moving.

Maggie reached up with her right hand and pulled the casket lid down tight. The padding from inside the cover pressed on her face. She couldn't breathe. She kicked and pushed against the cover. It opened and she took three deep breaths. *I'm not going to make it. I need another tranquilizer.* Maggie scrambled back out of the emerald casket and choked down one more pill.

The truck pulled slowly onto the street. Maggie swayed and felt light headed. *Get back inside. Breathe slower...breathe.*

She felt the truck turn again. One more turn into the cemetery. *Not much time. Unlatch the back door. Hurry.*

She pushed her legs back into the dark recesses at the bottom of the casket and laid back. The padding pushed on each shoulder and her head rested on the slippery pillow. She counted her bounding pulse as the darkness closed around her. She pulled the lid shut one last time.

#

Father Muldoon stood near the head of the grave next to the O'Reilly family monument. The deeply etched letters of Albert's name were half filled with gray lichens and debris from the past seventeen years. Maggie's grave was carefully dug next to his and the edges of the frozen hole were lined with green carpet. A wide brass casket stand was perched over the grave with straps to lower Maggie's casket the final six feet of its journey. The pallbearers slowly stepped around the stand and slid the casket into place. Mick and the O'Reilly family took their places in the folding metal chairs alongside the casket. Bishop O'Connor stood to the side watching the priest conduct the service.

Father Muldoon raised his right hand and as he stepped closer to the mourners. "In the name of the Father and the Son and the Holy Ghost. Amen"

"Amen."

"Ashes to ashes, dust to dust..." Father Muldoon read slowly, his voice choking with emotion. He looked up from his Bible, glancing from face to face reading the same pain and loss as he felt in his own heart.

There was a movement to the side of the family gathering. He turned his head to see Patrick Murphy limping toward the grave-side, using his walker to negotiate the frozen uneven ground.

Father Muldoon continued, "We commit our sister Margaret Rose O'Reilly-Torkelson to the everlasting…"

"He did it." Patrick yelled. "He took her away from us. He did it."

"Patrick!" Father Muldoon yelled.

"He's the one." Patrick leaned on his walker, his long black coat was unbuttoned and open in the front. "She would be alive if it wasn't for him."

"Patrick!" Father Muldoon stepped around the head of the casket and moved toward him.

Mick stood and took two steps in his direction.

"It's too late." Patrick reached into his coat pocket and pulled out his .38 revolver. His hand shook as he aimed it toward Mick. People screamed and ducked. A dozen people ran to their cars. Bishop O'Connor was pushed to the ground by his assistant.

Tommy and Father Muldoon lunged forward hitting Patrick as the gun fired. Patrick and Father Muldoon were thrown backward and their heads collided into a rough granite tombstone. Father Muldoon went limp and there was a cracking sound as Patrick's head hit the corner of the stone. Blood ran freely and his body jerked.

Tommy jumped back on his feet and turned toward Mick. A woman next to him screamed and fainted. Mary kneeled next to Mick and pulled his overcoat open. There was a large red stain forming on the front of his white shirt. His head bobbed and his eyes rolled back.

"Call an ambulance!" someone yelled.

The crowd scattered. Big Bert Griffin lifted Mick like a rag doll and tossed him into the back of his truck and raced toward the hospital. The ambulance and police arrived within fifteen minutes. Father Muldoon and Patrick Murphy were transported together, to Baxter Hospital.

The cold was raw and biting so the police took the witnesses back to St. Michael's Parish for questioning. The casseroles and gelatin salads were bundled up and whisked off to the hospital waiting area as people gathered to await news on Mick, Patrick and Father Muldoon.

Bishop O'Connor shook his head and said to his assistant. "It's a shame. I was going to give him a good report."

After the cars dispersed, Ross lowered the emerald casket into the darkness and filled the hole with frozen dirt. A volunteer drove the Ding-Dong ice cream truck to the big storage garage two blocks off main street and parked it inside. He hung the key on the nail in the office, turned off the lights and locked the doors.

CHAPTER 54

I always arrive late at the office,
but I make up for it by leaving early.
– Charles Lamb

Father Muldoon regained consciousness as the ambulance pulled into the hospital emergency room. He groaned and tried to sit up but the EMT's had a restraining belt in place holding him down.

"Take it easy Father." One of the EMT's gently pushed him back onto the gurney.

"How's Patrick?"

"He's still breathing."

Father Muldoon felt sick. The throbbing behind his eyes was like a jackhammer. He tried to recall what happened. He heard the gunshot and everything went black.

"Did anyone get shot?" he asked.

The two EMT's looked at each other but said nothing. One stuck a stethoscope in his ears and checked Patrick's heart and lungs. Father Muldoon closed his eyes and prayed.

#

The emergency room doctor flashed a bright light into his eyes. Father Muldoon blinked and tried to turn away.

"Do you know where you are?" he asked.

"Baxter hospital."

"Do you know what happened?"

Father Muldoon told the story as best as he could recall and then he asked, "Who got shot?"

"You know I can't tell you."

"Mick?"

He nodded. "He's in surgery now, but it looks like the bullet missed the big stuff."

"Patrick?"

"He'll be taking a helicopter ride to the big city." The doctor put the light back into his pocket and wrote some notes. "We're going to watch you for a couple hours. If everything's stable you can go home. There's some people here to see you."

Mary and the rest of the O'Reilly family filed into the observation room. Mary said, "Father, thank you for trying to stop Patrick."

"I wish I could have stopped the gun from going off." He rubbed his eyes. "Have you heard anything more about Mick?"

"We don't know any more than you do." Mary turned to her siblings. "If you guys want to leave, I'll stay and give the Father a ride back to town."

Each offered words of encouragement to Father Muldoon and left the room. When they were gone, he asked Mary, "What's next?"

"Mick is my step-father now. He's going to need some help." Mary reached out and squeezed his hand. "I'm going to miss Mom. If I had to do it all over again, I'd do it differently."

"What would you change?"

"Everything."

#

He was feeling much better and when the CT scan on his head didn't show any bleeding or brain damage, Father Muldoon asked to be released early. Mary drove him back to Peterville.

"Drop me at the church. The rectory is right next door anyway."

"Are you sure you don't need some help?"

"I'll be fine. Thanks."

It was 4 PM when Mary drove away. Father Muldoon stood alone in the church yard. The low afternoon sun glared off the crusty snow and hurt his eyes. He walked from the church into the cemetery and wound his way between graves until he came to the fresh dirt in the opposite corner. The chairs were gone. The grave was leveled and raked smooth, awaiting grass seed and a spring rain. He picked up a broken long-stemmed rose lying next to Maggie's headstone and carried it with him back to the church.

The heavy oak doors closed behind him and the noise echoed in the empty church. He walked down the aisle and sat in the third row on the right side where Maggie and Sally and Mabel sat every Sunday. *Bishop O'Connor was right. It's time to move on.*

He felt lost wandering about the empty space. He checked his watch. It was an hour past confession. As he did every Friday, Father Muldoon went into the small confessional and closed the door behind him. It was dark and comforting like hiding under a blanket during a thunderstorm when he was a child.

He held the rose in his hand. The stem was broken and it drooped to the side. He began to weep, softly at first and then his shoulders shook until he leaned against the wall to steady himself. He let the tears run free until there were no more and his eyelids felt sticky and swollen.

There was a sound in the church sanctuary. The main door closed softly and he heard someone step into the confessional. Father Muldoon cleared his throat and straightened his back. He rubbed his eyes and shook his head to clear his mind.

"Father forgive me for I have sinned."

There was a rustling and Father Muldoon heard the person shifting about on their seat. "Go on my child, what has the Lord laid on your heart?"

"Father, forgive me for I have sinned."

"Maggie?"

"I couldn't do it."

"You're dead. We buried you this morning." He pressed his face against the listening holes in the wall between them, desperate to see living flesh and not an apparition.

"I panicked when the casket closed over me. I was desperate. I couldn't breathe. I took another valium to calm my nerves and tried it again but I felt as if I was being swallowed up by the devil. I could hear the men coming to get me. At the last second, I climbed out of the casket and hid in the ice cream truck cabinet, but the double dose of the tranquilizer came over me and I fell asleep." She was quiet for several minutes.

"When I woke up it was quiet. I thought I was still in the casket. I pushed the door open and saw that the truck was parked in the town garage. I walked to the church."

"Do you know about Mick?"

"No."

"Patrick shot him in the chest." The priest pushed open the door of the confessional and stepped out. "He had emergency surgery."

"I need to see him." She sounded groggy from the pills and she struggled to keep her eyes open. "He was the only one who knew about the plan. I was going to jump out of the casket at the graveside and teach my children a lesson."

"If you had fallen asleep in the casket, you would have been buried alive." Father Muldoon shuddered.

"I'm afraid, I've destroyed the trust of my family, what little there was. And I doubt the people of Peterville will invite me to dinner."

"What were you trying to accomplish?"

"I wanted to hear the truth, not some mushy fake stuff buried in lies and manipulation. But I didn't know what it looked like."

"Did you find it?"

"The truth was disguised and I couldn't see it. Sometimes it looks like tough old men giving up their breakfast to carry a casket of a stranger. And sometimes it looks like potato soup."

EPILOGUE

Life would be tragic if it weren't funny.
-Stephen Hawking

The residents of Peterville never quite figured out what happened with Maggie. Rumors abounded about being an angel or being resurrected from the dead. They never asked and Maggie let them believe what they wanted.

St. Michael's Parish closed its doors for three weeks until Peterville hired a new village policeman with fifteen kids and a baby girl on the way. Father Shamus did his first baptism in seven years and started a catechism class. He refused Maggie's generous offer of support and never told anyone about it.

Maggie's children were another matter. After they recovered from the initial shock and joy of her survival, a new level of suspicion flared up. Maggie tried to redeem herself and made daily efforts to be honest and open with them, but forgiveness didn't come easily. Eliza returned to the west coast and opened a green burial service. It went well until Portland had the hottest summer on record. David went back to college and got a degree in family counseling. He wrote a best-seller about parenting even though he had no children of his own. Freddie and Therese filed for divorce and bankruptcy on the same day. Tommy lived in his mother's home and worked at Bert Griffin's hardware store, sharpening chain saws and lawn mower blades. Mary softened a bit but remained a younger version of her mother.

Mick recovered from the gunshot. He and Maggie started a new life together. He sold his house in the country and moved into town with Maggie. Their families were equally supportive. Mick's son, Larry recommended getting a lawyer to help with estate planning and suggested preplanning a funeral. Mick and Maggie crossed that item off the list.

Maggie agreed to follow through with the doctor's orders. The spot on her lung turned out to be cancer. The cardiologist cleared her for surgery. She had a small section of her lung removed followed by six weeks of radiation. Every day Mary drove her to the radiation oncology center and they spent plenty of time together.

"Mom, do you remember Olga Benson, from Brainard?"

Maggie was quiet for several minutes. "Sure. Kind of chubby with a hump back and a big nose."

"Who was she?"

"Velma Gladwell's sister."

"Did Velma have anything to do with great-grandpa Kurt from Berlin?"

"I'm not sure. Do you know Goldie Finkelstein?"

'No."

"When we get home, I'll make some potato soup."

##

If you've enjoyed this book, tell a friend and please consider posting a book review on Goodreads.com or Amazon.com.

Thank you

ABOUT THE AUTHOR

John W Ingalls MD is a small-town family physician in northwestern Wisconsin. He lives in the same area settled by his great-great-great grandparents, Lansford and Laura Ingalls who are grandparents to the famed and beloved author, Laura Ingalls Wilder.

Dr. Ingalls graduated from Webster High School, Webster Wisconsin in 1976. Following three years in the US Army-Infantry, he attended the University of Minnesota, graduating with a BS degree in biology. In 1985 he and his family moved to Madison,

Wisconsin where he attended the University of Wisconsin Medical School. He graduated in 1989 and completed a Family Practice Residency in Eau Claire, Wisconsin. Dr. Ingalls returned to his home town to practice medicine where he remains today.

Married to his wife, Tammy they enjoy all things related to the great outdoors, extensive travel, fine dining, and time spent with close friends. Together they have four wonderful daughters, married to gracious and loving husbands. Together they are now raising their own families and writing their own stories.

www.johningallswriter.com
Amazon.com
www.instagram.com/riverbend58

Made in the USA
Middletown, DE
17 January 2020

83124711R10150